R.I. Olufsen has a background in investigative journalism and broadcasting. She enjoys travel, good food, golf and literary puzzles. *Bogman* is her first crime novel.

BOGMAN

R.I. OLUFSEN

First published in the United Kingdom in 2015
by Crux Publishing Ltd.
ISBN: 978-1-909979-29-1
Copyright © R.I. Olufsen, 2015

Also available as an ebook:
eISBN: 978-1-909979-30-7
Requests for permission to reproduce material from this work
should be sent to
hello@cruxpublishing.co.uk

CONTENTS

1.

SUNDAY: WEEK ONE

East Jutland Police District

Tobias Lange was playing golf when he got the call about the body in the bog. The match, against his stepmother's fiancé, Norbert Fisker, was friendly but a little tense. The two men were wary of each other. Norbert had only recently got engaged to Tobias's stepmother. Tobias was checking him out at the request of his stepsister who lived in England. Tobias quickly realised Norbert knew he was being checked out. He was no fool. Tobias thought him pleasant, if a little dull. His stepmother, Inge, was a handsome, lively woman. Tobias wasn't surprised she was getting married again. But he couldn't work out why she had chosen Norbert who was no match for her, either in looks or in style.

"Your mother is lonely, Margrethe," Tobias had said to his stepsister when she telephoned demanding to know more about 'this man mother met on a cruise'. "She wants someone to share things with. She's been on her own for five years." A faint shock ran through him as he said it. His father had been dead five years. Five years! It still felt like a few months.

"She only met this man in February. It's too soon," said Margrethe.

"Not when you're sixty-two," said Tobias. "And Norbert is sixty-five. I think they just want to get on with it."

He had already run Norbert's name through the police computer and discovered nothing more than a fine for speeding some ten years earlier.

"Your mother is young at heart, Margrethe. As long as this man isn't a serial killer or after her money, or both, we should be glad she's going to have company in her old age."

Margrethe had made one of those harrumping noises that signify dissent. "We'll see," she said.

By the time they got to the ninth tee, Tobias had learned that Norbert's only interests, beyond running his waste disposal company, were golf and fishing; that his wife had died two years earlier; that he had a daughter who was divorced; that he was learning bridge to please Inge.

Tobias had already concluded that Norbert had plenty of money. Skovlynd Golf and Country club was frequented by rich people. A dark blue Bentley, so highly polished it reflected the smaller cars around it, dominated the car park. He hoped it didn't belong to Norbert. The green fee Norbert had insisted on paying for him – No, no, let me do this. You're my guest – was steeper than at any other course Tobias had played in Denmark. They'd had an excellent lunch. Norbert had been greeted by any number of expensively suited men, including a distant relative of the Royal Family.

Tobias liked the course – rated one of the best in the country. It hadn't rained. He had played well, despite losing a ball in the lake on the ninth hole, and now he had a putt on the eighteenth to finish the match all-square. That would be a satisfactory result. He was looking forward to a relaxing dinner. His stepmother was an excellent cook.

He was bringing the head of the putter to the back of the ball when the mobile phone in the back pocket of his trousers buzzed like a saw. He flashed an apologetic smile at Norbert.

"Sorry, I have to take this."

His ball trundled past the hole. He swore softly.

"Feel free," said Norbert. "Take the call. You're allowed."

"This had better be urgent," said Tobias into the phone.

Two men stood on the wide terrace outside the bar and restaurant overlooking the eighteenth green. One was blond and imposing. He wore plus fours in brown checked tweed. His companion was shorter, greyer and more muscular. He wore a discreet business suit and carried a briefcase. They both stared disapprovingly at Tobias.

Norbert saluted them with a wave of his hand and mouthed the word, "Police."

Doctors, priests and policemen were exempt from the prohibition against mobile phones on the golf course.

Tobias held the phone to his ear. He was as still as a hawk in a tree. After a few minutes he said, "Yes, yes, do that. I'll get over there before dark to take a look." He stowed the phone in his pocket.

"They've found a body in a bog west of the E45," he said. "A place called Roligmose. They think it could have been there at least a thousand years."

"A bog body. That's exciting." Norbert putted his own ball across the green and watched it drop into the hole. "I've only ever seen a bog body in a museum."

"Me too." Tobias had a sudden image of himself aged seven, gripping his father's hand, only letting go to press his hands and face against the glass case with the leathery brown body curled up inside as though asleep. He had been mesmerised by Tollund Man's eyelashes, the red stubble on his chin, the peaceful expression on his face. He lay on a mossy carpet, his cheek scrunched up against it as though resting on a pillow. Tobias remembered his shock at seeing the rope around Tollund Man's neck and felt again the pang of compassion that had blown his heart open. "I've never forgotten him," he said.

"There hasn't been a find in a long time," said Norbert.

"There were a couple of bog bodies in Ireland in the last ten years," said Tobias. "But nothing here since the 1940s."

They shook hands and walked off the green. The man with the briefcase had disappeared into the clubhouse. The man in the plus fours came down the steps from the terrace calling out, "I'm delighted to see you are on good terms with the police, Norbert."

Goldfinger, thought Tobias, from the James Bond film. The smooth-smiling man advancing towards them wasn't fat like the actor whose name Tobias couldn't remember, but he had the same what-I-don't-own-I-can-buy air about him.

"I'm being interrogated by my future son-in-law," said Norbert. "Chief Inspector Tobias Lange from the Criminal Investigation Unit in Aarhus."

"Kurt Malling," said Goldfinger. He shook hands with Tobias. "Welcome to the club. I know the Commissioner. I was chatting to him in Copenhagen last week." He clapped

Norbert on the shoulder. "We must have a game sometime, Norbert. I'll have a look in my diary. I'm tied up at the moment. I'm about to have my photograph taken. Advance publicity for the Hickory club competition I'm hosting in July. And I dare say you've heard I'm going into politics? But I'll pick out a few dates and get in touch." He nodded at Tobias. "Nice to meet you, Chief Inspector." He raised his hand in farewell and strode off in the direction of the car park.

Norbert said, "When I was a young man making my way in the waste disposal business, I hated people who told me they were friends with my boss."

Tobias immediately warmed to him.

"Maybe you'll be Commissioner one day," said Norbert cheerfully. He paused. "But maybe not. You don't strike me as much of a back-slapper. Kurt is a great back-slapper as well as a name-dropper. Hickory competition. That explains the fancy pants. And he's going into politics. I bet it's a fund-raiser. He's never asked me for a game before. I suppose he'll want a donation for the party."

They changed their shoes in the locker room and carried their clubs to Norbert's car.

"I'm sorry you have to dash off. I've texted Inge. She'll be disappointed you can't stay and have dinner with us." Norbert paused. "You know, I can't believe my luck in meeting her. I wanted you to see how happy we both are. I was devastated when my wife died. I thought I wouldn't be able to go on. I was like a zombie. The business kept me going. Then I met Inge and it was like coming to life again." He threw both sets of clubs into the boot of the car. "You never re-married, Tobias?"

Tobias hesitated. Words swam around in his head.

Hope. Duty. Love. Disappointment. Anger. Dislike. Had he known Norbert better, he might have attempted to string them together in a narrative. He shook his head.

"Not even tempted?"

"It would take a lot to tempt me."

They saw Kurt Malling again as they were driving out of the car park. He was standing beside the Bentley talking to the man with the briefcase.

"The last time I saw a man in plus fours like that with a man in a business suit they were in a James Bond film," said Tobias. "It was on television at Christmas. There was a scene on a golf course. The man in the suit was a killer called Oddjob."

Norbert laughed. "I remember. He decapitated people with a steel-rimmed bowler hat. I can't imagine Marcus Thomsen killing anybody. He's Malling's in-house lawyer. I often see them together. I hear Malling is building a golf resort in the Philippines. It's probably easier than building one in Denmark. The Lord knows they had a big enough problem with this one."

"I suppose raising millions is always a problem," Tobias said drily.

"Finance wasn't the problem," said Norbert. "Protestors were the problem. Eco-warriors. The kind of lunatics who chain themselves to trees. They were against the golf course being built."

Tobias turned to look back at the gently rolling, tree-covered landscape.

"You'd hardly know there was a golf course here," he said.

"Oh, there's still plenty of forest," said Norbert. "With plenty of my balls in it as well. And it looks like any other forest to me. But the green brigade argued it was home to some rare species of bat. Plus they wanted to stop all golf course development. Too many pesticides and so on." He shook his head. "I don't much care for Malling. He's an arrogant bugger. But he owns three courses, they're all good and they all provide employment."

"I don't remember any protests," said Tobias.

"This was about fourteen or fifteen years ago," said Norbert. "They went on for a couple of years. They set up a camp in the forest. They chained themselves to the trees. They lay down in front of the diggers. They drove equipment into the wall of the clubhouse. They drilled into the concrete lining of the lake on the ninth."

He turned into the driveway of a baroque-style manor house with two wings, a mansard roof, and a formal garden at the front.

"It's an exact copy of a manor house on Funen," said Norbert proudly. "I used to pass it on the way to my grandparents on the bus." He parked on the sweep of gravel near the wide steps to the front door and rested his hands on the wheel. "I grew up in a small flat in Odense. Three of us shared a bedroom. We played in the street. I swore if I ever got rich I would have a house like this with enough bedrooms and bathrooms for my parents, my children, their children, guests. I built it when I made my first five million kroner. Garbage disposal is essential and lucrative, but it's not fashionable, not nice." He wrinkled his nose and then smiled broadly. "One or two snobs I know look down on me. But I tolerate them."

Tobias began to like him even more.

"I'm thirty minutes from the office, fifteen minutes from the golf club. A hour to our summer house in Saeby," said Norbert. "It's perfect."

Inge came out to greet them. She tutted and clucked over Tobias. "The first time I've cooked for you in ages and you have to go and look at a set of old bones."

"If they're as old as they think," said Tobiás, getting into his car. "I might be back in time for coffee and aquavit."

2.

He was still some two kilometres from where the bones had been found when he drove over the crest of a hill and saw the police helicopter like a great lighthouse in the clouds, its beam sweeping across an expanse of flat, dark land. The horizon glowed faintly pink. He turned into a side road and bumped down an unmade track. A lone policeman stood where the track divided. Tobias rolled down the window, showed his ID and was directed left. The track petered out. Suddenly there were vehicles everywhere, parked at crazy angles. Katrine Skaarup, the fresh-faced recent recruit to the team was waiting to greet him.

"It's a real circus, boss," she shouted over the drone of the helicopter.

Tobias got out the car and looked around. The ground was lumpy and covered with rough grass, reeds and clumps of bushes. Half a dozen uniformed police were rolling out blue and white tape and pegging it at intervals around an area the size of a football field. The helicopter banked. The spotlight flashed across a black drainage channel, turning it into a white streak across the surface of the bog and illuminating two parallel lines of tape running towards a large white tent. A model aeroplane, painted yellow and white, its wings about a metre long, its undercarriage complete with neat black rubber wheels, rested between the lines of tape as though on a miniature, floodlit runway. Beside it, a man in a denim jacket was talking to a teenager who had some kind of tray harnessed to his chest. It took Tobias a few seconds to realise it was the control panel for the model plane. The man in the denim jacket was scribbling in a notebook. The teenager was gesticulating. A tall blonde in a red jacket and matching spectacles bounded purposefully towards them. A bearded man hoisting a television camera on to his shoulder scrambled after her.

The helicopter flew off towards the eastern horizon. The drone died away. Tobias blinked. His eyes adjusted to the gloom.

Katrine took her hands from her ears. "The guy who found the remains was flying a model aeroplane. He lost radio control. It crashed out there." She waved towards the tent. "He was looking for a bit that broke off. He called the press and a television station as well as the police in Randers. Arsehole."

She's trying too hard, thought Tobias with quiet amusement. She's beside herself with excitement and trying to hide it. Those little skips when she thinks no one is looking. What age was she? Twenty-two? Twenty-three? What had he been like at his first crime scene, at her age? Did he also try to sound offhand and professional without succeeding? Probably. He took a forensics kit from the dashboard locker of the car.

"He found a foot." said Katrine. "A foot like a bog body foot. So he called every Tom, Dick and Harry. Police, newspapers, television."

"Where is he?"

"Over by the Forensics van. He's called Kenneth Skov. Inspector Haxen is talking to him."

Tobias glanced over at the van. There was no mistaking Eddy Haxen's skinny frame and mop of flaxen hair. He was talking to a stocky man in a leather jacket who had a remote control panel hanging from a strap around his neck.

"The television guys called a professor from the university," said Katrine. "Which is just as well because he stopped them walking all over the place and contaminating stuff before Forensics got here."

"Where's the professor?"

Katrine looked around. "I can't see him. He might be in the tent. The guy talking to Eddy has been flying planes here for a while. The other one is his nephew. It's some kind of nature reserve but they've got take off and landing rights." She giggled.

Tobias crouched to pull on a pair of overshoes and hide a smile. He stood up. The cameraman and the blonde in red spectacles sprinted towards him. Tobias ignored them. He stepped over a stretch of tape and tramped past the model plane towards the tent. The ground sucked at his feet. The tent glowed in the dusk. When he finally reached it and ducked inside, he was dazzled by a spotlight. When his eyes adjusted, he saw the forensics team – all four of them – on their knees examining a taped-off area around a slight hollow in the ground. He glimpsed a scattering of bones covered in what looked like spiders' webs. A few metres away, Inspector Harry Norsk, the medical examiner, was standing over a folding table staring at a foot that seemed to be made of dark brown wood or leather, and a white skull. He greeted Tobias with an absent-minded wave.

"The foot is mummified. There's a split in the skull. It could have been caused by a blow with something like a rock. But God only knows when. Could be anything between ten and two thousand years."

"Is this one for us or one for the archaeologists?"

Harry shrugged. "I can't tell at this stage. We could be dealing with a bog body or with something more recent. I have no expert knowledge of how the bog affects bone and tissue, or anything else for that matter. You're going to need a forensic anthropologist."

Eddy Haxen came into the tent.

"Hi, Boss. Will I let the plane buffs go? They seem shocked by it all."

"Not too shocked to call up a television station," said Tobias. "Where's this professor?"

"Out there giving an interview to the press."

Tobias tramped back across the bog to a pool of light in which stood the be-spectacled blonde pointing a microphone at a tubby man wearing the same blue protective clothing as the forensics team.

"Strictly speaking," said the tubby man with the air of a lecturer addressing students, "this is mostly fenland, not bog. Like a lot of fens, it's on the edge of a bog and it looks and feels like bog but there's a crucial difference. Bog peat contains humic acid. It preserves body tissue. Bodies decompose in fen peat. It won't mummify bodies. But it has a high chalk content. It preserves bones."

A look of alarm crossed the interviewer's face.

"Can we keep it simple for now, Professor Brix? Why were these bodies buried in the bog, or fen?"

"It was once assumed that some of them were sacrificial victims in a pagan, Iron Age ritual," said the professor. "P V Glob famously posited that Tollund Man was killed in a ritualistic way."

"So this a ritual killing?"

Now it was the professor's turn to look alarmed. "I'm not saying that," he said. "I'm just explaining one theory about Tollund Man."

"So this is another Tollund Man?"

"I'm not saying that either," said the professor.

"Have you found anything with the body? Anything from the Iron Age?"

"One of the forensic team found a metal coin or button with what looks like a laurel leaf design. A laurel leaf typically..."

At which point Tobias intervened.

"Chief Inspector Lange from Aarhus Criminal Investigation Department. I must ask you to stop recording," he said. "This is now a police matter. We can't divulge any more details at this early stage of the investigation."

The blonde gestured to the cameraman and turned her attention to Tobias. "Are you investigating an Iron Age murder, Chief Inspector?"

"We don't know what we're dealing with at the moment," said Tobias, uncomfortably aware he was now on camera. "All I can say is that human remains have been found here. We need to establish how long they've been in the bog. That could take some time. There'll be a statement in due course. Now I must ask you all to leave."

He took the professor by the arm and led him aside. "I'm sorry, but we have to do things by the book. The forensics team know what they're doing."

The professor took a card from the breast pocket of his jacket and handed it to Tobias.

"Thanks," said Tobias. "We'll be in touch if we need you."

The camera crew had packed up. The blonde called out, "Can you come into the studio, professor?"

She threw a challenging glance at Tobias. "Do you have any objection to that, Chief Inspector?"

It was now dark. Tobias shone his torch on the card.

Professor Johann Brix
Forensic Anthropologist
Department of Forensic Medicine
University of Aarhus.

"I'm afraid I do," said Tobias.

He tramped back to the tent and said to Harry Norsk, "I think we've found our man."

3.

It was nearly ten o'clock when he got back to his flat. He was hungry. He could almost smell the roast pork loin, the cabbage with juniper and garlic, the roast potatoes, Inge's apple pudding. Too late for all that now. He went pessimistically to the refrigerator. A curled up lettuce, three eggs, a dried up slice of ham in an opened plastic packet, half an onion in cling film and a nugget of crumb-embedded butter on a saucer. He had the makings of an omelette at least. He cheered up. An omelette was a proper meal. It justified a glass of decent wine.

He laid the table beside the window leading to the balcony, adjusting the knife and fork to lie parallel to each other, equidistant from the sides of the table. He lit the single candle in the blue and white Royal Copenhagen pattern candlestick which sat in the dead centre of the table. The same candlestick had sat on the dining table in the house where he grew up. It had been ritually placed on the tiny fold-out table in the boat on which he spent endless weekends and holidays with his father after his mother died, because his father had not been able to bear being in the house without her.

He selected a bottle of Macon Villages from the temperature-controlled wine cabinet above the refrigerator, unscrewed the cap and poured himself a glass. He took a sip, swilled it around his mouth, savouring the taste before swallowing a mouthful. He took the omelette pan from a cupboard and began to cook.

He drank the Burgundy with the omelette. He washed up his plate, knife and fork and swept the remains of the lettuce into the compost bin. In the three periods in which he had shared his living space with a woman – including his ex-wife – he had found that they, not he, left dirty plates in the kitchen sink, scattered clothes about the bedroom, abandoned damp towels on the bathroom floor. The last woman in his life, Anna, a librarian in Silkeborg, had tried to persuade him to move in with her. To live in her cosy house with its fat cushions and swagged curtains and scented candles everywhere. But on the occasions when Tobias had stayed there he had felt suffocated. He preferred the spareness of his own flat. She had called him a dried up stick.

He poured himself a second glass of wine and carried it out to the balcony. He could just about afford the mortgage on the flat. It was worth it to be right in the centre of Aarhus. To see, over the rooftops, the cathedral spire soaring into the sky. To see below him in the space between the back of his own building and the next street, the neat gardens and patios of his neighbours with their budding lilac and cherry trees, their bicycles and their pots of tulips, his ground-floor neighbour's lily pond with its miniature fountain spouting from dawn to dusk. Thank God it was Sunday night. On Fridays and Saturdays there was always noise from the bars and cafés in the surrounding streets, sometimes making him nostalgic for the student life he had briefly glimpsed and left behind.

He watched his neighbour, Hilde, in the flat across from his balcony, moving about in her kitchen. He wondered if it was too late to telephone and invite her over for a nightcap. But that usually meant sex and he was enjoying being alone. He wanted to sip his wine and listen to music. Hilde was energetic and fun. She was married to the first officer on a cruise ship who was away from home for weeks at a time. She had exchanged glances with Tobias when they met in the street and, after several such encounters, had rung his doorbell on the pretext of asking him to help mend a fuse. He was both taken aback and aroused by the blatancy of her approach. She quickly abandoned any pretence of not being competent with fuses. She was more than competent in bed as well but she talked a lot and she liked Bruce Springsteen. Tobias was in the mood for something ordered and serene. Bach preludes, a Haydn sonata or a fugue by Arvo Pärt. Something cool and cerebral but full of beauty too. He stepped back into his flat. His phone rang. He picked it up and saw his daughter's number on the screen.

"Hi, Agnes. What's up?"

"Hi Dad. I saw you on the news. Another Tollund Man, maybe? Hey, that would be exciting."

"Well," Tobias sat down again at the table. "It's a bit early to say. It's not like Tollund Man. It's a mummified foot and a pile of bones. We've no idea how long they've been there. We've sent the lot to a forensic anthropologist."

"The fat guy who was interviewed?

"That's the one."

"And you really have no idea how long the bones have been there?"

"Not really."

"It might be the work of a serial killer."

Tobias laughed. "You've been watching too much television, Agnes."

"Well I hope the poor soul had some love in his or her life, whenever it was."

Tobias thought that was a good sentiment.

"So what else have you been doing, Dad?"

"Well, I've met granny Inge's fiancé, Norbert Fisker."

"What's he like? Aunty Margrethe thinks he's after granny's money."

"He doesn't need it. He's rich. He has a lot more money than granny Inge," said Tobias. "He seems nice. He doesn't take himself too seriously. He's sixty-five but he still goes to work every day. He has a waste disposal company."

"Landfill or incineration? How much recycling?"

"I've only just met the guy, Agnes."

There was a pause.

"I'm going on a protest tomorrow, Dad. I thought you should know."

Tobias sat up. "What kind of protest? Where? What about?"

"They're building a wind farm on the west coast."

"So what's the problem? You approve of alternative energy."

"They're cutting down a forest to build it. There's no sense in that."

Tobias thought there was probably a lot of economic sense in it, but he didn't say so.

"Magnus says there are other sites. They don't need to cut down the forest. I just wanted you to know in case the police got heavy," said Agnes.

"They won't get heavy if you stay within the law."

Tobias heard a derisive snort.

"The police get heavy whether or not we stay within the law," said his daughter.

"What exactly are you planning to do on this protest?" Tobias was immediately sorry he'd asked. If she were planning anything illegal he would have to warn the police in Esbjerg.

"Sometimes I wish you weren't a policeman, Dad," said Agnes.

"This has nothing to do with my being a policeman," Tobias said sharply. "It has everything to do with being lucky enough to live in a democratic country under the rule of law. It's the duty of every citizen, and that includes you, Agnes, and your boyfriend, to uphold the law. I have to warn you not to break it." To his own ears, he sounded like a prig.

After a few moments of silence Agnes said, "We're not breaking any laws. Unless climbing tress is illegal."

Tobias groaned.

"Don't worry, Dad. I'm not going to fall out of a tree. I'm going to be holding a banner at the bottom of a tree. Magnus is going to be in the tree. In fact he's there already. He's spending tonight in a tree in case they try to sneak the loggers in early."

"I bet it's cold and windy and you wish you were here."

"It's cosy in my tent," said Agnes. Tobias could hear the smile in her voice.

"It's not very cosy up a tree," he said drily.

"Magnus won't be up the tree all night." Agnes chuckled. "Aksel's here. He'll take his turn. And there'll be others tomorrow." Her voice changed. "You don't like Magnus, Dad. You don't like that he's an activist."

"I just wish he was a bit more active in looking for a job."

There was a pause. Tobias said in a more casual tone, "No lectures this week?"

"It's half-term, Dad. Don't you remember?"

Tobias smacked himself on the forehead. "Of course it is. Any chance of seeing you?"

"That ought to be the other way round, Dad. Last time we had a date for lunch you were called away, remember?"

"Sorry," said Tobias. "It's the job."

"We'll probably be here all half-term anyway," Agnes said. "You might even see us on television." She laughed, and rang off.

Tobias picked out a CD of Arvo Part and selected *Fur Alina*. Two minutes of perfection. He concentrated on each limpid, bell-like note. One hand, then the other hand, then two together. He'd played it for Hilde once. She had found it boring. When the last note sounded, he switched off the CD player and sat for a while picturing his brave, blonde idealistic daughter, wrapped up in a parka – he hoped she was wrapped up in a parka, it was probably blowing a gale on the west coast – standing vigil over a tree.

4

MONDAY: WEEK ONE

Chief Superintendent Jens Larsen, Head of Special Investigations, and the prosecutor, Renata Molsing, were examining photographs spread across a table in Larsen's office, when Tobias and Eddy Haxen arrived for a briefing.

Larsen looked up from the photographs. "So what do we know about this bog body?"

Not at lot so far," said Tobias. "Forensics are still at the crime scene."

"If it is a crime scene," said Eddy. "We might end up sending the bones to a museum."

"Well, at least we've shortened the process by giving them to Johann Brix," said Larsen. "He's good. We called him in to help after a multiple pile-up a few years ago. He can send the remains to the museum if it turns out they're from the Iron Age."

"It only becomes a matter for us if the death occurred within a time frame which means the perpetrator could still be alive." said Renata.

"So we could be looking at a ninety-year-old perpetrator? Assuming the death wasn't accidental," said Eddy.

"That split skull didn't look like an accident to Harry Norsk," said Tobias. "Nor to me."

"We could be looking for killer who's been dead for a thousand years," said Eddy.

"Let's wait to hear what Brix has to say," said Renata Molsing.

"In the meantime, I suggest you get back out there, Lange," said Larsen. "And keep me informed. Right?" He nodded his dismissal.

Katrine Skaarup was at her desk in the Investigations Room.

"So where do we begin?"

"We're waiting to hear how old the bones are," said Eddy.

"We could start searching for missing persons in the area," said Katrine. Her face shone, she flexed her fingers as though ready to strike the keys of the computer and summon up names, dates and circumstances.

"We could be wasting our time," said Eddy. "I've got a report to write up for Renata." He settled himself at his desk.

"I'm going back to Roligmose," said Tobias. He glanced at Katrine. Her face had fallen. "But it's a good idea to be up to date on missing persons, just in case. Start ten years back and make a list."

He thought he might enjoy being around Katrine for a while. Before her enthusiasm turned to cynicism and she lost the romantic notions he guessed had made her want to be a detective.

The sky was the colour of slate when he drove out of the city. Drops of rain spattered the windscreen. By the time he bumped down the track into the bog, a drizzle had become a downpour. He cursed a climate that even at the end of April could turn from sunshine and a light breeze to sleet and high winds in the space of a day. He parked between the forensics van and a solitary police car. The officer in the car lifted his head from the newspaper. Tobias gestured to him to stay where he was. The officer looked relieved. He returned to his newspaper.

Tobias pushed the car door open against the wind. Rain whipped his face. He put his head down, pulled up the hood of his jacket and squelched across the rough grass towards the tent. The model aeroplanes had vanished. The sides of the tent ballooned in the wind. Just as well they'd got it up when the weather was calm. He was glad to get inside it.

"Hi, Tobias," the head of the forensics team, Karl Lund, raised a hand in greeting.

"I reckon we've got every bone and fragment of bone," he said. "As well as this lot." He pointed to a row of see-though plastic bags on the trestle table. "We found fragments of metal and four metal buttons, a silver buckle and a bracelet which feels like it could be bronze or silver. We're still looking," he nodded at two white-suited technicians on their knees combing through the grasses.

The rain stopped beating on the canvas. The wind softened. Tobias looked around. The ground sloped almost imperceptibly. A trickle of water had entered the tent. He followed it with his eyes to where it ran out under the opposite flap.

"The aerial photos showed a pond," he said.

"Yeah. About ten metres away," said Karl. "It's cordoned off. We haven't searched there yet."

"I'd like to take a look at it."

Karl handed him overshoes and orange plastic gloves. "At least it's stopped raining."

He led Tobias to a small oval of dark water concealed by tall reeds and grasses.

"It's unlikely a body would be dumped on open ground, however remote," Tobias said. "I wonder if this pond was bigger at one time."

He crouched beside a tiny stream trickling through black earth into the pond.

"We can drag the pond," said Karl.

"Hardly worth it until we know what we're dealing with. I was just curious." Tobias stood up. His foot dislodged a section of turf. He looked down and saw a thin round object, like a coin or medal.

"Have you got tweezers, Karl?"

Karl pulled a plastic bag from his pocket, ripped it open and handed Tobias a pair of tweezers.

"Looks like you've found another specimen for Professor Brix," he said.

5.

TUESDAY: WEEK ONE

Johann Brix had analysed human remains in the aftermath of aeroplane crashes, factory explosions and exhumations. He had identified bodies from bone and tissue fragments. He'd spent time at the famous Body Farm in Knoxville, Tennessee, studying how bodies decompose at different rates in different settings. He was the author of several research papers on tissue and bone rot in dry and damp conditions. But he had never examined human remains from the Iron Age. When he took delivery of the mummified foot and the bones and artefacts found in the bog, he felt a rising sense of excitement.

He began with an inventory of the bones. By one o'clock in the morning he had assembled a near-complete skeleton. He began work again at eight o'clock. When Tobias and Harry Norsk arrived at his laboratory on Tuesday afternoon, he was using a ruler to measure the distance between the hip bones.

"Male," he pronounced. "Female hips are wider. I thought he'd turn out to be male because of the height. I measured the skeleton at 1.61 metres. If I add 10 or 11 centimetres to account for the missing tissue and muscle that makes him 1.71 or 1.72 metres tall. Not especially tall by modern standards, but tall in Roman times."

"Age at death?" asked Tobias.

"Probably between eighteen and twenty-eight. See where the clavicle, the collarbone, is joined to the sternum, the breast bone?"

Harry and Tobias leaned forward to look.

"You can see it's not yet completely fused."

Tobias couldn't see but he was prepared to take the professor's word for it. Harry was peering at the collarbone, nodding and muttering, "Yes, yes."

"It begins to fuse around age 20 in young males," said the professor. "Complete fusion occurs between age 26 and 30. This is nearly half-way there, wouldn't you say?"

Harry nodded agreement.

"So he died in his early twenties," said Tobias.

"He was killed," said Harry. "Am I right?"

"Yes," said Professor Brix. He took the skull into his hands and turned it so that Tobias and Harry could see the cleft at the back. "He was hit on the head with something like a rock or an axe." Brix replaced the skull and pointed to the ribcage. "See the fractures?" He picked up the right upper arm bone. "See the break?" He laid his hand gently on the right hand of the skeleton. "I took a long time putting this hand together. There were so many small bones fractured." He sighed. "The poor fellow was almost certainly beaten to death. Wouldn't you agree, Harry?"

"I'd say he was turning away from the blows," said Harry. "The injuries are all on the right side. The skull fracture is right side as well. When he fell, the murderer probably stamped on his hand."

The three of them stood in silence for a moment.

"Was he killed in the bog, or somewhere else?" asked Tobias.

"It's impossible to tell," said Brix. "Your guess that he was dumped in the pond, and that the water level subsequently dropped, is almost certainly correct. From the order and position in which the bones were found, I'd say he was lying on his left side with his left arm under him and his right arm extended. He was probably rolled into the water, near where it's fed by a small stream. The microenvironment around the stream is alkaline and preserved the bones. The ground near the feet is acid. It rotted the bones of the left foot but preserved the skin."

The professor's mobile rang. He held it to his ear. His face fell.

"One of my graduate students has managed to reconstitute the remnants of gauzy material found in the grave." He paused. "Polyethylene terephthalate. Otherwise known as polyester." He smiled ruefully. "I'd been hoping to hear they were from an Iron Age or Roman woven garment." Another pause. "The metal fragments are parts of a zip fastener."

His expression reminded Tobias of a child whose toy had been taken away.

"She's sent me some images." Brix moved to a desk a few feet from the stainless steel table on which the skeleton lay. He tapped the keys of an open laptop. "Take a look."

A pair of trousers that seemed to be made of gossamer appeared on the screen.

"The rest of his clothing must have been mostly wool or cotton," said Brix. "The synthetic fibres haven't decomposed. What you're seeing is the ghost of a pair of trousers."

Tobias thought of his daughter, Agnes, and her passion

for the environment. She would love the symbolism of the phantom trousers. He found himself smiling as he imagined telling her about them.

"Polyester has been around since the 1940s," said Brix. "But it wasn't used in clothing until the 1950s. It was used on its own at first. Then it became more popular in a blend."

"Presumably at least one of the buttons found is from the trousers." Tobias was already calculating that the death occurred within the prosecutor's time frame. He felt a rush of adrenaline.

Brix clicked on another image. Four buttons. He zoomed in. Four copper buttons with a laurel leaf design. Tobias moved his face closer to the screen.

"These are Levi buttons," he said. "My father had a vintage Levi jacket with buttons like this. He told me Levi Strauss made them during the war."

"So the victim was wearing a vintage denim jacket. But not denim trousers," said Harry.

"A cotton denim jacket. Probably a cotton vest or T-shirt as well. Polyester trousers. They probably had a belt," said Brix. "But it must have decomposed. All we have is the buckle."

"The ghost of a pair of trousers, four buttons, a zip fastener and a belt buckle. At least we know he was clothed when he died," said Tobias.

"But barefoot," said Harry. "We didn't find a boot or shoe for the left foot. Would the bog not have preserved that as well?"

"You're right." Brix scratched his head. "The body crossed at least two micro-environments. One foot is skeletal. The other is mummified. Yes, I'd expect the shoe on it to be preserved as well."

"He must have been barefoot," said Tobias. Why had he taken his shoes off? Was it summer?

"It's going to be difficult to date the bones," said Brix. "There's no bone rot. Normally I'd expect bone rot to set in around twelve years post-mortem. Fifteen years if the body has been buried deeply. But in this case..." His voice trailed off. He shook his head. "Even a Cat scan won't tell us much. All I can confidently say is that whenever this poor soul was killed, it was more than twelve years ago and after polyester cotton blends were used in clothing."

Tobias said, "What about the other things forensics turned up?"

"Birgitte, my graduate student, is working on them. She's very thorough."

He ushered them across a corridor to a smaller laboratory where a young woman with tight curly blonde hair tied back like a lamb's tail was perched on a stool at a desk, one eye closed and the other peering through a microscope.

"Hi, Birgitte. Meet Chief Inspector Lange and Inspector Norsk."

Birgitte waved unseeingly at them with a gloved hand.

"Nice to meet you," she called out. "The trousers, the zip fastener, the buckle and the buttons are on the table at the back. I did them first. I was going to do the bracelet or the medal next, but some stuff came in an hour ago that looked more promising. Especially this. I've put everything else to one side to work on it." She took her eye off the microscope. "I have more cleaning to do, but it's definitely a watch. A Seiko watch." She glanced at the label on the plastic bag beside her elbow. "It was found within a metre of the skull so it almost certainly belonged to the victim."

"That's lucky," said the professor. "I've identified a body by a Seiko watch. A train crash victim in Russia." He shook his head. "That was a terrible business. I still have the notes. As I recall, there should be a serial number on the back of the timepiece."

Birgitte slid the watch from under the microscope. The metal bracelet was broken in three places, but the timepiece and its glass case were miraculously intact. She picked up a tiny paintbrush and with careful, slow strokes removed specks of dirt from the back of the watch before slipping it under the microscope again.

"I can read the number," she said. "Six-eight-six-four-seven-three-five." She pulled a notebook towards her, scribbled down the numbers and passed them to Brix. "There are words engraved as well: Love from Famor and Mormor."

"Maternal grandparents," said Tobias. "A birthday present? Pity there's no date. That would help us identify him."

"As I recall, the first number is the number in the decade," said Brix. "Six? It can't be 2006. The body is older than that. It could be 1996, or 1986. Earlier than that, I'd definitely expect to see bone rot. The second number is the month. Eight," he paused to count.

"August," said Tobias. "So the watch was manufactured in August 1996, or August 1986?"

Brix nodded. "I can probably pin it down. But it will take me a day or two."

"We know the body was put in the bog at least twelve years ago," said Harry.

"So we're looking for a young man who went missing sometime between 1986 and 1999," said Tobias.

"That's about it," said Brix.

6.

Tobias drove directly from Brix's laboratory at the university to the restaurant at Risskov where he was meeting his stepmother, Inge, and Norbert Fisker. If he went back to his flat to change, he'd be late.

"We're making it easy for you," Inge had said on the telephone. "If we invite you to the house, you'll be detained at work, it will take you an hour to get here and we'll be lucky to eat before midnight. This way, we can have a nice relaxed dinner on the coast."

Tobias arrived to find her already seated at the table.

"Norbert has gone to chat to some friends," she waved vaguely in the direction of an alcove. "His daughter is with them. We didn't know she was going to be here." Inge fiddled with her bracelet. She sounded irritated. "I heard him on the telephone to her this morning. I'm sure he told her we were coming here for dinner."

"Maybe she didn't know she would be dining here," said Tobias.

"She doesn't like me," said Inge. "She makes it clear she doesn't like me. It's making Norbert unhappy."

"You have to give her time," said Tobias. "Put yourself in her position."

"She's young. She has plenty of men in her life. She doesn't want anyone else in Norbert's life. She just wants her father to herself."

"She was probably close to her mother. It's hard for her to see you in her mother's place."

"I'm not taking her mother's place. I'm just marrying her father. It's not as though she sees that much of him."

Tobias thought for a moment. "I don't think that affects how you feel about someone. You don't see that much of Margrethe."

"She's in England," said Inge. "If she was here, I'd see more of her and my grandchildren."

"Supposing Margrethe died, God forbid it, and Peter remarried less than two years later. How would you feel?"

"Your mother died and you accepted me, Tobias."

"I was seventeen years old, Inge. Mama died when I was ten. I had seven years of grieving."

"Sofie wouldn't like me whether it was seven years or twenty-seven years. She's the possessive type."

"Give her time. She'll see how happy Norbert is."

Inge shrugged. "She can do what she likes. I don't care." She brightened. Tobias followed her gaze and saw Norbert weaving through the tables towards them, smiling broadly. He shook hands enthusiastically with Tobias.

"Sorry I wasn't here to welcome you. I didn't know Sofie was going to be here. She's with Kurt Malling and the Thomsens. They're talking business." Norbert sat down and picked up a menu. "Malling's latest venture is a wind farm in Jutland. Sofie is doing the PR. The green brigades don't like it. God only knows why."

Tobias didn't feel like explaining. He felt like putting his head in his hands. He imagined Agnes in the wind and rain, hugging a tree. Worse. Hugging that bearded Tarzan with five – five! – gold studs. Two in each ear and one in his nose. He had opened his mouth only once that time he was briefly introduced, if you could call it an introduction. He just nodded and shook hands. At least it was a firm handshake. He'd yawned while Tobias was talking to

Agnes. There was a gold stud in his tongue as well! Don't even think about it. And that motorbike. He hated the idea of Agnes on the back of a motorbike. Was there a father in the world who didn't worry about his child or children? He wondered if he had spoken the thought out loud because Norbert was talking about somebody's daughter leaving home after an argument.

"Sorry, Norbert. My mind was on something else. What were you saying?"

"I was talking about Thomsen's wife, poor woman. My late wife knew her. They played bridge together. Her daughter left home around the time she got married to Marcus. They haven't heard from her since. Not a word. Apparently she went to Lapland with her boyfriend. She didn't like Marcus. Maybe she was jealous of him. Wanted her mother to herself. Who knows? I can't say I know Marcus well. But he's a good lawyer with sound commercial instincts. They had some kind of row. Marcus and the daughter, I mean. I never learned the details. I heard about it from my wife at the time. Maybe they'll all be reconciled in time. I hope so. It's a terrible thing when parents and children fall out."

Sofie came by their table before leaving the restaurant. "I'm stopping just to say hello," she said.

Norbert's dead wife must have been a beauty, thought Tobias. Sofie didn't get those dark blue eyes, those fine bones, from her father.

Inge greeted her with every appearance of warmth. She waved to Kurt Malling, half a dozen paces behind Sofie and grinning like a cat following a bowl of cream. He looked a bit drunk.

"Hello, hello. Still hanging out with the police, Norbert?"

Tobias wondered if Malling was sleeping with Sofie. Surely not. He must be sixty. And he dyed his hair. But you never knew. He was rich. Some women were drawn to money. Malling was talking about shooting clay pigeons. He was hosting some kind of charity picnic with a shooting competition.

"Sofie is coming. You're coming, aren't you, Sofie? Your father and Inge must come as well. Do you shoot?" He was talking to Tobias now.

"Only criminals," said Tobias.

Sofie laughed. Then Malling laughed.

"So you must come to my charity golf day instead." He was all joviality. "The Commissioner will be there."

There was nothing more likely to make Tobias turn down the invitation, except perhaps the dreaded words black tie.

"Golf in the afternoon, dinner and prize giving in the evening," said Malling.

Sofie was smiling at him. "I need a partner to make up a fourball." She had a glorious smile.

"Black tie for dinner," said Malling. "My wife likes to do things in style."

"Thanks for including me," said Tobias.

7.

WEDNESDAY: WEEK ONE

ddy Haxen and Harry Norsk were already at their
desks drinking coffee and reading newspapers when
Tobias walked into the Investigations room. He
nodded a greeting to them. Katrine Skaarup was helping
Karl Lund attach photographs to a folding screen at the
other end of the room. The photographs had also been sent
electronically to Tobias's laptop. He could enlarge them at
will. But he liked to see each photograph in the context of
all the others. He poured himself a cup of coffee from the
dispensing machine by the door and walked over to the
display. He gazed at it for a moment before straightening
three of the aerial photographs and standing back to take
in the whole sequence. A dozen aerial shots showed an
expanse of land with rough grass, clumps of bushes, narrow
drainage channels, the pond, the taped-off area with the
yellow and white plane looking as though it could take off at
any moment, the white tent. There wasn't a house in sight.
A second sequence of photos showed the leathery foot, the
skull and various bones with scale measurements. Tobias
adjusted the photograph of the skull and stood back again.
A third sequence, all straight he was relieved to see, included
several images of the watch, the metal parts of a zip fastener,

the four copper buttons, a metal buckle and the ghost of a pair of trousers.

"Good morning, everyone." Chief Superintendent Larsen bustled in. Eddy and Harry put down their newspapers and got to their feet.

"It looks like we have a murder investigation on our hands," said Larsen. "I take it there's no possibility this death could have been accidental? Harry?"

"Not a chance. You can see in the photographs, the skull was cracked open. The forearm was broken in two places. Three ribs were broken. The small bones of the right hand were smashed. There is no way all that could have happened accidentally in marshy ground. He was beaten to death."

"What do we know about the victim?"

"The remains are of a young male aged between 20 and 26. He was the same height as Chief Inspector Lange – give or take a centimetre. He was killed between 1986 and 1999. It's impossible to say if he was killed in the bog or somewhere else."

Tobias moved to stand beside the array of photographs on the screen.

"Our theory is that the body was dumped in the pond and that water drained away, the pond got smaller, over time," he said. "The spot where it was found is about 400 metres from where the track ends. As you can see, the track winds down from the road for about a kilometre. Then it splits. To the right, it continues for about 300 metres to a hut used by the model aeroplane club. To the left, it runs for only about 80 metres, widens a bit, and then disappears into the bog. But you can see from this photo," Tobias indicated a line of white dots on a wide aerial shot of the track, "that this section was once about 100 metres longer."

"The regional planning office should be able to tell us when that part of the track was overgrown," said Larsen. "You think the victim was killed elsewhere, driven to the bog in some kind of vehicle and carried from the track to the pond? To me that says two people, or one very strong person. Almost certainly male."

"He hasn't seen the new desk sergeant at Randers," whispered Eddy.

Larsen glared at Eddy. But his lip twitched when he turned away.

"The victim was barefoot," said Tobias. "That could mean he was already in the bog."

"Or barefooted when he was carried there," said Karl Lund. "We've not found any trace of shoes."

"So tell me what you found," said Larsen. "Anything useful?"

"The team did a great job, sir," said Karl. "As you can see, Brix was able to assemble a complete skeleton from the bones. You can read his report. I printed out copies." Karl pointed to a buff folder on the table. He turned back to the photographs. "We also retrieved a watch, a bracelet, four copper buttons, a metal badge or medal, most of the teeth from a metal zip fastener, a belt buckle and the remains of a pair of trousers. We should have photographs of the bracelet later today."

"Right," said Larsen. "Any other clothes, or traces of clothes?"

"No obvious trace. We can analyse the peat for traces of fibres but I doubt we'll learn anything useful."

"What about DNA? Fingerprints?"

"We can try," said Karl. "But there's not much to go on. We're going to drag the pond. It's muddy on the bottom and too shallow for divers."

"Right," said Larsen. "Lange will lead the investigation." He paused. "What's the latest on the Danske bank robbery?"

"At least one member of the gang was sprayed with SmartWater when they exited the bank," said Eddy. "We can't get DNA from the van that was torched. We're still looking for the car they switched to. If that's got SmartWater DNA we might get a match and nail them. Alsing is liaising with forensics on that."

Eddy Haxen and Soren Alsing, the other chief inspector in the squad, had been working together on the bank robbery.

"Right. Chief Inspector Alsing can stay with the robbery enquiry," said Larsen. "You can work with Lange on this investigation, Haxen, with Skaarup in support as well. Lund and Norsk will liaise with Brix on forensics. Uniformed support as and when required. Follow the usual protocol for media enquiries. There's been a lot of interest already. It would be good to get this one cleared up quickly, and preferably," Larsen became emphatic, "without involving Copenhagen. This is now a national story. But I want it resolved here. I'm glad to see you are all nodding your approval of that sentiment." He paused. "How soon will we get an identification? Lange?"

Tobias felt like saying the superintendent's guess was as good as anybody's. Instead he said, "Skaarup has already begun a search. We can match age, height, sex, for a start."

The superintendent gave a quick nod. "Right. I'll leave you to get on with it." The door swung closed behind him.

"In Denmark alone," said Katrine, "there are 50 males in that age group missing, not found, between 1986 and 2000."

"Good luck," said Harry. "I'm off. Call me if you need me."

"That goes for me too," said Karl. "I'm going back out to Roligmose. I'll let you know if we find anything in the pond."

Eddy filled three cups of coffee from the machine. He handed a cup each to Katrine and Tobias.

"So, Katrine, fifty males missing in this country alone? They won't all fit the profile," said Tobias. "Who's on the shortlist?"

"I started with this region," said Katrine. "Six of them disappeared in East Jutland, including a Swedish tourist who disappeared on a booze cruise here. The assumption was he got drunk and fell overboard."

"Coming or going?" said Eddy. "Morning or evening?"

Katrine checked her notebook. "Morning. The eight o'clock sailing from Gothenburg to Friderikshaven. It arrives at 11.15." She stopped. "Drunk at 11 o'clock in the morning?"

"Definitely Swedish," said Eddy.

"So you're xenophobic as well as sexist," said Katrine. "I heard your remark about the desk sergeant at Randers, who happens to be a very nice person. She was at school with me."

"Loosen up," said Eddy.

"Give it a rest," said Tobias. "I can't hear myself think. Go on, Katrine."

"Three are from Aarhus. One from Randers. One from Silkeborg. Of the remaining forty-four, one is from North Jutland, two from South Jutland. The others are all from North Zealand or Copenhagen and district."

"We'll divide them between us," said Tobias.

By lunchtime, they had narrowed the list to twenty males aged between seventeen and thirty, around six feet tall, who had gone missing in the time frame established by Professor Brix.

"I need a break," said Tobias. He stood up and stretched. "Your turn to get the coffee, Katrine."

Eddy wandered over to the window and stood looking out at rain falling from a grey sky.

"I'm glad I'm not dragging the pond," he said. "I left the merchant navy because I hated getting wet."

"Why did you join it?" asked Tobias.

"To see the world. I dreamed about the South Seas and girls in grass skirts with flowers around their necks. But I ended up sailing back and forwards between Esbjerg and Harwich, mostly in the rain. So I joined the police instead. Now I stand around in the rain instead of sailing in it. What about you?"

"I was twenty-one, I was married with a child on the way. I had no money and I didn't want to work for my father-in-law," said Tobias.

"I wonder how many people join the police because they have a burning desire to uphold the law," said Eddy.

They watched Katrine manoeuvre her way through the desks balancing three polystyrene cups of coffee.

"I bet Skaarup did," said Eddy. "But she's toughening up. She's OK."

"We were all rookies once," said Tobias. "But it feels like a long time ago."

He had the cup halfway to his mouth when the telephone rang. He set down the cup and picked up the receiver.

"Chief Inspector?" said Birgitte's voice in his ear. "I have good news for you. The professor got a reply from Seiko. The watch was made in 1995."

Tobias beckoned to Eddy and Katrine. They moved to stand by his desk, watching his expression as he listened to Birgitte.

"I've cleaned the badge," she said. "It's enamel. Most of the colour has worn off. There are traces of green. And three raised letters. S S N. Maybe you can find out what they stand for?" She paused. "But I've got even better news." Now there was a note of triumph in her voice. "I've cleaned the bracelet. There's a date on it. 1997. It's solid silver. One centimetre thick and fifteen centimetres in diameter. I'd say it was expensive, and almost certainly made to order by a silversmith."

"How can you tell?" asked Tobias.

"It's hand engraved. The design on the outside is actually an inscription. It's in Danish. *'Encircled by your love.'* It was definitely done by hand, not a machine. There are initials on the inside, probably the silversmith's. I've sent a set of images to you."

"Thanks, Birgitte." Tobias put the phone down. He punched his fist into his palm. "Great. We have a lead on Bogman. The bracelet has a date on it. 1997. We can eliminate everyone who went missing before then. And that's not all."

He sat down at his laptop and enlarged the images Birgitte had sent him. "Take a look at this."

Eddy and Katrine read the inscription over his shoulder.

"Encircled by your love," said Katrine softly. "That's beautiful."

Tobias enlarged an image of the inside of the bracelet. "B H 1997, inside a circle," he said. "Probably the initials of the maker."

"So we're looking for a jeweller or silversmith with the initials B H," said Eddy. He was already halfway to his desk.

By six o'clock that evening, Eddy and Tobias had spoken to the Danish Design Centre, the Danish Jeweller's Association and the Guild of Danish Silversmiths. They had checked the initials of every jeweller in the Danish Business directory and had found Benny Henriksen, Brigita Holm, Benny Hagen. None of them had created a silver bracelet inscribed, 'Encircled by your love', although all of them thought it sounded like a great design.

"Maybe they're the victim's initials after all," said Eddy.

Katrine winnowed the list of missing males to five who went missing after 1997.

"Three of them don't have either a B or an H in their initials. One of them has H for Hans. Hans Meyer. But one has both initials. B H. Bruno Holst."

She turned her laptop around so that Tobias and Eddy could see the full-screen image of a thin-faced, bearded young man in torn jeans and a t-shirt. He crouched beside a motorcycle with a spanner in one hand. He wore an over-large wristwatch. He looked surprised, as though he hadn't expected to be photographed.

"Bruno Holst, aged twenty-three when he disappeared," said Katrine. "Six feet tall. A techie in an Internet service company in Randers. He lived with his girlfriend, Hanna Jensen, in a rented house. He left the house on foot on the evening of July 10th 1998 to go to a friend's flat. Hanna Jensen reported him missing the following morning when she realised he hadn't come home. He had no criminal record. There was no reason to suspect suicide. He was the father of a three-month old baby. He played a lot of computer games."

"A geek," said Eddy.

"He doesn't strike me as the kind of man who would wear a silver bracelet," said Katrine.

Tobias frowned. "Why not?"

She shrugged. "Like Eddy, says, he's a geek."

"So geeks don't wear bracelets?"

"I've met geeks who wear tecchie bracelets with gizmos on them, and oversized watches like the one this geek is wearing," said Katrine. "I've met good-looking geeks and even sexy geeks. But I've never met a romantic geek. I've not met one who'd wear a bracelet with an inscription like "Encircled by your love.""

Eddy whistled. "I'd no idea you got around so much, Skaarup."

Katrine flushed. "I'm just saying Bruno Holst doesn't look the romantic type."

"Don't close your mind to possibilities or jump to conclusions," said Tobias. "People are full of surprises. You have to back up your assertions with something stronger than your dating experience with geeks."

Katrine flinched. She stuck her chin out. "It's also an age thing. If you don't mind my saying so, older romantics don't wear bracelets either."

"Older romantics?" said Eddy. "This guy was twenty-three."

"Of course he's not old. I meant as a general rule, older romantics don't wear bracelets either."

"She must mean you, boss," said Eddy. "All cynics are romantics at heart."

"Who says I'm a cynic?" said Tobias. He grew brisk. "Who was the investigator?"

Katrine scrolled down the screen. "Pernille Madsen."

Tobias had been at CEPOL, the police college outside Copenhagen, at the same time as Pernille Madsen. He remembered a tall, athletic blonde with a musical voice and a big smile. All of the male cadets, including Tobias who was already married, had fancied her.

"I'll find out where she's stationed now and give her a call," he said.

8.

North Jutland Police District

Detective Pernille Madsen, Aalborg special investigations unit, took four plain postcards from her jacket pocket. On one of them she had written YES in block capitals, on another she had written NO, on the third she had written MAYBE, and on the fourth, DON'T KNOW. She placed the cards on the hospital bed-table in front of the patient propped up on pillows, hooked up to a drip, unable to speak because her upper and lower teeth were wired together to heal a broken jaw. Her left leg was in traction. She had three fractured ribs, and black, purple and yellow bruises on her left side and arm. Her left eye was a brown button in a duvet of yellow and black flesh. Her right eye was covered with a patch.

Pernille said, in a low, calm voice, "I'm going to ask you a series of questions, Jolene." Jolene? What kind of a name was that? Not the one on her birth certificate, that was for sure. Dolly Parton hadn't been singing 'Jolene Jolene' when this one was born. Probably good-looking before her face was smashed up. "You can answer Yes, No, Maybe or Don't Know by pointing to the appropriate card. The duty solicitor, Nils Soderborg, is here to witness your replies." Did she understand? Was there a flicker in that button of an eye? "Do you understand, Jolene?"

A hand rose limply from the bed and pointed to YES.

Nils Soderborg, who looked as though he'd got dressed in a hurry, as indeed he had, finished tucking his shirt into his trousers, positioned himself by the bed, stifled a yawn and said, "My client answers, yes."

"Good. We want to find the person who did this to you, Jolene. We'll do our best to find him." And lock him away for a long, long time. And throw the key into the canal. Pernille signalled to Detective Peter Lundquist on the other side of the bed to begin recording the interview.

"Interview with Jolene Karlsson," said Pernille, briskly. "Present are Detective Pernille Madsen, Detective Peter Lundquist and Nils Soderborg, lawyer for Jolene Karlsson. Did a man do this to you, Jolene?"

The limp hand again indicated YES.

"Yes," said Nils Soderborg.

"Was it your boyfriend?"

Jolene pointed to NO. Nils Soderborg voiced it.

"A client?"

YES.

"Did you pick him up in the street?"

NO.

"In a club?"

YES.

And so the interview proceeded. After forty-five minutes, a nurse slipped into the room.

"Your time is up. We said half an hour. You've had more than that. The doctor is on his rounds. He'll be here in a minute. You have to stop now."

"Five minutes," said Pernille. "We'll be five minutes. I'll just summarise what we've learned so far. Then we'll stop recording."

"If that's all right with Jolene," said the nurse. She raised her voice. "Is that all right, Jolene? We don't want you getting overtired."

Jolene lifted her right hand and pointed to YES.

"You met your attacker in The Vikings nightclub," said Pernille, speaking quickly. "He wore casual clothes and looked to be in his late forties or early fifties. He said his name was Jon. He spoke to you in Swedish. You walked with him to the room you rent in the next street. You thought you were going to have sex but he said he just wanted to take photos of you naked. He took several photographs of you. When you asked for payment he hit you and banged your head against the wall. You fought back. He broke your jaw. He gagged you with your panties. He used your bra to tie your hands together. He spread-eagled your legs and tied your feet to the bed frame with strips of black cloth he took from a briefcase. He took more pictures of you with a smartphone. He punched you in the face. He stopped to take pictures. He punched you again. He raped you with his fist. You became unconscious. When you came round, you heard him taking a shower in the adjoining bathroom. You managed to pull your hands free and untie your feet. You got out into the back alley but you fell. He followed you. He was dressed by this time. He kicked you. You heard a police siren. He stamped on your hand. He ran off. You lay in the alley until the refuse collectors found you and called an ambulance."

Jolene pointed to YES.

"Jolene Karlsson says yes," said Nils Soderborg.

"Fuck me," said the nurse.

Pernille, Peter Lundquist and Nils Soderborg had breakfast in the hospital café.

"Poor bloody cow," said Nils Soderborg. "I came in thinking it would be the usual drunken fight outside a club. A couple of young lads. Maybe an assault on a policeman or bouncer. I've not had something like this before."

"You're not long qualified," said Peter Lundquist. "Give it time."

Pernille smiled to herself. She was older than both of them.

"Will she have any visitors, do you think? Has she anyone at all looking out for her?" asked Nils.

"Her pimp, I suppose," said Peter.

"We don't even know her real name," said Pernille. "Whatever it is, it's not Jolene."

"People give their children all sorts of names," said Nils. "I acted last week for a shoplifter whose child was called Nike."

"That's a Greek name," said Peter. "Meaning Winged Victory." He was the star of a pub quiz team.

"It was Greek to the shoplifter anyway," said Nils. "Why would you call your child after a shoe?"

"Jolene is a Dolly Parton number," said Pernille. "It wasn't recorded until 1974. Our victim is forty-two. That's what she told them in casualty, before they wired her jaw."

"I bet you didn't know that Pernille is a singer," said Peter. "She sings with the Police Swing Band."

"Sounds offbeat."

"Arresting, even," said Peter.

"The next bad pun is going to cop it," said Pernille. "I'm off."

She was playing back the recorded interview with Jolene when Tobias telephoned.

"Tobias Lange. What a surprise. I haven't spoken to you in, well, I don't know how many years."

"It must be at least ten," said Tobias, who remembered clearly his last glimpse of Pernille slipping into a bedroom in the Thon conference hotel in Oslo with a Swedish academic who had earlier given a paper on Crime and Ethnicity.

"Oslo, 2002, I think," said Pernille, whose memory was equally clear. "We bumped into each other at a conference. I saw you on television last week, looking much the same I have to say. I assume this call is something to do with the body in the bog?"

"Correct," said Tobias. "You were the investigating officer in the case of," Tobias glanced at his notebook, "Bruno Holst, aged 23, reported missing in July 1998."

"Remind me," said Pernille.

"He worked for a technology company. He lived in Randers. His partner reported him missing when he didn't come home from visiting a friend."

"I remember," said Pernille. "It was the first case I worked on after I was made inspector. They had a child." She paused, remembering the claustrophobic flat, the angry girlfriend and the crying baby. "We never got anywhere with the case. It turned out he never went to his friend's place. As I recall, the friend wasn't expecting him. My feeling at the time was he felt trapped and did a runner. They'd only been

together a couple of months when she got pregnant, and..."
She stopped. "Well, that was my impression anyway."

Tobias had a memory flash. A tender, drunken encounter
with Pernille in a club in Copenhagen after an exam at CEPOL,
when he'd confessed to her he'd abandoned university and
joined the police solely to support his girlfriend and his soon-
to-be-born daughter. She had disentangled herself and slipped
away to rejoin a noisy group of cadets at the bar.

Now she said, "We made extensive enquiries. He had
no criminal record. He had no debts. He didn't do drugs.
There was no suggestion he was seeing anyone else. He
seemed like a typically introverted tecchie. You think he
might be your victim?"

"It's possible. He fits what we know. Male and aged
between 18 and 29. He went missing around the right
time. Between 1997 and 2000. We're hoping to get a bit
closer on the date."

"Good luck," said Pernille. "You can call up the file on
the case. If you want anything more, just let me know."

"It would be a lot easier if he was our victim," said
Tobias. "He disappeared in the right area."

There was a pause. Tobias found himself reluctant to
end the conversation. He wasn't sure if what he was feeling
was nostalgia, or residual tenderness for a woman he had
fancied but couldn't have.

"So what's keeping you busy these days, Pernille?"

"A bugger of a case," said Pernille. "We had a body
washed up on Saltholm. A female. Although you couldn't
have told at first. She'd been in the water for weeks. There
was no one reported falling overboard from a boat. We
checked with the coastguards and got an oceanographer

to plot the tides and currents. He worked out she'd been dumped into the sea at Hamburg."

"Dumped?"

"That's what we assumed. She had a lot of head injuries which we thought were from buffeting in the sea. Then our pathologist found there was no water in her stomach, no foam in her airways. She was probably dead when she went into the water. We finally identified her as a prostitute. Her fingerprints were on file in Hamburg. She was Russian. Ludmila Akulova. She'd been arrested for shoplifting. We got in touch with the police in Moscow. She came from a small town, but nobody had reported her missing. Not in Germany. Not in Russia." She fell silent for a few seconds. "What a life."

"What a death," said Tobias.

"Plus I've just been interviewing an assault victim," said Pernille. "Another prostitute. Beaten up by a client. A really nasty piece of work. He gagged her with her panties and beat her to within an inch of her life."

There was a pause.

"How's Karren? And your daughter? She must be grown up by now. She was a year old when you were at CEPOL, as I recall."

"Agnes is nineteen," said Tobias. He cleared his throat. "Karren and I divorced eight years ago." Without being asked he added, "there was nobody else involved, on my part anyway." He hesitated. "What about you, Pernille?"

"I married Erik Gunnersen. Do you remember him? He was a year ahead of us." She paused. "We were married for six years and all that time he was seeing someone else."

"Idiot," said Tobias. "Him, I mean. Not you."

There was a longer pause.

"Well," said Pernille. "If there's nothing else I can help you with, I'd better be getting along. I'm meeting someone for dinner."

The gently bantering tone of their conversation changed to something more formal. Tobias thanked Pernille for her help.

"I've just remembered one thing," she said. "It might not be important. I saw a plane go over just now and that reminded me. Bruno Holst flew model aeroplanes in his spare time."

Tobias sat up. "The guy who found the bones flew model aeroplanes. Do you have DNA?"

"There didn't seem any point. We didn't have a suspect or a body."

"We do now," said Tobias.

9.

THURSDAY: WEEK ONE

East Jutland Police Station

I f Bruno Holst was the body in the bog, who killed him? Tobias ruled out Torben Skov, the teenage flyer of model planes. Torben was eighteen, which would make him six, or younger, when the body was dumped in the bog. His uncle, Kenneth Skov, on the other hand, would have been in his early twenties. Tobias knew it might only be a coincidence that Bruno Holst was a model plane enthusiast and that his remains had been found by another enthusiast of approximately the same age. But he thought coincidences should always be explored. Which is why on Thursday morning he and Katrine Skaarup spent an hour with Kenneth Skov going over exactly how he had found a mummified foot while searching for the missing tail fin of his crashed glider.

"We started over by the hut," said Kenneth Skov. He spoke quickly. "It's about a kilometre from where I found the foot. Torben landed his Supercub and then I got my Tigermoth airborne. It's a flat field glider so I can fly it with planes. You can't always fly both together. I got it up with a tug plane. It caught a thermal and rose very high. It flew well for about five minutes. I did a loop. Then I did a couple of somersaults. I was flying it east. Almost out of sight. Then it went into a cloud and I shouted to Torben could he see it and he said no. Then I thought bloody hell, I've lost it and it's going to crash."

"How far away was it?" asked Katrine.

"I already told you. About a kilometre, at least. I wouldn't normally go over there. The ground is marshy and most of the bushes have thorns." Kenneth here displayed hands covered in scratch marks. "But the tail fin was missing and I thought it might be in the bushes so I scrabbled through them. Nothing. But when I got through the bushes to the other side, I saw the foot. Dark brown. Like a big lump of liquorice. At first I thought it was a piece of bog wood, you know the way they have funny shapes sometimes? But when I looked more closely I saw it was a foot. I texted Torben and he came over. It took him a while because he had to go a long way up the bank of a stream to cross over to me. And when he saw it he said it was a bog body like Tollund Man in the museum at Silkeborg. So we called the police."

"You called the television people first," said Katrine. She was enjoying herself. Tobias was allowing her to lead the interview. Her first formal interview, with video recording, of a possible witness in a murder investigation. She couldn't wait to tell her parents.

"We thought he was going to be another Tollund Man. We didn't know the poor bugger had been done in."

"How do you know he was done in?"

"Because it said so on the television."

"We haven't released any statement yet," said Tobias.

"They were speculating. I definitely heard them speculating he was murdered."

"How do you know it was a he?" asked Katrine.

"There aren't many women flying model planes."

"So you think he was a member of your club?" said Tobias.

"Maybe. I don't know. Until I know who he is I won't know if he was a member or not, will I?"

"Has any member of the club gone missing?" asked Katrine.

Kenneth shrugged. "Not that I know of. I've been a member for ten years. People come and go all the time."

"How many members are there?"

"I don't know. Maybe about forty? There isn't a formal club with meetings and agendas and stuff. People just turn up. It's usually a mixture of the same faces. I've told you everything I know. If I remember anything else, I'll tell you. All right? Can I go now?"

Katrine glanced at Tobias.

"Yes. You can go," said Tobias. "When you've given us all the names and addresses of everyone you know in the club."

"I don't know their addresses. I fly with Torben and a couple of mates. I know where my mates live. But I don't know about the others. You can't keep me here."

"So who knows? Isn't there a club secretary or someone?"

Kenneth Skov looked blank for a few moments. "There might be names and addresses on the petition," he said.

Tobias sat forward. "What petition?"

"About ten years ago. Before I started flying there. They were going to put restrictions on people who used the bog. The club sent a petition to the Regional Council. But I told you. That was before my time. Now can I go?"

"Yes, yes," said Tobias. "But tell us if you're planning to fly off anywhere."

Kenneth Skov gave him a look, but Tobias had a straight face.

When he left the interview room, Katrine said, "Do you think it's possible Bruno Holst killed someone in the model aeroplane club and that's the real reason he disappeared?"

"Motive?"

"Maybe they committed a robbery together. Maybe they used model planes to smuggle stuff?"

"You wouldn't fly stuff far in a model plane."

"You know what I mean. Where do they buy the planes? Maybe stuff comes through customs in a model plane." Her shoulders slumped. "No. That doesn't work. Those things are expensive. They wouldn't be buying them all the time."

"Check the details of the other missing males who match the victim's description," said Tobias. "Could any of them have known Bruno Holst? Were any of them model plane enthusiasts? And get a copy of the petition the model aeroplane buffs sent to the planners." He smiled. "Imagination is a good thing in a detective, Katrine."

There were two petitions about Roligmose. One from the model aeroplane club and one from a hunting club. The Planning Department emailed the documents to Katrine. She was checking the names and addresses on the petitions against the list of missing persons when Eddy tapped her on the shoulder.

"That can wait, Skaarup. Get your coat. We're going to the hospital. The Sexual Assault Centre."

Katrine snatched her jacket from a hook on the wall and hurried after him.

10.

They were met by the doctor on duty, Josefine Bro. She had round glasses and a ponytail. Eddy thought she looked about the same age as his daughter who was sixteen and still at school.

"I've worked here for the last three years," she said. "I've seen victims of rape and domestic violence. But I've not seen anything like this. She has serious, multiple bruising. Nearly all her ribs are broken. She has a black eye." Dr Bro suddenly looked and sounded a lot older. "She has internal injuries as well."

"Has she said who did it?" asked Eddy.

Doctor Bro shook her head. "She was left at the door of the Emergency Room. Dumped like a sack out of the back of a van, according to the ambulance driver who saw it. She was naked, except for some kind of kimono. She won't say who beat her. It was probably her husband or boyfriend. It usually is. But at least she consented to photographs. We always take photographs in case there's a prosecution. Come and take a look."

In her office, she touched the screen on her computer. An image flashed up. Katrine felt a rush of vomit into her throat. She turned away and put her hand over her mouth. She swallowed bile and made herself look at the screen. Her mouth dried.

"She is wearing a bracelet with the name Girlie," said the doctor. "She answers to that name, but she won't tell us anything else. She has no bag, no purse, and no identification. She has only a few words of Danish. She can speak a little English."

"Did anyone get the number of the van?" asked Eddy.

"Maybe the ambulance driver," said the doctor. "I don't know."

She led Eddy and Katrine to a room where a small figure sat bunched in a high-backed chair, motionless as a doll. She looked less bad in the flesh than in the photographs. A hospital social worker had given her tracksuit trousers, a T-shirt and a thick woollen cardigan which concealed the bruises on her body. She had regained some colour in her cheeks. The swelling around her right eye had subsided, although the eye itself was still puffy and closed.

Eddy positioned himself against the back wall of the room and nudged Katrine forwards.

Katrine crouched and put one hand on the arm of the chair. She said slowly, in English: "My name is Katrine. I am a police officer. Your name is Girlie. Is that correct?"

The doll-like figure's lips moved. Katrine leaned closer to hear the whispered, "Yes."

"Who did this to you, Girlie?"

A tear trickled from the unswollen eye. Girlie lifted her hand to wipe it away. She wore a wedding ring.

"Did your husband do this?'

Girlie whispered, "No."

"Whoever did this is a very bad person. We need to stop him doing this again."

Girlie closed her good eye. Her mouth tightened.

"If you tell us who did this, we can stop him doing it again to you or anyone else."

Girlie turned her head away.

Eddy slipped out of the room to speak to the doctor hovering in the corridor.

"She's frightened of whoever did it," he said. "Probably her husband. Although she denies it."

"Almost certainly her husband," said Doctor Bro. "I've seen this kind of thing before, although not as bad as this. They won't leave their husbands until they get residency. They're afraid of being deported."

"She could be an illegal," said Eddy. "Either way, we need to tell Immigration."

"What will happen to her?"

"If she's illegal, she'll be deported," said Eddy. "If she tells us who did this, we'll arrest him. If it's her husband and she's been here longer than two years, she might be allowed to stay."

He went back into the room. He stood over the crumpled figure in the chair.

"It's an offence to withhold information about a crime," he said in a stern voice. "Assault is a serious crime. Who did this to you, Girlie?"

Girlie bit her lip and looked away.

"We have to tell Immigration about you," Eddy said.

He saw her body stiffen.

"It will help you if you talk to us first," he said in a softer tone.

He thought there was a flicker of response. But Girlie didn't speak. She closed her eyes.

Eddy and Katrine exchanged glances. Eddy shrugged. Girlie gave a little snore. Her body was limp.

"We could be here all day," Eddy muttered. "We have to speak to the ambulance driver and I still have that report to finish." He shepherded Katrine into the corridor. He had his phone out, ready to call Immigration.

They called into Doctor Bro's office before leaving the Sexual Assault Centre.

"She's asleep," said Eddy. "And she's not any more helpful when she's awake. An Immigration officer will be here in about twenty minutes to interview her. And we'll send a uniformed officer to keep an eye on her."

"You hardly need to," said Doctor Bro. "She's not fit to go anywhere at the moment."

"In that case," said Eddy. "We'll leave you in peace."

They found the ambulance driver enjoying a quick cigarette in the parking bay outside the emergency room.

"It happened so fast," he said. "The van pulled up. She was pushed out. I was coming on duty. I rushed over to her. I didn't have time to check the number plate. It was a white van. Not new."

Eddy said, "Did you see the driver? Was he alone?"

"There was a woman with him," said the driver. "White van. White driver. Black woman in the passenger seat. Big shoulders. She was the one who did the dumping."

"You're sure it was a woman?"

The ambulance driver cupped his hands at chest level and winked. "I'm sure."

"But she didn't get out of the van?"

The ambulance driver shook his head. "Just pushed her out." He sucked on his cigarette. "Maybe she was an illegal. You see a lot of things in this job. We got called out to an emergency last year. There was no one at the address when we got there except a woman with a burst appendix. Everyone else had scarpered. Illegals, every one of them."

Eddy glanced around the parking bay. No CCTV. Pity. The driver was probably correct. The victim was an illegal, beaten up by her husband or boyfriend and taken to hospital by a friend, also an illegal.

"Immigration will probably want to speak to you," he said.

"They know where to find me," said the driver. He extinguished his cigarette with a flick of his thumb and threw the stub into a bin. "Pity they're not better at finding illegal immigrants."

Katrine was scrolling through the Missing Persons list when Eddy took a call from Immigration. Katrine heard him groan and slap his desk.

"You can add another missing person to the list," he said. "Girlie disappeared from the hospital before Immigration could speak to her."

They tossed for which one of them was going to tell Larsen. Katrine lost.

Larsen was icily angry. "You're only here a week and you manage to fuck-up. I should send you straight to Traffic Control. I have enough politicians bleating about immigration. I don't need them to know we let an illegal slip out of our hands."

"She might not be illegal, sir."

"And pigs might fucking fly, Skaarup. She could have helped us find out who got her into the country. Why weren't you watching her?"

"A constable was on the way, sir. But she was gone when he got there."

"Why didn't you wait for him?"

"She was asleep and the doctor thought she was too injured to go anywhere. She never moved while I was there. I'm amazed she could walk."

"Blood lazy of you. Bloody careless of you. I don't need lazy and careless detectives. This is a black mark against you. And Haxen as well. I suppose you tossed for who was going to tell me and you lost? Screw up once more and you're off my team. That goes for both of you."

"I'm sorry, sir."

Larsen calmed down. "If these people don't have the wit to see that they're better off talking to us and getting the abusers locked up, then I don't know what we're supposed to do. Now bugger off. And don't fuck up again." He waved her away.

Katrine spent five minutes in the washroom dabbing her tears away.

"Why do you want to join the police?" Katrine's best friend had asked in astonishment when Katrine confided that she wanted be a detective. "It's not a flattering uniform. Especially with those bulky vests. You have a nice figure, Katrine. But I suppose if you're a detective you can wear your own clothes." Linda had tossed her hair back and adjusted her skirt. Linda was now assistant manager of a hotel in Skagen. They were still good friends.

Katrine's parents were equally puzzled by her choice of career. No member of the family, for as far back as they could remember, had been in the police force or any other job in a uniform. They were all independent-minded dairy farmers.

"At least it's a good job with a pension," said her father. "But it's a pity you have to leave the island."

Since leaving Bornholm had been Katrine's primary ambition, she just smiled and promised to come home as often as she could. She was a dutiful daughter. She'd been a diligent student. She was determined to be a good detective. But in her first few weeks in the Investigations Unit, she had felt as though she was always missing the point, was trying too hard, was patronised by Tobias and Eddy. Larsen's threat rang in her ears. She looked at herself in the mirror. Pull yourself together, Skaarup. She checked her eyes in the mirror. Her face was white but her eyes were only slightly pink. She straightened her shoulders and made her way back to the Investigations room.

Eddy looked up when she came in. "How was it?"

Katrine shrugged. "Not too bad."

"So he shouted and raged and threatened to fire you if you fucked up again?"

Katrine smiled. Her eyes were bright with unshed tears.

"Well done," said Eddy. "You've survived your first bollocking." He stood up and clapped her on the back. "Join the club."

Katrine felt it had almost been worth it.

11.

FRIDAY: WEEK ONE

Tobias carefully arranged the photographs of the skull, bones and mummified foot to make a complete skeleton in the centre panel of the screen. He closed the other two panels. He straightened the photograph at the top. A white skull with a fan of white teeth, and black holes where once there had been eyes and a nose. He stepped back and stared at it.

"Who are you, Bogman?" he questioned silently. "Who killed you? Why?"

The skull grinned back at him.

"'Encircled by your love.' Who felt like that about you?"

He had given Karren a silver bracelet for her twenty-first birthday, not long after they were married. He couldn't afford gold. He'd noticed Agnes wearing it a few times. He supposed Karren had given it to her. Not wanting to wear the memory of a marriage gone sour.

The file on Bruno Holst had arrived on his desk. He squared the buff coloured folder and opened it. Pernille had stuck a post-it note to the opening page. "Nice to be in touch again. Good luck. P". He tidied the note into the section of a desk drawer in which he filed personal notes and reminders. He read each page in the folder.

Bruno Holst and his girlfriend had a three-month-old baby girl. What age would she be now? He sat back and closed his eyes, remembering Karren's angry shouts, four week old Agnes crying in her cot, the bills spread out on the kitchen table, his overwhelming impulse to run out of the flat and take great gulps of air. He was unaware of the background noise in the office, of Katrine's curious stare at his closed fingers clenched against the edge of the desk. He opened his eyes. He flicked back through the file to the statement by Bruno Holst's mother, Hannelore Schmidt. The marriage was unhappy, she'd said. But she was sure her son would not have killed himself. She had no idea where he was. She'd given her statement to police in Germany. She had re-married and moved to Berlin some years before Bruno went missing. There was an address and a telephone number. On an impulse, Tobias picked up the telephone and tapped out the number. A woman's voice answered.

"Schmidt."

Tobias, in German, asked to speak to Bruno Schmidt.

"Wer spricht?"

Tobias said he was from the flying club and was calling about a model aeroplane.

Hannelore Schmidt tutted annoyance and said she didn't know why he had given her number when he knew he was only staying with her for a few days. She dictated Bruno's mobile phone number and said a brisk goodbye.

Tobias dialled the number she had given him.

"Schmidt."

"Bruno Schmidt?"

"Ja."

"Bruno Holst Schmidt?"

Silence.

"It is not a criminal offence to run away from your girlfriend and your child," said Tobias. "It is, however, a criminal offence to withhold information from the police. I am a police officer investigating a murder committed around 15 years ago. Are you Bruno Holst who went missing from Randers fifteen years ago?"

Silence.

"The body of a man was found in East Jutland on Monday. The body fits your description. I merely want to establish that you are not the victim. That you are alive."

"I'm alive," said Bruno Holst.

12.

"So we're no further on than we were yesterday." Eddy stared despondently at a yellow crane hovering idly over an empty dock in the harbour.

"On the bright side," said Katrine, "Bruno Holst's case is closed and there's one less person on the missing list."

"Big deal," said Eddy.

"At least I'm getting on with stuff. I'm working my way through the petitions to the Planning Department. From the model aeroplane club and from a hunting club. Checking the names and addresses against missing persons. Apart from Bruno Holst, no match so far."

"No surprise, and not much use," said Eddy.

"Not much use being negative either," said Katrine.

Harry Norsk, Karl Lund and Professor Brix arrived for a three o'clock briefing. They gazed silently at the skeleton, now flanked by photographs of the watch, the bracelet, the buttons, the badge, the gossamer trousers and aerial photographs of the bog.

"We know Bogman was aged between 20 and 28 and was about 1 metre 70 tall," Tobias began. "He wore a Seiko watch, an expensive silver bracelet and an enamel badge, presumably pinned to his shirt or jacket, with the letters SSN. The jacket had vintage Levi buttons and was most likely made of cotton denim. His clothing was cotton or wool, except for his trousers which contained some polyester. He was probably in barefoot when he was beaten to death. Why wasn't he wearing shoes?"

"Maybe he wasn't barefoot," said Harry. "Maybe he was wearing some kind of canvas shoe that decomposed."

"He wore mostly cotton," said Katrine. "He might have had concerns about the environment. Maybe he was a vegetarian. Some of them won't wear leather shoes."

Tobias nodded. "Good thought. Suppose he was wearing something like canvas deck shoes, or espadrilles? Would they have decomposed, Professor Brix? "

"The left shoe, if it was biodegradable, could have decomposed. You might find metal eyelets if it was a shoe with laces, but not if it was all cotton and rope, like an espadrille. On the mummified foot, I'd expect to find something. But there wasn't even a microscopic trace of any material on it."

"Why would he be barefoot?" asked Eddy. "Was it summer? If he was killed in the bog, what was he doing there?"

"Maybe he was flying a model plane," said Harry.

"The petition from the flying club to the Regional Council, about access to the bog, is dated 23rd June 1998," said Katrine.

"That fits the time frame for the murder," said Tobias.

"I've spoken to all the signatories except for six who have moved away. I'm still tracing them. The ones I've spoken to all say the same thing. They don't recall any member of the club going missing. Two of them think they remember Bruno Holst. But people came and went all the time. Just like Kenneth Skov said."

Professor Brix glanced at his phone and slipped out of the room.

"What was the reason for restricting access to the bog?" asked Tobias.

"Otters," said Katrine. "Conserving the otter population. The flyers won their appeal."

"Maybe he was hunting otters. Or trying to photograph them," said Karl."

"The hunting club lost their appeal," said Katrine. "The club was disbanded afterwards."

"Did they have a badge or logo?" asked Tobias.

"There was a shield with Randers and District Sporting Association on the letter header. The letters on the shield are R D S A."

"The letters on the badge are S S N," said Tobias. "Let's assume Bogman belonged to, or supported some kind of club, or team or organisation with those initials."

"There's nothing I can find in this country with those initials," said Eddy. "Nothing with a website, nothing on any list of organisations. There's a Dutch economic association, an American publishing company and a Norwegian bank. They all have the initials S S N."

"Contact all of them. Find out if they have a member or employee who went missing," said Tobias.

"It's unlikely. But we should cover all possibilities." He paused. "Let's concentrate on the bracelet. Who gave Bogman the bracelet?"

"A girlfriend or wife. Someone who loved him enough to give him an expensive bracelet engraved with 'Encircled with your love,'" said Katrine.

"But she didn't report him missing," said Eddy. "If she loved him that much, why didn't she report him missing? What about the Swede who went overboard?"

"He doesn't have either of the initials on the bracelet," said Katrine. "Only one missing male who fits the profile has either of those initials. H. Hans Meyer. Went missing in July 1998."

"Maybe the letter B is his girlfriend's initial," said Eddy.

"There's no mention of a girlfriend in his file."

"So maybe he's an arse bandit," said Eddy.

"I'll check if he had a male partner," said Katrine.

"Girlfriend, boyfriend," said Tobias. "It makes no difference. The point is, whoever gave Bogman the bracelet didn't report him missing."

"Maybe they'd split up," said Katrine. "Maybe he's not Danish. I'll check Interpol for missing persons as well."

"Maybe he or she killed him," said Eddy.

Professor Brix came back into the room. He was bouncing with satisfaction. "Birgitte has cleaned and identified coins found when the pond was dragged," he announced. "Two kroner," he paused. "And two Swedish decimal coins dated 1997 and 1994."

"A Swedish silversmith," said Eddy.

"Or victim," said Katrine.

"I'll tell Larsen," said Tobias.

13.

"A foreign national," said the Chief Superintendent. "That's all we bloody need. A foreign bloody national." He drummed his fingers on the desk. "Can you be sure there are no missing Danish nationals who fit the victim profile?"

"None that has been reported missing, sir," said Tobias.

"Any other reason, apart from the coins, to indicate he's Swedish?"

"Not yet. The letters on the badge don't fit any organisation, here or anywhere else in Europe. We found Danish as well as Swedish coins. He could be a Swedish national reported missing in Sweden but not in Denmark. Presumably because no one knew he was here."

"No one knows anything, as far as I can see," said Larsen.

Tobias knew better than to say they knew more than they'd known at the beginning of the week.

"Get in touch with the Swedish police. I'll speak to Foreign Affairs," said Larsen. "But if any Swedish nationals went missing in Denmark, I'd expect the name to be on every region's list of missing persons. That kind of thing is always circulated." He glanced at the clock. "They'll all have gone home. And it's Friday. Well, the poor bugger has waited fifteen years to be found and identified. He can wait until Monday. Enjoy the weekend, Lange. Anything planned?"

"I'm going to a charity event, sir," said Tobias. "Raising money for street children in the Philippines and a drop-in centre here."

"Good, good," said Larsen. "The commissioner likes us to get involved in charity work. That reminds me. Did

Immigration find that woman Skaarup and Haxen let slip out of their hands at the hospital?"

"I'm not sure, sir."

"Keep an eye on it, would you? She might be an illegal, but an assault is an assault and I don't like it on my patch."

Katrine and Eddy had already left when Tobias emerged from Larsen's office. He picked up the telephone and tapped in Peter Karlssen's number in Immigration.

"If you mean the Filipina who was dumped at the Assault Centre, the one called Girlie, your lot aren't the only ones in trouble over that. I'm in the doghouse as well," Karlssen told him. "We searched the hospital and found her hiding in a storeroom in the basement. We took her back to the Assault Centre. The doctor said she was too weak to be interviewed. I was waiting for uniform branch to turn up and keep an eye on her. I can only have turned my head for a couple of seconds."

"You mean a nurse turned your head." Tobias had worked with Karlssen before. "You were chatting up a nurse."

"OK. I was chatting to a nurse. Long legs, big tits. We were only a few metres away. I looked in to check on her and she was gone. Vanished. Searched the hospital again. Gone. I got a right bollocking for it."

"Are you still looking for her?"

"We're checking the usual places. Refugee support centres, homeless charities. Nobody knows anyone called Girlie. Officially, we're still looking. Unofficially, I think she was working in an illegal brothel. We could go looking for it but what's the point? We have enough work on our hands."

"Let me know if she turns up," said Tobias. "Have a good weekend."

He telephoned Pernille Madsen. There was no answer. He sent an email: "You'll be interested to know Bruno Holst is alive and living in Germany. Your instinct was correct. I've amended the file. Tobias."

The evening stretched out in front of him. He wondered if his father's dinner jacket would still fit him. He hadn't worn it since his stepsister Margrethe's wedding party in London. He could ask Hilde to tell him if he looked alright in it. That would make a change from the usual invitation to join him for a glass of wine. Same message, different code. He took his mobile phone from his pocket.

"Hi, Hilde. Can you take a look at a dinner jacket I'm having to bring out of hibernation?"

"Sure," said Hilde. "Bring it over tomorrow morning around ten o'clock. Erik's here, which was a nice surprise for me. He'll give you an honest opinion as well."

So her husband had come back earlier than expected. He was almost certainly in the room with her, maybe able to overhear the conversation as well.

"Thanks, Hilde," said Tobias.

He felt unsettled. He'd been relying on the energetic Hilde to fill his evening. He glanced at the sky. It would be dark in an hour. There wasn't the time to drive out of the city and play a few holes of golf. He saw he had a text message from Eddy. "Outside bar Friederiskgade. Join us?"

His spirits lifted. He fancied a bit of company. He could probably persuade Eddy and whichever woman was with him – Tobias could not keep up with Eddy's chronic pursuit of unsuitable women – to go somewhere quieter than one of the noisiest streets in Aarhus.

It was a dry, sunny evening. The wind ushering high clouds across the sky had a hint of warmth in it. The riverside bars and cafés were filling up. He found Eddy sitting outside a bar contemplating a pint of lager. Tobias looked around. The other outside tables were occupied by couples.

"Who's 'us'? I thought you were with someone."

"Skaarup's inside," said Eddy. "There's a Swedish Country Band playing tonight. They haven't started yet. The bar manager is Swedish. He says there'll definitely be Swedes turning up to hear the band. Katrine thinks there's a chance some of them, or one of the musicians, might recognise the badge. Good idea, isn't it?" He grinned and raised his glass.

"You can buy me a Pils," said Tobias.

Inside the bar, Katrine was seated at a table, trying to get a half-sober Swedish musician to look again at the picture of the badge. He didn't speak Danish so they communicated in English.

"It is a little familiar," he said, with reasonable enunciation. "But I don't know what it is. Will you have a drink?"

"Try to remember. Is it the badge of a football team? Or a sports club?"

The musician shook his head. He had reddish-blond hair that tumbled to his shoulders.

"I think I saw it somewhere, maybe a long time ago," he said. "But I don't remember where. My name is Dusty Svenson. What is your name?"

Katrine handed him a card with her name, rank and mobile phone number.

"Call me if you remember," she said.

"May I call you even if I don't remember?" said Dusty Svenson. He winked, slid the card under his glass on the table, picked up the guitar he had put to one side and began to pick out a tune.

Katrine pushed back her chair and stood up. "We're investigating a murder," she said sternly. "We don't know the victim's identity but we have reason to believe he might be Swedish."

Dusty Svenson put aside his guitar.

"He was beaten to death about twelve or thirteen years ago," said Katrine. "We need to find out who he was and who killed him. He was wearing this badge when he died. You said you might have seen it before."

Dusty closed his eyes and beat his fists against his head. "It's no good. It will not come to me. If I remember, I call you for sure." He stowed the photograph in the inside pocket of his jacket. "Good luck."

Eddy was standing at the bar. Katrine joined him.

"I've shown the badge to every Swedish person here. I've pinned a photo of it up there." She pointed to a noticeboard on the wall.

The barman slid two glasses of beer towards Eddy.

"The boss is waiting for his beer," said Eddy. I've bought you one as well, Skaarup."

They went outside.

"Well done, Skaarup," said Tobias. "Good thinking." He raised his glass in salute. "Cheers."

From inside the bar came the sound of a band tuning up.

"I like country music," said Eddy. "Gambling, cheating, drinking, jealousy, murder, loss."

14.

SATURDAY: WEEK ONE

Tobias needed luck to get out of the steep-sided bunker guarding the ninth green at Skovlynd. He had driven his ball safely over the lake, only to see it drop into the sand. Sofie, his playing partner, had driven two balls in succession into the water before giving up with a shrug and a cheery call to Tobias, "It's up to you now, partner." The other two golfers in the four-ball – Norbert and a former colleague of Sofie's called Hannah who was an excellent, if taciturn, golfer – had driven their balls to the rough grass at the edge of the green and were still a long way from the flag. Tobias steadied himself, hovered the club over the sand behind the ball, muttered to himself, "keep your head down," and swung the wedge. The ball flew up in a flurry of sand, cleared the edge of the bunker, landed on the green and rolled to within half a metre of the flag.

Hannah and Norbert chipped their balls to within two metres of the flag, but missed their putts. Tobias confidently sank his ball.

"Good par," said Norbert. "Keep this up and you'll win a prize."

"Only in the raffle," said Tobias.

But from then on, every ball he hit flew straight and true. He had never played better. Four hours later, he and Sofie stood on a podium to receive third prizes in the competition – a pink cashmere golf sweater for Sofie, a navy cashmere golf sweater for Tobias, a bottle of Louis Roederer Cristal each – from one of the stars of a television soap opera who now shook Tobias vigorously by the hand. Tobias had seen the man's face in the newspapers but had never watched the show. A photographer bounded forward to capture the actor kissing Sofie on the cheek.

Sofie blew kisses, smiled and acknowledged congratulations as they weaved their way back through the tables to their seats.

"You seem to know everybody in the room," said Tobias.

"Of course I do. I'm in PR. It's my job." Sofie returned a wave from the deputy leader of the Centre party.

When they finally got back to their seats, there were more congratulatory hugs and handshakes from Norbert and Hannah.

The dining room in the clubhouse was laid out in long rectangular tables each seating twelve guests. Tobias sat opposite Sofie at one end of a table. Norbert and Hannah sat beside them. At the other end of the table, Tobias recognised the mayor of Aarhus and a politician in the Green Party called Nicholas Hove who exchanged a cordial salute with Norbert.

"Hove has changed his tune," said Norbert quietly. "He was one of the protesters who wanted to stop this golf course being built."

Tobias glanced at the apple-cheeked man in the too-tight dinner jacket.

"Kurt invited him because of his wind farm project. And also because he's going into politics," said Sofie. "You never know whose support you're going to need in a coalition."

"True enough," said Tobias, absentmindedly. He was thinking about Agnes. Was she still camping out in the forest? At least the weather was better. It hadn't rained all day and the wind was from the south.

"If the way to a man's vote is through his stomach, Malling will do well in politics," said Norbert. "That was an excellent dinner."

"Kurt always puts on a good spread," said Sofie. "He understands the importance of public relations. Which is why he's such an easy client. Wouldn't you say, Hannah?"

A burst of applause signalled the end of the prize-giving. Talk broke out. The mayor beckoned to Norbert.

A small dance band – piano, trumpet, double bass and drums – set up on the podium and began playing a rhumba. Tobias tapped his feet under the table in response to the beat. They met Sofie's feet.

"Sorry," he made a little gesture of apology.

Sofie smiled. She moved her shoulders with the music.

The actor led an elegant blonde in a long black dress to the space created for dancing. Chairs scraped on the floor. Tobias moved to get up, but Kurt Malling was already drawing Sofie to her feet. She sashayed away from him.

"The early worm catches the bird," said Hannah.

Tobias glanced quickly at her. Her expression was as innocent as her tone but he thought she was secretly laughing at him.

"It happens all the time," said Hannah. "It's been happening since I was in Kindergarten with Sofie. The boys queued to walk home with her."

Tobias couldn't stop himself. "Did she prefer the rich ones then as well?" To his own ears he sounded churlish and sulky, as though he was four years old instead of forty.

"Kurt Malling is our biggest client," said Hannah. "Sofie is an excellent business woman."

Tobias got to his feet. "Would you like to dance, Hannah?"

"I'm not a consolation prize."

Hannah's tone was light but her cheeks were flushed. Tobias saw he had hurt her pride.

"I hate all this black tie, stuffed shirt hoo-ha, but I love dancing. Humour me."

She shrugged. "If you like."

Tobias studied her face as they danced.

"Well? What do you detect in my features?"

"I haven't seen you smile," he said. "You didn't smile on the golf course."

"My game wasn't up to scratch."

"You play well," he said.

"I'm out of practice."

"So am I," said Tobias.

"Really? I'd never have guessed." Her lips twitched. Her eyes were definitely laughing at him.

She was really rather attractive, Tobias thought. Big breasts. Easy company. He glanced at her hands drumming the air. No wedding ring. No ring of any kind. The music stopped

"Maybe we could have dinner some time," he said.

Hannah smiled. "I'd like that. But my girlfriend might object."

Before Tobias could add words to his apologetic shrug, she slipped away to speak to a friend.

He made his way back to the table. Sofie was already seated. Malling was on his feet, talking to the police commissioner.

"Ah, Lange," said the commissioner. "Working hard I see," he laughed genially and clapped Tobias on the shoulder. "I like to see my officers enjoying themselves, mixing with the wider world. You can get too narrow and jaundiced a view of life when you're only dealing with criminals."

Tobias felt like saying there were criminals in all walks of life. Fortunately, the commissioner had already turned away and was busy greeting another politician whose face Tobias recognised but whose name he could not recall. He sat down.

"That will have done you no harm," said Sofie.

"Dancing is good exercise," he said blandly.

Sofie stared at him. "You know exactly what I mean, but you deliberately misinterpret me. Meeting the commissioner socially is good for your career. You know that perfectly well. But you won't admit it. You think you're above that kind of thing. You want to be promoted entirely on your merits. Well, the world doesn't always work like that."

Tobias flinched inwardly. She had touched a nerve. He glanced around. There was no one else at the table.

"Any man who's good at his job wants to be promoted. To go as far as he can," said Sofie.

"At least you think I'm good at my job."

"Well, aren't you?"

There was no right answer. If he said no, he'd be lying. If he said yes, he would have to concede that he wanted promotion.

"If you're too proud for office politics," said Sofie, "you should run your own business."

"Like you?"

She shrugged. "I'm my own boss."

"And Hannah?"

"We started the business together. She looks after all the sports clients. I look after business and politics."

"Which are often connected," said Tobias. "Which is how the world works." He felt dispirited.

"Denmark is probably the least corrupt country in the world," said Sofie sharply. "All I do is smooth the path of business. I persuade people to listen to my clients and persuade my clients to listen, or at least give the appearance of listening to their opponents."

Tobias couldn't help glancing at Kurt Malling, now dancing with the blonde woman in the black dress whom he took to be the Mrs Malling who liked to do things in style.

"Kurt is a case in point," said Sofie. "There was a lot of opposition to this golf course. I was still at college at the time, of course. But I gather Kurt met it head on at first. Bad idea." She shook her head. "There were arrests and demonstrations. That isn't the way to do things. Now there's opposition to the wind farm on the west coast. My advice to Kurt is, listen to the arguments, be nice to the protestors, invite them to lunch. If you use the velvet glove you shouldn't need the iron hand."

"I'm glad to hear it." Tobias smiled. He didn't think either Agnes or her boyfriend would be easily bought for the price of a lunch with Kurt Malling.

There was the plinking of a fork rapped on a glass. The dancers returned to their tables. Silence fell. Kurt Malling thanked the guests for their support. The draw for raffle prizes had taken place. The winning cards were pinned to the prizes on the table in the entrance hall. He wished his guests a safe journey home. Sofie was spending the night at her father's house. Hannah was going to her parent's house in Silkeborg. Tobias was driving back to Aarhus.

"We should have driven up together," said Sofie. "I could have been company for you on the way back."

And something more, her demure tone seemed to imply.

High maintenance, thought Tobias. Great fun, but high maintenance. Did he have the energy for her?

"Another time, perhaps" he said.

Sofie and Hannah went to get their coats. Norbert lingered in the dining room for a last word with the mayor. Tobias glanced at his raffle card, the Six of Hearts. He joined the guests milling around the long oak table in the hall, uttering little cries of delight or moans of disappointment. He cast his eye over the cards attached to sets of wine glasses, bottles of champagne, golf bags, golf shoes, golf caps and mysterious envelopes. To his surprise, for he could not remember ever having won a raffle prize, the Six of Hearts was pinned to an important-looking envelope. Inside, were two tickets to Rigoletto at the opera house in Copenhagen.

He tucked the envelope into the pocket of his dinner jacket. He thought he might give the tickets to Norbert and Inge. His stepmother loved opera and would appreciate the gesture. Norbert, Sofie and Hannah were now checking their cards against the last four prizes on the table. Hannah picked up a red and black golf umbrella.

"At least one of us has won a prize," said Sofie. "Did you have any luck, Tobias?"

"I never expect to be lucky in raffles," said Tobias. Which was true.

"Lucky at cards, unlucky at love," said Sofie. She smiled.

Tobias thought he might have the energy for her after all.

15.

He felt wide awake driving back to Aarhus. He liked driving at night, especially when he was alone. It was one o'clock in the morning. The roads were almost empty. There was a pleasing rhythm in the way occasional headlights glittered in the distance, grew brighter and flared as they passed, briefly illuminating a fine drizzle of rain. The windscreen's wipers rose and fell occasionally. His mind was like that. Empty for long periods. On screensaver. Then a flash of thought. Life was strange. Few women had quickened his interest since his divorce. You wait a long time for the bus then three turn up at once. He corrected himself. Two. Hannah preferred women. A pity. She was restful and focused. Curvy. Soft. She was probably swatting men away all the time. Sofie was playful and teasing but no fool. She would keep him on his toes. If he could afford her. He ought to telephone Pernille Madsen. She'd get his report on Bruno Holst. Case closed. But he'd telephone anyway. She'd been right. Holst walked out. Just like that. Left his partner and their daughter. Without so much as a note. Would Holst get in touch with them now? They'd have moved on. What would have happened if he'd walked out on Karren and Agnes? Karren was happy now. Hans Frederik was a better husband for her. Agnes liked her step-father well enough. Agnes and Magnus in a tent in the forest. When did he last sleep in a tent in a forest? In the scouts? There was that week in Crete with Karren. Beside a beach. Toes full of sand and a sky full of stars. Not many stars tonight. The clouds are moving fast across the sky. There's the moon. Nearly full. Roligmose. Left, 5 kilometres. Who was Bogman? Was he killed on a night like this? Shadowy figures moving in the moonlight. A hand raised to strike. Was he killed in the bog or somewhere else? Who carried him to the pond? Two men? Or one strong man? Not a woman. Unless she was built like the desk sergeant at Randers. She could throw a body over her shoulders like a sack. Was she gay? Was Bogman Swedish? A tourist unlucky enough to meet a psychopath? He must have been travelling alone. Or with a friend. Maybe someone he picked up. There was something pathetic about that naked, leathery foot. Tollund Man in his glass case. A sacrificial victim, resigned, calm. Katrine said what they'd all been thinking. Was some sick bastard fixated about bog bodies? Was another one going to turn up? A bright girl, Katrine. Not a girl. A young woman. Long legs. Pert breasts. She was going to be a good detective. Sign for the University of Aarhus Department of Anthropology on the right. Good work by Brix and Brigitte. Another attractive woman. Blonde springy hair. Two tickets for the opera. Maybe he should ask Sofie after all. She wrong-footed him. He was out of practice on the niceties. Hilde didn't bother with all that. She said what she wanted. She didn't flirt. She probably couldn't be bothered. Maybe she saved eyelash fluttering and sideways glances for Eric. She was probably asleep beside him now. Eric the cuckold. Maybe they made energetic love all night when he was at home. Eric the absent. Hilde didn't talk about him much. He was overworked. Maybe he was always tired when he got home. I didn't bring my dinner jacket over. Didn't want to meet him. Too guilt-inducing. Has that made Eric suspicious? Maybe he'll ring my doorbell and punch me in the face. I wouldn't blame him. I didn't punch Hans Frederik when he told me he was sleeping with Karren. That's when I knew there was no spark left. Only ashes.

Tobias parked the car in the square and automatically glanced up at Hilde's flat. No lights. On the other side of the square, drunk students swarmed below the glaring lights outside the café bar. Raucous laughter. Shouts. He could still hear the roar when he walked up the stairs to his flat. The lights were on when he opened the door. He smelled toast.

"Hi, Dad," said Agnes. "You look nice in a dinner jacket. Had a good time?"

Tobias looked around quickly, half-expecting to see Magnus sprawled on the sofa.

"Classes start on Monday. I thought I'd call with you on my way back." Agnes dropped another slice of bread into the toaster.

"Where's Magnus?" He stopped himself adding, "Still up a tree?"

"He's gone to talk to the group about tactics. The company building the wind farm has invited us to a meeting. A lunch meeting, no less. What do you think, Dad?" Agnes carried her plate to the table. She had lit the candle and poured herself a glass of wine.

"It can't do any harm to listen, Agnes. And you can put your side of the argument to them." Tobias took another wine glass from the cupboard.

"They're not interested in our side of the argument,"

said Agnes. "They're going to go ahead whatever we say." She brushed a crumb from her mouth and grinned. "On the other hand, a free lunch is a free lunch."

Tobias nearly voiced the old cliché, 'there's no such thing as a free lunch'. He said instead, "Lunch isn't much of a bribe."

"That's what Magnus says. He says if they want to bribe us they should offer to give money to a green charity."

"If they did that, would Magnus accept it? Would you accept it? Would you call off the protest?" Tobias was immediately sorry he'd asked. If he saw Sofie again, he would feel uncomfortable knowing something that could affect her business.

"They'd never give money to Greenpeace," said Agnes. "It's far too political. But there are other charities. Saving whales, saving dolphins, saving lots of species. Bechstein's bat lives in that forest, you know."

Tobias didn't know. Where had he heard something recently about bats and forests?

Agnes propped her chin on her hands and gazed at the moon through the window. "Would we stop the protest if they gave money to a green charity? I don't know. It's a difficult ethical question, Dad."

"I quite agree," said Tobias. "Finish your toast before it gets cold."

"And maybe play a duet? You choose."

The flat wasn't big enough for a piano. Tobias had an electronic keyboard. It sat on a stand against an inner wall. Above it hung a portrait of J S Bach. In front of it sat the double piano stool in whose depths Tobias kept his sheet music, arranged alphabetically. He picked out Ravel's piano suite for two hands, *Ma Mere l'Oye*. He had played it with his mother. Agnes loved it too. And it was a quiet piece. There was no need to listen in headphones.

They played the first part, *Pavane for Sleeping Beauty*, sitting side by side at the keyboard. In perfect harmony.

16.

SUNDAY: WEEK TWO

Tobias drove Agnes to the station after breakfast. "Concentrate on your exams. Leave all the protest stuff for a while." He hugged her.

Agnes adjusted the rucksack on her shoulders. It was covered in badges and stickers. "I'll be OK in the exams, Dad. Don't worry."

"I worry. It's what fathers do."

A man with reddish-blond curls and a guitar case strapped to his back was walking towards the station. He stopped and stared at Agnes. Tobias recognised him as a Swedish musician who'd approached Katrine outside the bar on Friday evening and asked for a date. She had been more amused than bothered by his extravagant compliments and had gently shaken him off. Now he was walking towards Agnes with the same furrowed intensity. What was it with Agnes and all these alternative types who looked as though they hadn't washed in a week? At least this one didn't have studs. Not anywhere visible anyway. Tobias planted himself like a guard in front of his daughter.

The man with the guitar addressed Tobias in English: "Good morning. I think you were with the fuckable policewoman on Friday night?"

"Police officer," Tobias corrected. "You are referring to Detective Skaarup."

"Detective Skaarup, yes. The badges on the rucksack reminded me. My name is Dusty Svenson. She asked me about this." He pulled a crumpled photo from the back pocket of his jeans and handed it to Tobias. "This image. I remembered where I saw it."

Behind him, Agnes said, "I don't want to miss my train, Dad."

Tobias put his hand on Dusty's arm. "Wait a moment." He hugged Agnes. He watched her until she disappeared through the portico.

Dusty stared after her. "Another fuckable woman."

"She's my daughter," Tobias said curtly.

Dusty put his hands up. "Sorry."

"So you've recognised the badge," said Tobias.

Dusty nodded. "I am almost sure. I will write it. Do you have a pen?"

Tobias patted his pockets and found a pen. He gave the photo back to Dusty. "And write down where I can reach you. I might need to speak to you again."

"I texted my number to the good-looking detective."

"She might have deleted it," said Tobias, smiling now.

"There," Dusty handed back the photo. "I move around with the band. The bar knows how to contact me. Dusty Svenson. Country singer." He swept a mock bow.

Tobias smoothed the photo and read the words "Sami Saga Nej". In Swedish it meant "Sami Says No." Who or what was Sami? Was it a Turkish name? Or Palestinian? He might have to call in counter-terrorism. There'd be endless meetings and paperwork. He groaned. "Is it political?"

"It was a green protest in Sweden," said Dusty. "We played a concert for it. I have to go. I will miss my train."

Tobias drove straight to East Jutland police headquarters in Fredensgade and headed for the Investigations room. Eddy Haxen was fiddling with the coffee machine.

"I've been up since five o'clock this morning," he said. "I'd hardly got into bed when I had to get out of it again. Alsing's on leave this weekend. A stolen car. We think it might have been used by the Danske bank gang. It went missing near where the getaway van was torched. It's been found in the car park at Skolebakken. It's with Forensics now. But I bet it was wiped clean before it was abandoned. Katrine is still over there. What brings you in?"

"S S N. Sami Saga Nej." Tobias typed the name into an Internet search engine. "I met the guy who was making sheep's eyes at Katrine on Friday night. He remembered where he'd seen the badge. It's the logo of a bunch of greens in Sweden."

Eddy clapped his hands softly. "Well done, Skaarup."

"Get me a coffee, would you?"

Eddy gave a mock salute. "Yes, boss."

"Bugger off."

The Internet search brought up several links. The first one took Tobias to the website of an umbrella organisation for environmental groups in Sweden. He scanned the page looking for Sami Saga Nej. He scrolled through several pages.

"Got it."

Eddy set a cup of coffee in front of Tobias and read the screen over his shoulder.

Sami Saga Nej was formed in 1996 to fight for reindeer winter grazing rights for Sami herders and to oppose plans to dump nuclear waste at Mala in Sweden. S S N favoured direct action such as sit-ins and demonstrations. It raised money through both organized and impromptu music concerts. Their opposition to the nuclear waste facility was successful in 1997 when the plans were abandoned. The group also campaigned for the return of a sacrificial stone from the museum in Skelleftea to its original site near Mala. The stone was returned in August 1998. The occasion was marked by a special ceremony. The S S N continue to support the Sami reindeer herders' rights to winter grazing.

"A Laplander," said Tobias. "What was a Laplander doing in a Danish bog?"

"Sounds like the beginning of a bad joke," said Eddy. "Ever been to Lapland, boss?"

"I went there once for cross-country skiing," said Tobias.

"What was it like?"

"White," said Tobias. "Frozen lakes, lots of trees. There was a blizzard. We didn't leave the hotel for two days." They'd left Agnes with Karren's mother and gone away for a few days in the faint hope of mending their marriage. He'd felt trapped. Karren had spent most of her time in the sauna, emerging only to announce that she was leaving him.

"Should be nice at this time of year," said Eddy. "Land of the midnight sun."

Katrine came into the Investigations room. She dropped her jacket on the chair at her desk and skipped over to join Tobias and Eddy.

"Forensics have taken the car to the garage, Eddy. You were right. All the surfaces were wiped clean. No prints. But there's a tiny trace of SmartWater on the floor under the driver's seat. Enough for a DNA match anyway."

Eddy and Tobias acknowledged her with a wave. They were concentrating on the screen in front of them.

"The boss bumped into the musician who wanted to fuck you on Friday night," said Eddy. "He remembered what S S N stood for."

"He was OK," said Katrine. "I thought he was nice. Hey." She brightened. "So what does it mean, S S N?"

"Samis Say No," said Tobias. "A Swedish conservation group."

"Laplanders," said Eddy.

"I don't think you're supposed to call them Laplanders any more," said Katrine.

"The group was active from 1996 to 1998," said Tobias. "The coin is 1997. So when did Bogman come to Denmark?"

"Brix thought he died no later than 1999," said Eddy. "So Bogman must have been here between 1997 and 1999. He could have come earlier than 1997. If we had a name, we could check airline and ferry records. If we check airline and ferry records we might find a name. If he went by road there'd be no record at all. Do you ever feel we are going around in circles on this one?"

"Start looking for Swedish and Sami silversmiths with the initials B H," said Tobias. "I'll call Larsen."

Katrine found three silversmiths with the initials B H on a website featuring Swedish designers. Three of them had the initials B H: Benedict Huss, Bo Holgersson and Berit Hansdatter. Only Benedict Huss and Bo Holgersson had their own websites. Benedict Huss could be contacted only by email. But Bo Holgersson had posted his telephone number as well. Eddy telephoned him.

"I don't make much jewellery," he said. "Only the necklaces you can see on my website. I can give you the telephone number for Benedict Huss. I don't have a number for Berit Hansdatter. Maybe Benedict knows how to contact her. Maybe Benedict is the guy you're looking for. He had some bracelets in his last show."

Benedict Huss told Eddy he made jewellery, but nothing like the bracelet Eddy described to him. "It's a nice idea. But not mine." He didn't have a telephone number for Berit Hansdatter. "I was at college with her but we've lost touch. She lives up north somewhere. She doesn't sell her stuff in any of the Stockholm galleries."

Katrine found an art gallery in Northern Sweden which included Berit Hansdatter in the list of artists it represented.

"She lives in an artists' community about twenty kilometres from Vilhelmina," Katrine told Tobias. "They make a lot of traditional Sami stuff. Reindeer horn necklaces, braiding, some pewter. Most of the pictures on the gallery website are that kind of thing. Except for a necklace of engraved silver beads by Berit Hansdatter. There's no telephone number listed for her, but there's an address, and a map with directions from Vilhelmina."

Tobias booked a flight to Ostersund, the nearest airport to Vilhelmina. He would have to leave Aarhus before six the following morning. He went home to pack a bag.

He was arranging a pair of socks to fit exactly into the fold of a sweater – he expected northern Sweden to be colder than Jutland, and it was cool in Aarhus despite the lilac blossom in his neighbour's garden – when his phone buzzed. It was his ex-wife.

"I'm busy, Karren."

"This won't take a minute. I need to speak to you about Agnes."

"I dropped her at the station this morning. She seems fine."

"Did she tell you about this crazy encampment in Jutland? Demonstrating against a wind farm? If she gets arrested you have to promise you'll get her unarrested."

"I can't do that," Tobias said. "I can't interfere. And it's not my district."

"What's the point of being a policeman if you can't even help your own daughter?"

Tobias was silent. He could have reminded Karren that he'd joined the police because he'd been a penniless student and she was pregnant. That he'd wanted to get a job on his merits and not as a gift from his father-in-law. He sighed.

"Well?" demanded Karren.

"Agnes promised me she won't do anything illegal."

"What about that crazy boyfriend with the tattoo?"

Tattoo? Tobias hadn't noticed a tattoo.

"I don't care if he gets arrested," said Tobias.

"Or some of the other eco-lunatics?"

"They're not my problem, Karren. They're not your problem either."

"Why does Agnes have to be an activist? Why can't she be green silently, like the rest of us? Hans Frederik's father is furious."

"Silently green?" Tobias wanted to laugh. Karren drove a sports utility vehicle, a real gas guzzler. Hans Frederik shot pretty much anything that moved and he thought climate change was a left-wing plot.

"We have solar panels, we have a ground heat exchanger," said Karren. "Agnes approves of those. She believes in alternative energy. So what's wrong with a wind farm?"

"They're cutting down a forest to build it. It's a save the trees thing. Plus there's some kind of otter that needs protecting."

"It's her future Agnes needs to protect."

Tobias made soothing noises. He promised to speak to Agnes about sticking to her studies. He thought he might ask her about Sami conservation groups as well.

17.

MONDAY: WEEK TWO

North Jutland Police District

Chief Inspector Pernille Madsen and Inspector Peter Lundquist stared at four plastic bags laid out on a desk in the Forensic Science Laboratory.

"Is that all?" said Pernille. "You've been in that flat for three days and that's all you've found? It's not much for the file."

Magda Johanssen, who'd supervised the team which had searched the studio flat in which Jolene Karlssen had been assaulted, held up her gloved hands.

"We went over it twice. There wasn't much to go on. They didn't have sex. He didn't jerk off. There's no semen. Jolene's panties have her saliva, vomit and blood. There was urine on the mattress. She wet herself. The poor woman was terrified. We swept the bedroom and the bathroom for prints. Nothing. Every surface had been wiped clean," said Magda.

"He must have cleaned up before he followed Jolene into the alley," said Peter Lundquist.

"She thinks she was on the ground for no more than five minutes before he came after her," said Pernille. "Five minutes to clean up? He's done this before. He's got it down to a fine art."

"Item one," said Magda, holding up a bag containing a scrap of blue fabric and a button. "Jolene had this in her hand. He was wearing a blue shirt. If we can find the shirt, we can match the threads."

"Half the men in Sweden wear blue shirts," said Peter Lundquist. "I'm wearing one myself."

"This is from a high quality shirt." Magda held the bag up for inspection. "It's very fine cotton and best quality thread. The button is pure bone, not plastic, and nicely finished around the edges."

"Not like one of mine, then," said Peter.

"Item two," said Magda. "Jolene's bra. I'll send it to the national lab. If there's anything on it, they'll find it. But he was wearing plastic gloves, wasn't he?"

"According to Jolene," said Pernille, "he wore clear, skin-tight, plastic gloves. She didn't notice them at first. Pity. They'd have warned her she was dealing with a pervert. Who knows how to remove all trace of himself."

"He didn't manage to remove all trace of himself," said Magda with a satisfied air. "Item three."

She held up a plastic bag containing a skein of grey-blond hairs. "They were pulled out, roots and all. Jolene had them in her left hand. They were bagged and kept by the ambulance crew. We found other hairs in and under the bed but they'd been shed naturally. You can't get DNA from them. You need follicles for DNA. So, well done, Jolene. It will take a bit of time, but I think we'll get DNA from these." She waved the bag in triumph.

"He picked the wrong victim," said Pernille. "Tenacious woman, Jolene. Did you know she used to be a female contortionist until she broke her leg?"

"I thought that stuff was all faked," said Peter Lundquist.

"She tripped over a rope in a circus tent about ten years ago," said Pernille. "Discovered there was more money in prostitution. What's item four?"

"I'm not sure." Magda opened the bag and tipped a round metal object, the size and thickness of a coin, into her gloved hand. One side was enamelled pale green. The other side had a clip.

"We found it in on the second sweep. It was in a gap between two floorboards. There was fluff and dust underneath it so it was dropped recently. It's some kind of badge or clip. There are three initial letters embossed on it. I can make out an S but the surface is worn and there are scratches." She slipped it under a microscope. "Have a look. See what you think."

Pernille peered through the eyepiece. "It looks like the badge of some institution or club. I think the third letter is N."

Peter took his turn at the microscope. "Yes. Some kind of badge." He took his eye away from the microscope and blinked before taking a second look. "It could also be a golf ball marker."

"Golf ball marker?" said Pernille.

"You use it to mark the position of your ball on the green." Peter straightened up. "I've often pulled something out of my pocket and my ball marker has dropped out as well."

"Jolene's attacker was wearing chinos," said Pernille.

"He might have been wearing them for golf," said Peter. "He might have had a ball marker in his pocket. The initials could identify the club. And some companies give out golf ball markers with their company logo. It's a form of advertising."

"So he's a member of a company, or organisation, or golf club with first and third initials S and N," said Pernille.

"If it's a golf club, he mightn't be a member," said Peter. "He might just have played there and bought the marker, or been given it on a corporate golf day, or just played at the club and picked up the marker on the course. I'm always finding markers."

"That's a big help," said Pernille drily. "Tell me something useful."

"You can also buy simple plastic markers with no logo," said Peter. He dodged the fake punch Pernille threw at him.

"I'll tell you something useful," said Magda. "There's half a thumb print on it."

18.

Tobias picked up a hire car at Ostersund airport and programmed the satnav to take him to where Berit Hansdatter lived in Vasterbotten county. Aarhus to Copenhagen, then Copenhagen to Ostersund. Four hours. Now he had a long drive to northern Sweden. Three and a half hours the satnav told him. And it was almost lunchtime. At least it was spring. It would stay light until well into the evening.

He drove through what seemed to him a haphazard sort of area. He was on a dualcarriageway lined with factories and housing estates interspersed with forest. After about half an hour, the forest appeared to be winning. Instead of factory buildings and blocks of houses, there were clearings with cabins. Then there was only forest. The road wound round a lake. Then forest again. Forest and lakes. Forest and lakes.

He played over in his mind the information he'd gleaned from a search for persons missing in Sweden. Three men had gone missing between 1997 and 1999. One was fifty and an alcoholic. One was from Pakistan. One was twenty-six, but he had an artificial leg. The bones of Bogman's legs were intact. There were no Swedish citizens reported missing in Denmark, or in any other country.

He stopped the car in a quiet town and parked outside a lakeside bar. The interior was dark and cool. The barman handed him a menu. Tobias, who was curious about food, ordered a suovaskebab from the "local specialty" section, and a glass of beer. He usually had beer at lunchtime – and smorssbrod with herring and pickle and hard-boiled egg and salad. He looked doubtfully at what seemed to be a pitta bread sandwich when it arrived. It didn't look very Lapland-like.

Tobias spoke reasonably good Swedish. "What's in it?" he asked the barman.

"Smoked reindeer, cucumber, salad and garlic dressing," said the barman. "Sami fusion cooking."

The combination was surprisingly tasty.

Tobias sipped his beer and reviewed what he knew about Bogman. He wore a bracelet inscribed 'Encircled By Your Love.' He wore the badge of an environmental group. And yet no one reported him missing. Had his lover killed him? That was possible, yes. His lover, or maybe someone he picked up. But if it was some casual pickup, why didn't the person who gave Bogman the bracelet report him missing? It didn't make sense. He thought about the bracelet he had given Karren. She probably had more expensive jewellery now. He would know if Karren disappeared. Bad example. What about the women he'd been involved with since his divorce. If any of them went missing, would he know about it, if he wasn't in the police? Hilde, of course. She was a neighbour. Of course he'd hear about it if she disappeared. Marli Andersen, with whom he was still on friendly terms. But the others? He wouldn't notice if the librarian at Silkeborg disappeared – unless it made headlines. He'd given a necklace to a girlfriend at college. Mette Svensen. L O V E in gold letters linked by a gold chain. He'd been crazy about her for at least six months. Where was she now? He had no idea. But somebody cared enough about her, he was sure, to report her missing if she disappeared. Why had nobody cared enough about Bogman? Maybe he was a vagrant after all, and had stolen the bracelet. They'd have to trawl through all the stolen item reports in Denmark. The thought wearied him. Agnes didn't know anything about S S N, or any other Sami group. But she'd heard that one person in the wind farm protest had been in northern Sweden helping Sami protect their reindeer herding rights. That might be worth following up, if he had no luck with the silversmith. He drained his beer glass. Here's to Berit Handsdatter. His best bet so far.

He got back into the car and headed north again. The countryside changed from lake and forest to tundra. The sky was grey. A wide plain spread out before him. It looked empty, until he noticed reindeer grazing beside a lake, and one or two low wooden cabins. He passed a signpost for Asele and Umea. Less than a hundred kilometres to go.

Just before Vilhelmina, he stopped the car beside a lake and got out to stretch his legs. The landscape looked flat, dull, unexceptional. He was about to get back into the car when the sun came out. The air was suddenly crystal clear, luminous. The black lake turned from oily black to glittering turquoise. The grass sparkled. Yellow lichen on the grey rocks gleamed like gold. The forest looked almost fluorescent.

Tobias thought about Agnes protecting trees in West Jutland. Was it warmer there than it was here? The air had a definite chill in it. He could see snow on the mountains in the distance. He shivered and got back into the car. Only another fifty kilometres now.

The desk sergeant in Vilhelmina was expecting him.

"Chief Inspector Lange? Grete Lindberg. I'm the duty sergeant today." They shook hands. "I've read the file you sent us. It's an interesting case." She sounded envious.

"Let's go." She picked up a set of keys. "It's not far as the crow flies but the road is bad for the last ten kilometres." She ushered Tobias out of the police station and locked the door behind them.

"There are only four of us," she said. "My colleague on duty is helping to get a cow out of a ditch. The others are on the late shift. But not much happens up here. Whatever turns up can usually wait until morning. To tell the truth, I'm glad of something interesting to do."

Berit Hansdatter's house was a single-storey wooden house painted dark red, in a lakeside clearing. Further along the lake were four similar houses, two painted in the same red, two painted sky blue. A shared landing stage jutted into the lake. Five rowing boats rested on the water. Tyre tracks were clearly visible in the damp ground around Berit Handsdatter's house, but there was no sign of a vehicle.

Tobias parked where the forest ended and the clearing began. He and the sergeant got out of the car and walked towards the house. Poppies and marguerites fluttered in the window boxes on either side of the front door. A white card with a telephone number and message in Swedish – "If I'm not here, call my mobile!" – in bold black handwriting, was sellotaped to a window.

Tobias was tapping the number into his phone when an elderly red Saab came bumping down the track and parked at the side of the house. A wide-shouldered, tousled-haired woman, a good head taller than Tobias and Grete, got out. She raised the carrier bag in her hand in a kind of greeting. "Come in."

They followed her into the house where she shook their hands and introduced herself – "I'm Berit" – without waiting to hear their names, not seeming to notice the police badge on Grete Lindberg's jacket.

"I assume you've come to collect the rings? They're on the blue cloth. Take a look at them. I'll just take these things into the kitchen and make coffee. When's the wedding?"

She disappeared into the kitchen before either Tobias or Grete could speak.

Tobias looked at Grete and raised an eyebrow.

"We're not here about wedding rings," Grete called out. "We're here about something else."

Berit appeared in the kitchen doorway. "So it's something else? Did you make an appointment? Did I send

you a design? I'll be in with coffee in a moment. Sit down."
She disappeared again.

Grete and Tobias took seats at a long pine table by the
window. Berit returned, carrying a tray with a coffee pot,
mugs, milk jug, sugar bowl and a plate of spiced biscuits.

"I don't have a website. People steal your ideas. I send
out designs on request." She put the tray on the table and
poured coffee into the cups. "Milk? Sugar? I made the
biscuits this morning." She settled herself at the table. "Now,
what can I do for you?"

"We're police officers," said Grete without preamble.
"I'm Sergeant Lindberg from Vilhelmina and this is Chief
Inspector Tobias Lange from Aarhus. He is investigating
a murder committed in Denmark." She looked at Tobias
to continue.

"The victim was a male aged about twenty. We have not
yet identified him," said Tobias. "We hope you can help us."

Berit rocked forward in surprise. "Me?"

"We think you made a bracelet found with the," he
hesitated, "remains." He took a photograph from his
briefcase and handed it to her. "Do you recognise it?"

Berit studied the photograph. "Of course," she said. "I
made this bracelet about ten years ago. I remember it well.
Encircled by your love. In Danish. The words were her idea.
She wasn't sure if it should be a necklace with the letters in
silver, then they both decided on a bracelet instead."

"She? Both?" Tobias and Grete spoke in unison.

"They were a beautiful couple," said Berit. "Very much
in love. You could see it in their eyes. It was shining out of
them. I met them at a concert in Fatmomakke. They were
musicians. She played the guitar and he played the fiddle.

They picked up tunes as though they had heard them in the womb. She was full of life. I saw a lot of them at that time. They played many concerts. It was during the protests against nuclear waste dumping. They were involved in demonstrations about Sami grazing rights as well."

She paused for breath.

Tobias said quickly, "What were they called?"

"Emily and Lennart," said Berit. "I liked them very much."

"What were their surnames?"

"I don't remember," said Berit. "I don't know if anyone knew their surnames. We all knew them as Emily and Lennart or the Danish pair. You never saw one without the other. They were so attached to each other. They drove an old ambulance. It was painted sky blue with clouds and a rainbow. It was highly visible on the roads around here. You must have noticed it, Sergeant."

"I've only been here two years," said Grete. "In fact none of us in Vilhelmina were here at that time."

"You made the bracelet," said Tobias. "Who asked you to make it? Who paid for it? How did they pay? Cash or card, or cheque?"

"Oh, I don't take credit cards," said Berit. "I don't have the machine for that. People give me a cheque, or cash."

"So you keep a record of payments and receipts," said Tobias. "For tax purposes. With names and addresses." He held his breath.

"I tell the taxman my income and I keep receipts," said Berit. "But only for seven years. I don't have any receipts going back further. Or if I have, I don't know where they are." She paused. "I think I only asked Lennart to pay for the silver in the ring and not the workmanship. He didn't have much money."

"Just a minute," said Tobias. "You made a ring as well as a bracelet?"

"I made a ring for Lennart. For him to give to Emily. He couldn't afford a bracelet like the one she gave him. So he asked me to make a ring for her instead, engraved with *Together Forever* in Danish. You could read it both ways. Together Forever. Forever Together. Wasn't that a wonderful idea as well?"

"It looks like an expensive bracelet," said Tobias.

"It was," said Berit. "Solid silver, hand engraved. But Emily had the money. She insisted on paying me what I'd normally charge. She said she could afford it. I think her people were well-off. She had some kind of allowance."

A rich drop-out, thought Tobias. Plenty of money and no inclination to work.

"Emily was a waitress in a fishing hotel for a few months and Lennart had a summer job in a bar," said Berit. "They played music in the bar as well."

"The bracelet is dated 1997," said Tobias.

"So long ago?" Berit shook her head in wonder. "It seems like yesterday."

You might remember a bit more if it was yesterday, thought Tobias. No records. He kept the irritation out of his voice. "Do you remember when and for how long they were here?"

"I can't be sure about that," said Berit. "They were definitely here for at least one summer because I remember going to visit them at the campsite and thinking they were lucky it was a warm summer and it didn't rain. So that must have been 1996 because that was a good summer. And they must have been here in 1997 because the last thing I do is engrave the date."

"You were friendly with them," said Grete. "Did you never send a letter or postcard or email to them? Did you never ask them for an address?"

"I don't remember them leaving," said Berit. "They were probably gone before I had time to get an address. I didn't have email then. Maybe someone else has an address for them."

"Who might that be?"

Berit made a helpless gesture. "I don't know," she said. "But they were well known around here."

They heard the sound of a car drawing up outside, the murmur of voices, the slamming of a car door, a shout of "Bye now, thanks."

"That'll be Jossi back from Dorotea," said Berit. "He was getting a lift from our neighbour."

The front door opened. A thin, bony-faced man came in. "Johan wouldn't stay for coffee. He says hello to you, Berit." He stopped abruptly, on seeing Tobias.

"These are police officers, Jossi," said Berit. "They're asking about a Danish couple that used to come here. Emily and Lennart."

"Those two were not criminals," said Jossi immediately. "Two more honest souls you will not find between here and heaven. They were warriors for the environment. But neither of them would hurt a fly. They had only gentle bones in their bodies."

He darted forward and shook hands with Tobias and Grete.

"I'm afraid I bring bad news," said Tobias. "Your wife has identified a bracelet we found with the remains of a body in Jutland. We think the remains might be those of your friend Lennart."

Jossi looked shocked.

"We think he was murdered," said Tobias.

Jossi pulled out a chair from the table and sat down.

"We lost touch with them," he said. "I'm sorry about that." He shook his head. "Why would anyone want to kill Lennart?"

"That's what we're trying to find out," said Tobias. "First, we need to be sure it was Lennart. Do you know any person who had an address for him or for Emily? Who knows their surnames?"

"Maybe the Lake Hotel," said Berit. "Emily worked there for a while."

"I know it," said Grete.

Tobias took a card from his briefcase. "Here is my number. Contact me if you remember anything more. Thank you for the tea and delicious biscuits." He added casually, as though he had just thought of it, "Did either Emily or Lennart do drugs?"

Berit and Jossi exchanged a quick glance.

Jossi said, "If you mean did they smoke the occasional spliff, yes, they did. And dropped a tab or two of Ecstasy, probably. If you mean were they seriously into drugs? Definitely not. They weren't even big drinkers. They were more the herbal tea type."

Berit said, "When you find Emily's address, let us know. We'd like to be in touch with her again."

Tobias looked back as he turned the car in the clearing Berit and Jossi were standing contentedly, hand in hand, in the doorway, gazing at the lake. He remembered holding hands with Karren at the northernmost point of Denmark. He saw again in his minds eye the ripple where the North

Sea meets the Skaggerak. He recalled his sense of wonder when he looked at Karren, thinking "we're going to have a baby," and the rush of tenderness that led him to clutch her hand more tightly, led him to say, "let's get married". Where did all that tenderness go? He had reached the main road. Two cyclists, riding abreast, their jackets floating in the wind, dropped into single file to allow the car to overtake them and raised their hands in salute. They looked flushed and happy. Should he telephone Sofie when he got back?

He realised Grete was speaking to him. "We don't have a big drug problem up here," she said. "Alcohol, yes. There's not much to do except get drunk. I'm hoping for a transfer to Ostersund."

Tobias thought there probably wasn't much to do in Ostersund either.

A sign for the Lake Hotel loomed up. Tobias drove along the shores of the lake to a three-storey building overlooking a marina. Waders and fishing rods were stacked on the long wooden veranda. They were greeted by a young dark-haired girl with a foreign accent, Spanish? Portuguese? Tobias wasn't sure. They showed their ID. The receptionist picked up the telephone.

"There are two police officers here who wish to speak to you, Hanne."

A moment later, a harassed looking woman wearing a white chef's bonnet and apron appeared in the lobby. She ushered Tobias and Grete into a small office behind the desk.

"You have come at a bad time," she said. "Why did you not warn me you were coming? We could have fixed a better time. What do you want?" She was cross and abrupt.

Tobias and Grete mollified her with explanations and apologies.

"I'm sorry I was abrupt with you," she said. "I remember Emily. Emily Rasmussen. A hard worker. She was here for a couple of summers. It was before we built the extension so it must have been before 2001. I don't know if I had an address in Denmark for her. She lived on a campsite. There might be an address in our records but I haven't the time to go through them." She pulled open the bottom drawer of a filing cabinet. "The ledgers from 1990, the year we opened, to the year we did the extension are all in here. You can go through them yourselves."

She left like a whirlwind.

Grete took the ledger for 2000 and sat down at the desk. Tobias balanced the ledger for 2001 ledger on the top of the filing cabinet. They worked in silence.

"No Emily in this one." Grete swivelled round and replaced the ledger in the drawer.

"Or in this one," said Tobias.

They had no luck with 2000 and 1999 either.

Grete was running her eye down a page in April 1997 when she heard Tobias exclaim, "Got her. June 16, 1998. Emily. 15 hours. No address. There must be an address somewhere. Maybe with the first entry." Tobias flicked back through the pages. "Emily. Emily R. Emily R." He closed the book.

"Maybe there's one here." Grete leafed through the ledger for 1997. "Nothing in April." Pause. "Nothing in May." She gave a cry of triumph. "Here she is. June 22. It must be the first day she started working here. Emily Rasmussen. And there's an address in Denmark." She gave the ledger to Tobias.

They grinned at each other. Tobias glanced at the address for Emily Rasmussen.

"Skanderborg. Our lake country. But not as much water as around here." He fished out his phone and composed a text.

"Bogman Lennart. No surname. Girlfriend Emily Rasmussen. Skandeborg address. Will go there." He sent the text to Eddy and pushed the phone back into his pocket.

19.

Eddy was sitting outside a canal-side café in Aarhus. He was enjoying the last of the evening sun and drinking beer with a Pilates teacher he'd met three months earlier while investigating a series of robberies at an expensive private gym. The stolen items – money, watches, jewellery – were found in the flat of a part-time receptionist who'd been copying the locker keys. The Pilates teacher, who, along with the rest of the staff had been under suspicion, showed her gratitude, and continued to show it in an enticingly physical way. She was young, blonde, slim and sexually adventurous but, as Eddy soon discovered, otherwise boring and humourless. He was wondering how much longer they were going to sit staring at the canal before one of them suggested going back to his or her flat – and somehow the idea didn't thrill him as it should – when the text from Tobias flashed up on his phone. Eddy read it with a sense of release. He had an excuse to leave.

"Urgent request from my boss," he said, trying to sound disappointed. "I have to go back to work." He drained his beer, gave the Pilates teacher a quick hug and sprinted away.

Katrine was at the reception desk in headquarters talking to a man in blue overalls and an orange visibility jacket when a ptinkle sound from the phone in her right pocket told her she had a text message. She ignored it because she was holding in her right hand, at arms length, a clear plastic bag containing what appeared to be two dirt-encrusted bones. One was approximately 20 centimetres long and 5 centimetres in diameter, the other was shorter, thinner and appeared to be jointed. The man in the blue overalls and visibility jacket had just handed the bag to her. His name was Carl Andersen and he was a supervisor at the city's waste disposal depot.

"I didn't know what else to do with them," he said. "One of the team saw them when he was emptying one of the underground containers. Orvik, he's a sensible sort, very reliable. He called me over. They weren't in a bag. It's mostly household waste in plastic bags in that sector but they weren't in a bag. They were just mixed in with a lot of other rubbish."

"What sector?"

"Gellerupparken. It looked like someone had just chucked them into one of the bins. We thought at first they might be rubber bones. Some kind of joke. But it isn't anyone's birthday. Nobody was leaving the team or getting married. When I picked one of them up, even with thick rubber gloves on, I could tell it was a real bone. It could be an animal bone I said to Orvik, but I've never seen a dog with a femur that length. Unless it's a bone from a deer. They could be human bones we'd best take them to the police, I said. I put them in a bag for him to take them down here. But he was in the middle of his shift and there was another truck coming in with a load so I brought them here myself. What do you think?"

"I think you should stop unloading until we know if these are human bones or not," said Katrine decisively, although inside she was thinking what if I get bawled out for stopping the whole system when the bones turn out not to be human after all?

"I stopped everything before I left," said Carl Andersen. "They're waiting to hear from me."

"Good," said Katrine. That was a relief. But what if she couldn't get hold of Harry Norsk? And even if he came straightaway, could she order the city's waste disposal system to stop – at who knew what cost and consequences for the always delicate relations between the police and the city council – until Harry decided if the bones were human or not?

She stood holding the bag and its grisly contents at arms length, wondering if she should telephone the Chief Superintendent whom she knew was addressing a conference in Copenhagen that evening because he'd told the whole office about it, and imagining a range of consequences from Larsen's endorsement of her decision to Larsen's rage at having his attention deflected when he was in the middle of a talk about budgets and accountability. And supposing the bones turned out to be from a horse or a deer?

At which point Eddy Haxen loped into the building.

Katrine hurried towards him with relief. "I've just been given two bones in a plastic bag. They were found at the waste disposal centre. The supervisor," she gestured to Carl Andersen, idly swinging his orange helmet and staring at his boots, "brought them here. I can't decide what to do."

"Have you stopped all the waste dumping?"

"It's stopped. But how long can we stop it for?"

"As long as it takes," said Eddy. He smiled at her. "Don't worry. I'll take responsibility for ordering a shut-down." He put his hand on Katrine's arm. "It's my turn to take the flak. Call Harry Norsk. I'll speak to the waste disposal chap."

Harry Norsk came in straightaway. Katrine and Eddy met him in the pathology room. Eddy gave him the bag with the bones. Harry pulled on a pair of gloves, lifted the bones from the bag and laid them on one of the stainless steel tables.

"They're definitely bones. You can never be certain until you get a closer look. I've had wood and ceramics brought to me because people think they're bones. These look like radius and ulna to me."

"We shut down everything," said Eddy. "The place is sealed. Forensics will go through it all in the morning."

Harry picked up each bone in turn and weighed it in his hand. "They could be human. Animal bones are denser and heavier. And the radius and ulna are usually fused. These are separate. I can't be certain. Karl will want to look at the dirt traces. They might tell us something. I'll wash them and run a few tests. Any more where these came from?"

"We'll soon find out," said Eddy.

20

TUESDAY: WEEK TWO

Karl Lund and his team began at six in the morning and spent five hours sorting through the contents of the underground bin. They found twenty-three ribs and dozens of smaller bones which looked like finger bones. They scraped off the dirt for analysis, bagged the bones and sent them to Harry Norsk. The bin was sealed again until the rest of the contents could be analysed.

Harry washed the bones with boiling water and detergent. He was putting them on steel trays when Eddy and Katrine came into the lab.

"The rib bones are from pigs," he said. "Human ribs look pretty much like pork ribs. Haven't you ever noticed that?"

Katrine thought it might be some time before she ate pork ribs again.

"The little bones are chicken bones," said Harry. "It's hard to tell the difference between chicken bones and human finger bones. I put them under the microscope and ran a couple of tests. They're chicken bones all right."

Katrine glanced at Eddy. He gave her a rueful smile.

"So I've shut down the entire waste disposal organisation of the city to find the remains of a barbecue," he said. "At who knows what cost," he added miserably.

Katrine turned to him in sympathy. She was already bracing herself for the shouts, the storming up and down, the angry questions from Larsen.

Harry picked up the two bigger bones. He held them up, one in each hand, like trophies. He smiled broadly.

"These are definitely human. I can't tell either age or sex. Not yet anyway. But some person or persons put the arm bones of a human being in a rubbish bin."

Katrine felt like cheering.

She and Eddy spent the next two hours contacting all the hospitals and clinics in Aarhus to ask if any bones intended for an incinerator might have accidentally ended up in a city refuse bin. It was unlikely, but they checked anyway. A team of uniformed police went from door to door questioning the residents of the housing blocks who used the bin in which the bones had been found.

"No one admits to putting the bones in the bin. Not that I'd expect whoever did it to say so," Eddy told the Chief Superintendent. "Nobody saw anything suspicious. No one on the list of missing persons comes from that neighbourhood. It's a mystery, sir."

"Then get on with solving it, right?" said Larsen.

21.

Tobias was at Stockholm airport, distracted by a bottle out of line with its fellows on a shelf in the duty-free shop. He stopped on his way to the departure gate to push it back into place.

"Hello, Inspector," said a musical voice behind him. "What brings you to Sweden?"

Tobias knew it was Sofie before he turned around and saw her, head to one side, smiling at him. He felt wide awake. He felt like buying a bottle of whiskey. His hand was still on the bottle. He picked it up. There was something about Sofie that made a man think he needed a drink.

"I could ask you the same question," he said.

"I was here for meetings about a mining development up north. So what about you, Tobias?"

"I came to interview someone about the body found at Roligmose two weeks ago."

"Dad told me you were at Skovlynd with him when you had to rush off and investigate. He was very excited about it." Her eyes danced. "Are you getting closer?"

"I hope so," said Tobias. "Maybe we can sit together on the plane."

"I'm in business class," said Sofie.

"I'm in economy."

"I don't mind slumming it, if there's a spare seat beside you," said Sofie. "I'll see you at the gate."

Tobias realised he still had the bottle of whiskey in his hand. He took it to the till.

The plane was full. There were no spare seats in either class.

"Bad luck," said Sofie.

"Maybe we could have dinner sometime," said Tobias. "Are you free this weekend?"

Sofie shook her head. "I'll be in France. Kurt bought a chateau last year. It's going to be a hotel with a golf course and vineyard. He's got a good course designer. I think you'd like it."

"What part of France?" He wanted to prolong the conversation.

"Between Lyon and Avignon. Near the Rhone."

The last business class passengers were boarding. Sofie surprised Tobias with a quick hug. "I'll call you when I get back."

He walked past her on his way to the economy seats at the back of the plane, but she was looking out of the window and didn't see him. When he disembarked at Copenhagen there was no sign of her. He made his way to where he had parked his car the previous morning. On the motorway, he was overtaken by a Bentley. He caught a glimpse of two passengers in the back seat, heads down, perusing documents. One of them was Sofie. The other looked like Kurt Malling.

Tobias picked up a hire car and drove to the address he'd got for Emily Rasmussen. It was a tall, detached house with a large garden on a leafy avenue on the northern outskirts of Skandeborg. A man, carrying a trowel and a tomato plant, stood gazing into a lily pond set into the lawn at the side of the house. Tobias walked towards him. The man looked up.

"Bloody heron's been taking the carp again."

"Mr Rasmussen?"

The man looked surprised. "You've come to the wrong house. Nobody called Rasmussen lives here." He paused before adding, "I don't live here. I'm the gardener. The Hendriksens are on holiday in South Africa. This is their property. I know they've been here for at least five years because I've been doing this garden for five years and the same bloody heron has been taking the fish." He absentmindedly sniffed the tomato plant.

"Do you have contact details for the Hendriksens?"

"I thought you were looking for people called Rasmussen," said the gardener in a suspicious tone.

Tobias produced his ID. "They might know where I can find the Rasmussens."

"Wait a minute," said the gardener. He put down the tomato plant, rapped on the nearest window and signalled to someone inside. "My wife will meet you at the front door. She does the cleaning. She's been with them longer than I have."

They walked round to the front of the house. The door opened and a woman came out.

"This is a policeman, Birgit," said the gardener. "He wants to get in contact with the Hendriksens."

"They said not to call unless it was urgent."

"This is urgent," said Tobias.

Birgit went back into the house and reappeared with a sheet of paper. Tobias already had his phone in his hand. Birgit dictated the number to him. He put the phone to his ear.

"Arne Hendrickson," said a sharp voice. "I don't recognise this number. Who are you? Is something wrong?"

"Nothing is wrong," said Tobias. "I'm Inspector Tobias Lange, Criminal Investigations Department, Aarhus. I need to contact a person called Emily Rasmussen. Your house is the last address we have for her."

"We are about to leave for a game drive," said Arne Hendrickson. "Can you call tomorrow?"

"I'd prefer to do this now," said Tobias. "It won't take long. Do you have an address or telephone number for Emily Rasmussen who lived here in 1997? I believe she can help us with an urgent enquiry."

"Is this a joke? I should warn you, I know the National Commissioner. How do I know this isn't a joke?"

"You could call the Commissioner," said Tobias drily.

Silence. A woman's voice said, "This is Sarah Hendrickson. We bought the house from people called Thomsen. We don't know anyone called Emily Rasmussen. Perhaps our neighbour will know. She has lived in Strandvejen for at least thirty years."

Silence again. The man's voice said, "We have to go now. Sorry." The line went dead.

"Mrs Hendriksen thinks one of the neighbours might know," said Tobias. "Do either of you know which neighbour has lived here for thirty years?"

"That'll be Mrs Jacobsen," said the gardener. "I look after her garden as well. She's probably at home. She doesn't go out much any more."

The elderly woman who answered the door to Tobias was leaning on a Zimmer frame. It seemed to Tobias that her initial surprise gave way to pleasure at a visitor. She brightened when he showed his ID and said he was making enquiries about Emily Rasmussen.

"Why? What do you want to know about her? She hasn't got herself into some kind of trouble, has she?"

"I think she can help us with a line of enquiry," said Tobias.

"Well, don't loiter on the doorstep," said Mrs Rasmussen, already moving down the hallway. "Shut the door behind you."

Tobias followed her into a conservatory flooded with sunshine. Mrs Jacobsen manoeuvred herself into a high-backed cane chair and indicated to Tobias to sit in the matching chair opposite it.

"I knew Emily when she was a little girl. They lived next door. Then Jens died," Mrs Jacobsen paused, "it must be nearly twenty years ago. How time flies. Emily was devastated. Astrid too, of course. He was only forty-two. He had a heart attack. And he always seemed such a healthy man. He swam all year round, right here." She turned her head and shaded her eyes against the dazzle of the lake. "But he smoked, of course." She swivelled her gaze back to Tobias. "I hope you don't smoke, young man."

Tobias shook his head, smiling inwardly at being described as a young man and resigned to waiting for Mrs Jacobsen to tell him more about Emily. He risked a prompt.

"Did Emily's mother remarry?"

Mrs Jacobsen nodded. "She was a pretty woman. Fluffy blonde hair and big eyes. The kind of woman men want to protect. She met him at a bridge tournament, about a year after Jens died. They got married a year after that. Bridge," she added, "is the widow's friend. I don't know what I'd do with myself if I didn't play bridge. But when you get to my age, there aren't many men playing bridge. They've all died off." She sighed. "Are you married, Inspector?"

"Not at the moment." Get her back on track. Get her talking about Emily again. "I have a daughter. I think she'd be upset if I died. What age was Emily when her father died?"

"She was seventeen or eighteen, I think. She had such a shock. They were very close. She never took to her mother's new man. I met him a few times. He seemed nice enough to me. But Emily never liked him. She didn't want her mother to marry him. I remember one time we had them over for summer drinks in the garden. 'I don't like him,' she said to me. 'I don't want Mum to marry him.' She was fierce about it. She didn't like it when he moved in."

"And then they moved house?" Steady now. We're getting there.

Mrs Jacobsen nodded. "I don't suppose the new husband liked being in a house full of memories of the previous one. I assume Astrid is still married to him. I haven't seen or spoken to her for years. Although we still exchange Christmas cards."

Great. She has an address for Emily's mother.

"Poor Astrid," said Mrs Jacobsen. "So sad about her and Emily."

Take it easy. Don't rush her. "Why do you say that?"

"Emily left home and never came back. She and Astrid had some kind of argument. Emily went off with her boyfriend. Astrid was distraught. She couldn't stop crying. Her husband was upset as well. I wish I could remember his name."

"Do you remember the name of Emily's boyfriend?"

"I never met him," said Mrs Jacobsen. "I don't think either Astrid or her new husband approved of him. He was some kind of drop-out."

"Was he called Lennart?"

"I don't remember," said Mrs Jacobsen. "Astrid might remember."

At last. "Do you know how I can get in touch with her?"

"If you'd be kind enough to bring me that address book on the table beside the telephone, I'll tell you where she lives now."

Tobias found the fat, leather-bound book and brought it to Mrs Jacobsen. She turned the pages carefully.

"Here she is. Astrid Thomsen." She handed the book to Tobias. "You can write down the address. I don't have the telephone number."

Tobias copied the address and replaced the book on the table.

"Do you have any idea what Emily and her mother argued about?"

Mrs Jacobsen shook her head. "I wondered if it was something to do with Emily's boyfriend." She paused for a moment. "I remember the police came to the house a couple of times. Astrid was upset. She wouldn't tell me why the police had been there. She said she didn't want to talk about it." She added darkly, "Drugs, probably."

"You've been a great help, Mrs Jacobsen. I'll not trouble you any more."

"No trouble at all," said Mrs Jacobsen. "It's quite made my day."

22

WEDNESDAY: WEEK TWO

North Jutland Police District

So how are you this afternoon, Jolene?" Pernille Madsen dragged a chair towards the hospital bed in which Jolene sat propped up with pillows. "Have you remembered anything more about your attacker?"

Jolene shifted position and groaned. "I've been trying. I've been going over it all again in my mind. Why didn't I realise he was pervy? He must have been wearing the plastic gloves when he picked me up. I never saw him put them on. They were clear plastic. Hard to see. I couldn't tell he was a perv. Even when he said he just wanted to see me naked. Some clients are just strange." She shook her head. "They only want to gawp at you. Harmless voyeurs. Pathetic really. I thought he was one of those. I thought the briefcase was because he was a businessman. I wasn't expecting the punch." She put her hand on her stomach and winced.

"Did you notice anything about him? Had he any distinguishing marks? Think about it. Take your time," said Pernille.

"He didn't say much," said Jolene. "He just asked me to take my clothes off. He didn't take off any clothes himself.

Only his jacket. That's why I thought he was just a looker. Although most lookers are a bit older. The kind that can't get it up anymore. They don't want you to see their pathetic little dicks so they keep their clothes on. He had an ordinary kind of face. No beard, no moustache. Blondish hair." Jolene lay back, closed her eyes, put her hands to her ears and screwed up her face in concentration.

"Age?"

"Hard to tell." Jolene opened her eyes. "After he punched me, he pulled on a mask."

"Was he Danish?"

"I think so. He didn't say much. Just grunted. Especially when he was hitting me."

"Did he get blood on his clothes?"

"There was blood on the gloves," said Jolene. Her head snapped back as though she was re-living the assault. "I don't know if there was blood on his clothes."

"Did he take his clothes off before he went into the bathroom?"

Jolene thought for a moment. "I don't know. I must have passed out for a few minutes. I heard the shower running. I turned my head. I saw he wasn't in the room. I just tried to get myself free as quickly as possible. I fell in the alleyway. I could hear him coming down the stairs. I thought I was going to die. Then I heard the police siren. He stamped on my hand. She held out her bandaged hand, like a great white paw. I heard the bones crack." She shuddered. "Then he ran off. I think I passed out again. The next thing I knew, I was in the ambulance."

"But you managed to hold on to the hairs you pulled out of his head," said Pernille. "That's what will put him away for a long time." Under her breath she added, "but we have to catch him first."

None of the sex offenders whose prints were on file matched the partial thumbprint found on the badge or ball marker – Pernille still wasn't sure which it was – found at the crime scene. And it was possible the print was from one of Jolene's earlier clients. DNA was a better bet. If Magda succeeded in extracting it.

Pernille went to see the department's profiler, Matt Erikksen.

"I've looked at the file," he said. "You're right, Pernille. He's done this before. There's a clear modus operandi. The black strips of cloth, the plastic gloves, gagging the victim with her panties, taking pictures. Picking on prostitutes. He has a pattern. I've had a look through the database for Scandinavia. I didn't go back further than ten years. Look."

He handed a printout to Pernille. "Same pattern. Prostitutes, plastic gloves, panties, taking pictures. Except ten years ago, he was using a camera. In the last two attacks he used a smartphone."

"Three attacks in the last ten years," said Pernille. "But only the first one in Denmark. A year later, Swedish Lapland. Then a gap of seven years before Stockholm, two years ago. Norway last year. He's been getting about recently."

"I bet there were more attacks," said Matt. "I doubt if he waited seven years between attacks. The kind of rage he shows can't be suppressed for long. He's done this more often. My guess is not all the victims went to the police."

"It's possible," said Pernille. "Illegals wouldn't go to the police."

"He may be posting the pictures on Internet porn sites," said Matt. "Or he could just be wanking over them in private."

"I've sent Jolene's photo to the porn squad," said Pernille. "In case they come across a film of her attack. I'll send them photos of these other victims as well."

"You might get lucky," said Matt, in a tone which implied the opposite.

"Jolene managed to grab some hairs when she fought back," said Pernille. "When we get a DNA profile I can check it against known offenders. But…" she shrugged.

"…he's unlikely to be someone we already know about," said Matt. "And we need to find him before he does it again."

"So what's the profile?"

"He gets about. Probably for work. He's angry, but conceals it. He's very controlled in everyday life."

"We know most of that already," said Pernille impatiently. "What else can you tell me?"

"He'll do it again," said Matt. "And one of these days he'll go too far and kill someone."

23.

East Jutland Police District

Eddy Haxen was staring at his computer screen when Tobias got back to the office.

"Hi boss! Take a look at this." Eddy clicked the mouse.

Tobias peered over Eddy's shoulder at what looked like part of a rib cage. Eddy clicked the mouse. The bones swam closer.

"Two ribs. Definitely human, according to Harry," said Eddy. "They were found at six o'clock this morning in a litter bin. It's the second lot of bones in as many days. Some sicko dumped two arm bones in a bin at Gellerupparken on Monday night. Harry confirmed they were human. We shut down the city waste disposal for twenty-four hours. The rubbish collectors are all on special alert. One of them spotted these bones this morning in a bin near the harbour. We're going to have to shut the whole damn system down again."

"That will please Larsen," said Tobias.

"He doesn't want the media to get hold of this," said Katrine. "He's thinking maybe Bogman was killed by a psycho and the bones are from another victim. He doesn't want any panic about serial killers."

"I assume we have the bin and the rest of the contents," said Tobias.

Eddy nodded. "They're in the lab. Forensics are swabbing everything for prints and DNA."

"Let's have a look then," said Tobias.

They found Karl Lund in the laboratory steadying a pipette over a glass jar containing a cigarette butt. "It's all over there," he said, pointing to a random display of the contents of the rubbish bin. Each item had been bagged, labelled and laid on a table. There were five more cigarette butts, two cigarette packets, the remnants of a hamburger, three beer cans, four torn envelopes, a parking ticket, four bus tickets, three polystyrene coffee cups, half a croissant and a golf ball, cracked open. Tobias arranged the bags in two straight lines and alphabetical order.

"We should get prints from the cans, cups and cigarette packets, and maybe the golf ball," said Karl, "and DNA from the hamburger, the croissant and the cigarette butts. If nothing urgent comes in before the end of the day, I should have the results in time for tomorrow's briefing." He bent his head over the glass jar and released a drop of liquid from the pipette.

"Strange to find a golf ball in the city centre," said Eddy.

"It's a duff ball," said Tobias. "Maybe thrown out with rubbish from a car."

"There's parking not far from the bin," said Eddy. "I reckon it's about two kilometres as the crow flies between the bin in Gellerupparken where the arm bones were dumped and the bin at the harbour. Katrine is checking the bus routes."

"A bus goes past both bins," Katrine told them. "Maybe the perpetrator lives somewhere along the route. He takes the bus because he has no car and he's carrying stuff that's too heavy or awkward for a bicycle."

"The bones aren't that heavy," said Tobias. "What about CCTV?"

"Nothing near either of the bins," said Katrine. "Whoever is dumping the bones is choosing his spot."

"It could be a woman," said Eddy. "Remember Freja Frimand? She poisoned her husband with paraquat then cut up his body and dumped it, one piece at a time, in the canal?"

Katrine shuddered. "Before my time," she said. "How was she caught?"

"She hadn't put enough weights on the bits. They floated to the surface. We identified him from a tattoo. 'Freddy and

Freja forever'. She'd chopped through it but we found both pieces. We traced Freddy and Freja to an address in Randers. We found minute traces of his blood on a meat chopper. She hadn't cleaned it properly, the slattern."

"One other thing," said Karl. "We've scraped dirt off the bones. It's mud. Acidic mud."

"The same as the pond where we found Bogman?" asked Tobias.

"The PH is different," said Karl. "Maybe some kind of wet environment. Soil near a river, or a lake. There were salt traces as well."

"So the bones could have been in the sea?"

"Maybe near mudflats. But I think some kind of wet soil is more likely."

"Rivers, lakes, mudflats. The whole of Jutland," said Eddy. "The whole of bloody Denmark. Thanks a lot."

Tobias, Eddy and Katrine went back to the office.

"How was Lapland, boss?" asked Eddy.

"Interesting," said Tobias.

"What was the sergeant from Vilhelmina like?"

"Competent and intelligent."

"Not your type, then, Eddy," said Katrine.

Eddy made a face at her but couldn't stop it turning into a smile.

"We interviewed Berit Hansdatter," said Tobias. "The bracelet was a specially commissioned gift for a young Danish national called Lennart. She didn't remember his surname. The bracelet was ordered by his girlfriend, Emily Rasmussen, also Danish. According to Berit, they were devoted to each other. She gave him the silver bracelet. He gave her a ring."

"Even more strange she didn't report him missing, then," said Katrine.

"Maybe she killed him," said Eddy.

"What were they doing in the bog?"

Eddy grinned broadly and bounced his pelvis against the desk. Katrine's face reddened. She felt like an idiot again.

"A bog seems an odd place to choose," she said.

"Not if you were parked there for another reason," said Tobias slowly. "Didn't the flyers send a petition to the regional council? About not restricting access to Roligmose? There was a reason for the restriction. Protecting something. Bats or something. Remind me."

"Otters," said Katrine. "There was a threat to the otter population."

Tobias snapped his fingers. "That's it. They were protecting the otters. Just the kind of thing Emily and Lennart would get mixed up with. That's why they were there."

He now saw in his mind's eye the blue ambulance parked in the bog. Emily and Lennart walking through the reeds in moonlight. Getting into an argument.

"Why would she have a rock or a blunt instrument in her hand?" Tobias spoke this last thought aloud. "Imagine they were in the bog because they wanted to save otters. Imagine they were walking in the bog. You've seen the file. The pond where Lennart was found is a kilometre from where you could park a vehicle. Lennart was killed by a blow to the head with a blunt object. Why would Emily go walking in the bog with a blunt instrument?"

"Because she intended to kill him?" said Eddy.

"A blunt instrument is not the usual weapon of choice for a woman," said Tobias.

"Maybe they put up a tent in the bog," said Eddy. "They had an argument in the tent. She hit him with a hammer. The kind you use to drive in tent pegs."

"She'd have had to dismantle the tent, carry it all the way back across the bog to the van. Plus drag Lennart's body to the pond," said Katrine. "And why would she kill him?"

"Maybe he attacked her and she killed him in self-defence," said Eddy.

"Then why wouldn't she go to the police?"

Eddy shrugged. "People act stupidly all the time."

"I think if she killed him, she'd have needed help to move a tent, if there was one, and move the body as well," said Katrine.

"That's two people who need a motive," said Eddy.

"We'll know more when we've spoken to Emily Rasmussen's mother," said Tobias. "I've got the address. "He sat down and brought a map up on his screen. Larsen loomed behind him.

"I've been looking for you, Chief Inspector. I hear, from the National Commissioner no less, that you've been disturbing politicians on holiday. I hope it was worth it."

"The Hendriksens live at the address I'd been given for Bogman's girlfriend," said Tobias. "I had to speak to them to get the correct address."

"Oscar Hendriksen was elected to the Folketing last year," said Larsen. "He's a former judge. He's tipped for Justice Minister."

"It was crucial information, sir."

"I have enough people on my back," said the chief superintendent. "Thanks to Skaarup and Haxen letting that illegal at the hospital slip away, I'm still dealing with

Immigration. I've got the City Council complaining about the cost of holding up refuse collections. I don't need politicians as well. I expect progress by the end of the week. Ten o'clock briefing, Friday." He gave a curt nod and strode off.

"No pressure, then," said Eddy.

24.

Tobias took Katrine with him to interview Emily Rasmussen's mother. Her former neighbour in Skandeborg, Mrs Jacobsen, had talked about tears and arguments. He thought Katrine would handle tears better than Eddy. Better than himself, for that matter.

They approached the house along a stately avenue lined with poplars. The house was modern and built on a grand scale. The lily pond at the side of the house was the size of a tennis court.

"She must have married money both times," said Tobias.

"That's sexist," said Katrine. "She might have earned the money herself. Seventy per cent of women in Denmark work." She glanced around as they waited at the oak and glass-pannelled front door. "I wouldn't mind living here."

"You'll have to marry a rich man, then," said Tobias. "And that's not sexist. I know what a detective earns." He straightened his cuffs and grinned at Katrine.

A thin, smartly dressed blonde with dark eyes opened the door. Her face was matt smooth, her hair shone. Her coral lipstick exactly matched her shirt. Those immaculately manicured hands never did a day's work, thought Tobias. Mrs thirty per cent.

"Mrs Thomsen?" he said.

The woman nodded. "I'm Astrid Thomsen."

"I am Chief Inspector Lange and this is Inspector Skaarup. We are trying to contact Emily Rasmussen."

Astrid Thomsen's hand flew to her mouth.

"I understand that she's your daughter," said Tobias.

"What has she done? Has she been in some protest? Why do you want to speak to her?"

"We think she can help us with an investigation," said Tobias.

"What kind of investigation?"

"A murder investigation," said Tobias.

The colour drained from Astrid Thomsen's face. Tobias thought she was going to faint. He put out his arm to catch her. She clutched at it, steadied herself and said in a hoarse whisper, "Has something happened to Emily?"

"We have no reason to think so," said Tobias. "We would just like to speak to her. Do you know where she lives?"

Astrid Thomsen shook her head slowly. "I wish I did." She hesitated. "You'd better come in."

The house smelled of lavender and beeswax with a hint of cigarette smoke. The rugs in the vast sitting-room were thick and silky. The sofas were deep and soft. Katrine had never seen such a luxurious interior.

"Take a seat," said Astrid.

Katrine and Tobias perched on the edge of a sofa to avoid sinking into it. Astrid stood pulling at the sleeve of her silk shirt. She picked up a packet of cigarettes and a silver lighter from the coffee table. Her hand trembled as she lit a cigarette. She inhaled deeply before offering the packet to Tobias and Katrine. "Do you smoke?"

They shook their heads.

"I haven't seen Emily for nearly fourteen years," she said. "It eats me up, not knowing where she is." She drew nervously on her cigarette. "She sends me an email, once a year, on 12th April. I always reply, begging, pleading with her to get in touch, but she never answers. I sent her this address. We were living somewhere else when…" Her mouth trembled. "It's been thirteen years and seven months since I saw her, or heard her voice."

"Why the 12th April?" asked Tobias.

"It's the anniversary of my first husband's death," said Mrs Thomsen. "And Emily won't let me forget it." She ground her cigarette into an ashtray. "Wait here." She hurried out of the room. Minutes later, she returned carrying a box file. "All I have of Emily is in here." She sat down and cradled the box.

Katrine waited a moment before saying, "Do you have a photograph of Emily?"

"I have plenty," said Astrid. "And I have not enough." She opened the box and spread its contents on a glass table. Photographs, papers, a pink ribbon, a brown velvet rabbit, a necklace of red beads. Astrid touched the rabbit, almost surreptitiously, before she picked out a photograph and gave to Tobias. It showed Astrid with a blonde teenager – a younger version of herself, but with a stronger jaw line – sheltering under a golf umbrella on a beach near the water's edge. They were both smiling. The wind crumpled the sea behind them. The girl had her hand up to stop strands of hair blowing across her face.

"That was at Skagen," said Astrid. "We went there for Emily's 21st birthday. Just her and me. She loved the seaside. We asked a tourist to take the photograph."

"What's her date of birth?" asked Katrine. "And we need a photograph of Emily. Can we keep this one? We will have it copied and sent back to you."

Astrid shook her head. "That's my favourite." She selected another photograph from the box. "You can have this one instead." It was a head and shoulders photograph and looked as though it had been shot professionally in a studio. "Emily was born on 23rd March 1976. This was taken on her eighteenth birthday. Three weeks before her father died." She handed the photograph to Katrine and lifted a sheaf of papers from the table.

"These are print-outs of the emails she sent me. They're all the same, except for the first one."

She gave the pages to Tobias. They were fastened together with a paper clip. The most recent one was on the top.

"Hello Mum. I'm thinking about Dad and you and the wonderful life we had together."

Tobias leafed through the emails. They were exactly the same, except for one dated 24th September 1998.

"Dear Mum, I'm going away with Lennart. It's for the best. Sorry for all that's happened. I love you, Emily : ((:

"That's the first one she sent me. Just after she went away," said Astrid. "I thought the colon and brackets were a typing error but my husband said they meant something."

"They're an emoticon," said Katrine. "Meaning sad, very sad."

Astrid began to cry. Katrine hunted in her pockets for a tissue. Tobias produced a neatly folded, clean white cotton handkerchief and handed it to Astrid. She dried her eyes, sniffed, and composed herself.

"Thanks." She moved to give the handkerchief back to Tobias. He shook his head.

"Keep it. I have another."

"I'm sorry," said Astrid. "It just brings it all back to me. It was a horrible time. Completely horrible." She twisted the edge of the handkerchief. "Emily said unspeakable things about my husband. They were all lies. Terrible lies. The police said so."

"The police?"

"They came to the house and they took away his computer and his laptop." She paused and took a deep breath. "Emily told the police he had pornography on it."

Katrine exchanged a puzzled glance with Tobias. "Pornography is not illegal in Denmark," she said.

"That kind is," said Astrid. "The kind Emily accused him of having."

"Can you be more specific, Mrs Thomsen?" said Tobias.

"I don't want to talk about it," said Astrid. "It distresses me even to remember it. Anyway it wasn't true. The police said so. It was a wicked thing to accuse him of. Wicked. They arrested Marcus and took his laptop." She beat her fists together. Her shoulders shook. "And there was nothing on it!" she shouted. "No pornography. Just his business stuff." She grabbed another cigarette and lit it. "I was so angry with Emily." She jumped to her feet and began pacing the room, alternately puffing and waving her cigarette about. "We had a terrible argument. The police were going to charge her with wasting their time, but Marcus persuaded them not to. He said Emily was disturbed and possessive about me. He was kind and tolerant to her. She was horrible to him. She made those dreadful accusations. And he made excuses for her. And what thanks did he get? Not a word. It was the same when she and her friends were protesting about the golf club. Marcus persuaded the owner not to charge Emily with criminal damage. Even when she drove a mechanical digger into a wall." Astrid collapsed into an armchair.

Tobias remembered his golf day with Norbert. The day Bogman was found. Hadn't Norbert said something about green activists and a digger being driven into a wall at Skovlynd? Was that Emily?

"Do you mean the clubhouse at Skovlynd?" he said. "Owned by Kurt Malling?"

Astrid nodded. "Emily and her boyfriend said it was the habitat of some rare otter or something." She shook her head wearily.

"Where was Emily living?" asked Katrine.

"In our house in Skanderborg. She had her own room and study. But she didn't like it when Marcus moved in. It was only for a short time. Until this house was built. A year, maybe a bit longer. But she spent more and more time with her boyfriend. They were always travelling and protesting. Here, there and everywhere." She waved her cigarette dismissively. "Sweden, Estonia, Germany, you name it. He had some kind of mobile home." Astrid gave a little shudder.

"What was his name?" asked Tobias.

"Lennart. I thought he was quite a nice boy when I first met him, despite his being left-wing and always protesting about something. Marcus thought he was a bad influence on Emily. It turned out he was right. Emily put off going to university. She had this ridiculous idea that she could make a living as a musician." Astrid jumped up and began to pace the room again, sucking on her cigarette. She swirled around to face Tobias and Katrine. "Why exactly do you want to speak to Emily?"

"We found the remains of a young man at Roligmose," said Tobias. "We traced a bracelet found with the remains to a jewellery designer in Sweden. She told us the bracelet was ordered and paid for by your daughter."

Astrid went rigid. "What happened to him? How did he die?"

"We think he was murdered," said Tobias.

Astrid gasped. "Why was he murdered? Was it about drugs?"

"We are trying to find out," said Tobias. "We hoped Emily could tell us if he had any enemies. If anyone had a motive for killing him."

"What was his surname?" asked Katrine.

Astrid put her hands to her temple and shut her eyes in concentration. She opened her eyes and shook her head. "I can't remember. I don't know if I ever knew it. I only met him a few times. Emily told me his mother was a drug addict. She was banned from Christiana for selling hard drugs. Imagine. She died when Lennart was young. I don't think he ever knew his father. I felt sorry for him. But Marcus thought he was after Emily's money."

"Emily had money?"

"Her father, my first husband, wrote jingles for advertisements and was very successful. Emily will inherit his money when I'm gone. Maybe she'll come back to Denmark then," she added bitterly. "When I'm cold and in my grave."

"You say 'come back to Denmark,'" said Katrine. "Do you think she is in another country?"

"I know she is," said Astrid. "She's in Sweden. It says so on her Facebook page."

"When did you find out she had a Facebook page?" asked Katrine.

"Last week." Astrid brightened. "It made her seem closer somehow. I know that's absurd. But it gives me hope."

"How did you find out?"

"A young friend suggested it. I don't know about that sort of thing. I don't do much on the computer, except receive and send emails."

"Have you tried to contact Emily through Facebook?" asked Katrine.

"I asked my friend to help me. She said the way the page was set up meant I couldn't send Emily a message."

The door opened and a broad-shouldered, balding man in a well-cut business suit came in. "I saw you had visitors," he said. "I hope I'm not interrupting something."

"My husband, Marcus. Back from Stockholm," said Astrid. She jumped up to greet him. "How was it?"

"Fine, fine." He kissed his wife on the cheek and shook hands with Tobias and Katrine.

"Our visitors are from the police," said Astrid. "Chief Inspector Lange and Inspector Skaarup." She took her husband's hand. "They've been asking about Emily."

He stiffened. "What has she done?" He patted his wife's hand. "Don't get upset. We'll sort it out whatever it is." He sighed. "Tell me what she's done."

"Nothing," said Astrid. "She's done nothing."

"We'd like to speak to her," said Tobias.

"So would we," said Marcus. "Do you know where she is?"

"We were hoping Mrs Thomsen could tell us," said Tobias.

"We've had no contact with Emily for a long time," said Marcus. "Apart from an email once a year. But we don't give up hope, do we darling?" He patted Astrid's hand again. "Why do you want to speak to Emily?"

"We believe a body discovered in a bog at Roligmose is that of Emily's former boyfriend," said Tobias. "His first name is Lennart. We were hoping Emily could tell us his second name so that we can inform his next of kin." And find out who murdered him, he added silently to himself.

"That's terrible," said Marcus. "I can't say I liked him. I thought him a bad influence on Emily. But all the same…" He shook his head. "What happened to him?"

"He was murdered," said Tobias. "Beaten to death."

Astrid gasped and hid her face in her husband's shoulder.

"My wife's upset," said Marcus. "This is a great shock to her. She's naturally worried about Emily."

"Just one or two more questions," said Katrine quickly. "I understand Emily is on Facebook."

"I don't know much about that kind of thing," said Marcus. "The daughter of a friend said Emily might have a Face page or whatever it's called."

Astrid raised her head. "Sofie was a great help."

"Sofie?" Tobias had spoken before he realised it.

"Sofie Fisker," said Astrid. "Marcus plays golf with her father."

Tobias was briefly flummoxed. Katrine voiced the question he was about to ask.

"Was Sofie friendly with Emily?"

"Not really," said Astrid. "But she knows how much I'd like to find her. She was trying to help. I'm grateful for that."

"But you discovered you couldn't contact Emily via Facebook," said Katrine.

"Sofie said Emily had arranged it so that no one could contact her unless she asked them to."

"You're certain it's Emily's Facebook page? I assume you recognised the photograph," said Katrine.

"There's no photograph," said Astrid. "But she's the only Emily Rasmussen in Lapland. It says Sápmi, but I know that's Lapland. Emily liked Lapland. She told me she liked it. I think she went back there with her boyfriend. I think she's there now."

"You think, but you don't know," said Tobias.

"I know it in my heart," said Astrid. "I know it in my bones."

Marcus Thomsen accompanied Tobias and Katrine to their car. He glanced back at the house. Astrid was at the window, white-faced, puffing on a cigarette.

"My wife is distraught about all this," said Marcus. "I have to say, given all the grief Emily has caused us, if and when she gets in contact, I'd cheerfully wring her neck." He held up both hands and smiled. "I don't mean that seriously of course. But between you and me, she was difficult. She was jealous of me and possessive about her mother. Came and went without telling us. Used the house like a hotel. Astrid would go to make dinner and discover Emily had raided the fridge and the cupboards."

"Emily made some accusations against you," said Tobias.

Marcus waved the unspoken accusations away. "I forgave her," he said. "She suffered from depression after her father died. He died suddenly. It came at a bad time in her life. Frankly, she didn't like me taking her father's place and her mother's attention. I could understand. I did my best, but," he shrugged, "my best wasn't good enough."

"Was Emily ever violent?" asked Katrine.

Marcus thought for a moment. "There was a bit of door banging. Some sulks. Nothing more. I'm sorry we can't be more help. There's nothing Astrid and I would like more than to see Emily again."

"We might be able to trace her through Hotmail and Facebook," said Katrine.

"I hope you find her," said Marcus.

"So do we," said Tobias.

He was silent on the way back to Aarhus. If Agnes went away and never said where she was, his heart would break. How did Astrid Thomsen bear it? When he brought the car to a halt in the car park at headquarters, he took his phone from his jacket and gestured to Katrine to go ahead. He called Agnes. There was no reply. He texted her. "Thinking about you, Pumpkin. Hope all well." He got out of the car and stood for a moment gazing at a small patch of blue in an otherwise grey sky. What was it his father used to say? Enough blue for a sailor's trousers? A message flashed up on his phone. "Hi, Dad. All well. X." His heart lightened. He put the phone back in his pocket and switched his thoughts to Emily Rasmussen and the fastest way to find her.

When he got back to the office, Katrine was searching for Emily on Facebook.

"There are dozens of Emily Rasmussens," she told him.

"But I think this is the right one."

She swivelled the screen so that Tobias could see a postage-stamp sized, faceless, head and shoulders image, and the name Emily Rasmussen. The only other words on the screen were "Emily lives in Sápmi."

"The privacy setting is high," said Katrine. "It's one way traffic. Emily can find friends and get in touch. But they can't contact Emily."

"Get me the file on Emily's complaint about her stepfather," said Tobias. "There might be something useful in it. But I'm not holding my breath."

"I've checked the National Register," Eddy called out to them. "The only address for Emily Rasmussen, date of birth 23rd March 1976, is the Skovlynd address where she was living with her mother and stepfather, before they moved."

"Ask the best people-tracer in Denmark," said Tobias. "The taxman."

25.

THURSDAY: WEEK TWO

Two sets of bones in two weeks?" said Larsen. "First Bogman, now this lot. I don't like it. I don't like coincidence. I want the same team to work on both cases. Right? So let's get on with it. What can you tell us, Harry?"

"The bones," Harry Norsk pointed to a row of photographs displayed on a screen in the Incident Room, "were found in two different places. The arm bones were dumped in an underground bin in Gellerupparken." He put his forefinger on a red dot on the street map of Aarhus next to the photographs. "The ribs were found in a bin here," he stabbed a second red dot on the map, "at the harbour."

"You have no idea where they came from or who put them there, right?" said Larsen. "And they're definitely human bones."

"No question," said Harry Norsk.

"Are they from the same person?" asked the prosecutor, Renata Molsing.

"I think so," said Harry. "But I'm waiting for Brix's opinion. He's sent them for carbon dating."

"More cost," said Larsen. "Carbon dating isn't cheap. Have you any theories on how or when this person died, assuming the bones are from the same person?"

"There's a crack in one of the ribs and a fracture in the ulna. I can't say what caused these but they were ante mortem. The breaks weren't caused by being in the rubbish. They occurred when the person was alive. Brix will be able to tell us more. And we should have the carbon dating results next week."

"We could be wasting our time as well as our money," said Larsen. "What crime are we investigating?"

"It's a crime if the bones have been stolen from a hospital or museum," said Renata Molsing. "It's a crime to dig up a grave, unless it's an official exhumation."

"I've checked with all the hospitals in the city," said Katrine. "I'm searching for reports of graves being dug up or disturbed. Nothing in the last two weeks. That's the longest rubbish is left before being collected."

"Maybe whoever did this has dumped bones before and they weren't spotted by the waste collectors," said Renata.

"Where are we on Bogman?" asked Larsen.

Tobias got to his feet and stood to one side of a screen displaying an enlarged photograph of Emily.

"Emily Rasmussen," said Tobias, "former girlfriend of Bogman and the key to identifying him. We know his first name is Lennart. A Swedish silversmith made the bracelet found with his remains. It was ordered and paid for by Emily Rasmussen. The bracelet is dated 1997. We know Emily and Lennart were together then in Northern Sweden, in Vasterbotten county, Lapland or Sapmi as we're supposed to call it. We know they were there in the summers of 1997 and 1998. They took part in a protest against a nuclear waste facility. They played at a concert. They drove a converted ambulance with a rainbow design. In fact they lived in it. We know they came back to Denmark at the end of the summer of 1998 because Emily had an argument with her mother and left home in September 1998." Tobias paused. "Emily is estranged from her mother. They haven't spoken in the last fourteen years. They fell out because Emily told the police her stepfather, Marcus Thomsen, had illegal porn on his computer. We don't know if it was kiddy porn but it's a fair guess. Emily's mother wouldn't talk about it. She says the police took away the computer and found nothing. No charges were brought. She says the police were going to charge Emily with wasting police time but Thomsen asked them not too. I've asked for the file." He glanced at Katrine.

"I sent the request yesterday," she said. "Registry said it might take a day or two. They're understaffed."

"If Emily was jealous enough to accuse her stepfather of being a paedophile and was possessive about her mother," said Eddy. "How would she have reacted if Lennart went off with someone else?"

"Badly," said Katrine.

"You think Emily Rasmussen might have something to do with Bogman's murder?" asked Larsen.

"It's possible," said Katrine.

"The silversmith said they were in love," said Tobias. "Inseparable."

"Then why didn't she report him missing?" asked Eddy.

"Perhaps they fell out of love," said Katrine. "Or one of them fell in love with someone else. It happens."

"Even so, you'd think she'd hear on the grapevine that he'd gone missing," said Larsen.

"Suppose they'd split up," said Renata. "He stayed in

Denmark. She went back to Sweden. She didn't know he was missing. She doesn't know he's dead."

"That's also possible," said Tobias.

"At the very least, she's a witness. We need to find her," said Renata.

"I've asked Sweden to put out a general alert," said Tobias.

"She hasn't filed a tax return," said Eddy. "Inland Revenue have her listed at the Skovlynd address. She has a passport issued in 1996. It hasn't been renewed. She has claimed no benefits, committed no traffic offences."

"She must have kept in touch with somebody," said Katrine. "She must have some friends here."

"Presumably they don't know Lennart is dead," said Eddy. "There's been no report in the newspapers. This all happened fourteen years ago. No instant messaging then. Not so many people had email. It was easier to lose touch with people."

"Emily sends emails once a year from a Hotmail address and she has a page on Facebook," said Tobias. "Can we trace her that way, Renata?"

"It's complicated, and costly," said Renata. "Where's Facebook based?"

"Seattle," said Eddy.

Renata groaned. "And Hotmail is also based in the United States. I wish she used a Danish or any European-based site. There'd still be a lot of procedure to go through but it would be easier than trying to get information from a server in the United States. There are different privacy laws, international treaties, protocols. I have to ask the Ministry of Justice to approve an approach to the American authorities.

The Ministry will have to issue a warrant. We need to show good cause. The Americans have to agree good cause before they approve a warrant to disclose data. Plus, most of this stuff is held remotely."

"Data tracking is done by civilian specialists," said Larsen. "They don't come cheap."

"And they need time," said Renata. "There's so much stuff out there in cyberspace, it's like looking for a needle in a haystack."

Larsen tut-tutted. "We need to justify all this expense. There must be other ways of identifying Lennart."

"They were both members of an environmental protest group," said Tobias. "They tried to stop the development of a golf course at Skovlynd. There should be newspaper reports, television coverage."

"Then start with that," said Larsen.

26.

Tobias and Katrine spent the rest of the day at the television station viewing the available footage on the demonstrations against the Skovlynd golf development. Most of it showed demonstrators with placards – "*Stay Green – Say NO to Golf*"; "*Skovlynd Forest. Home to Bechstein's Bat*" – sitting down in the road to block the path of machinery and being removed by the police. There was no violence. There was no Emily either.

The edit suite was hot, dark and untidy. Tobias was uncomfortable. The bin overflowed with paper, there were empty paper cups on the floor and the remains of a hotdog on a paper plate at the elbow of Oscar, the technician, who was chewing gum. Tobias tried not to look. He was about to suggest they take a break, go outside, feel the breeze, maybe have a cold beer, when Katrine said, "Hold on, a moment. Can you stop it? Can you go back to the guy with the moustache talking to the reporter?"

The pictures reversed with the chipmunk squeaks of speech played back at speed, and stopped. An earnest looking reporter held a microphone to the moustachioed mouth of a young man with a pale face and long dark hair.

"Look," said Katrine, leaning forward. "Behind his left shoulder. There's a red car and next to it a blue van sticking out. Can you zoom in? There. You can see the wheels and handlebars of two bicycles on the top and a bit of rainbow on the back door. And the number plate. Yellow and white. Can you enlarge it?"

"I can freeze the frame and you can look at it on a bigger screen," said Oscar.

A fuzzy image of the number plate flashed on to a screen in the bank of monitors in front of them.

"This is as good as I can get it," said Oscar. "The first letter is S."

"The second is N," said Katrine.

"You two have good eyesight," said Tobias. "Sort it out. I'm taking a breather." He stepped into the sunlit corridor. The building had an empty, weekend feel. He opened a window and inhaled fresher air into his lungs. The phone in his pocket vibrated. He pulled it out and read the text message. "Back Tuesday pm. Dinner? Sofie."

He felt invigorated. He went back into the edit suite.

Katrine waved a piece of paper. "We're not sure if the

last number is 5 or 3 but we've got the rest. I've texted Eddy. With both 5 and 3 as the last number."

Tobias sat down, grinning. "Thanks. Good work. Who's the guy with the moustache?"

Oscar glanced at a sheet of paper. "Interview at 49 seconds. Nicholas Hove."

Tobias remembered the plump, clean-shaven man he'd seen talking to Kurt Malling at the Skovlynd charity dinner. Could this be the same man? "I saw him just over a week ago," he said. "What a difference fourteen years makes. He's twice as heavy and has half as much hair."

He scanned the faces of the demonstrators sitting on the road behind Nicholas Hove. They were young. The girls had long blonde hair and serious expressions. They reminded him of Agnes. None of them was Emily. The boys looked relaxed. They grinned at the camera. Was one of these grinning boys Emily's boyfriend, Lennart?

"Is Hove the only interviewee?"

Oscar checked a print out. "It looks like it. There are only two more reports. April 26th and 27th 1998."

Tobias settled into his seat. The next sequence of soundless pictures began.

Tobias recognised a side entrance to the golf course, near the ninth hole. He presumed it was the entrance used by the trucks and diggers during the construction of the course. There was a shot of a digger scooping out earth from what was going to become a lake. The shot changed to Kurt Malling watching a yellow dumpster tipping sand into a bunker. Next, a dozen demonstrators blocked the path of a yellow Hydrema digger. Then Kurt Malling confronted two demonstrators chained to a digger. The last two film sequences showed Kurt Malling with group of uniformed police, and Emily Rasmussen being escorted to a police car.

"Hold it there," said Tobias. "Can you enlarge that?"

The picture flashed up on the bigger screen.

"It's definitely Emily," said Katrine.

"Just as well," said Oscar. "There's no more footage."

"Thanks," said Tobias. "We've got what we needed. I'll set up a meeting with Nicholas Hove."

Eddy was the only person in the Investigations room. He looked up as they came in.

"A Mercedes van was registered in March 1997 in the name of Emily Rasmussen," he said. "At an address in Skandeborg."

"That makes sense," said Tobias. "Emily was the one with the money. She paid for the van."

"How old was the van when she bought it?" asked Katrine.

"Old enough," said Eddy. "It was registered as an ambulance in 1987. But it's a Mercedes. She could still be driving it."

"It would have to pass roadworthy tests if it's in Denmark," said Katrine.

"Other countries have regulations too," said Eddy. "She must have tax and insurance as well. But there's nothing on the register since 1997."

"Maybe it's permanently parked up somewhere and she's living in it," said Katrine. "Maybe she's abandoned it and bought a new one."

"I've checked all the Emily Rasmussens who registered a vehicle or applied for a driving licence," said Eddy. "None of them fits Emily's profile. They're all ten years older or younger."

"It could be in Sweden," said Katrine. "Or anywhere."

"Being driven illegally," said Eddy. "Her licence would be out of date by now."

"She might have a Swedish licence," said Katrine.

"Send the details to Europol and Interpol," said Tobias.

"I've done that," said Eddy. "With two versions of the plate. One with last number 3 and one with 5."

"Any newspaper reports on the golf club protests?"

"The newspaper archive isn't digitised that far back," said Eddy. "There's nothing online. The librarian at Jyllands Posten has gone home. I've sent requests to the big five dailies but tomorrow is Great Prayer Day, remember? And the librarians don't come in at weekends. We won't see anything until Monday."

"Any sign of the file on Astrid Thomsen's husband?"

"They haven't found it yet," said Eddy. "Cutbacks. Plus the weekend. We should have it by Monday or Tuesday." He paused. "It's a nice evening. Tomorrow is a holiday. This is the first decent weather we've had for weeks. Unless you have something urgent for me, boss, I'm going sailing tonight." He picked up his car keys and added in a casual way, "Would either of you like to join me?"

Tobias thought about endless days in the boat with his father, of sadness as deep as the ocean, of longing to be steady on his feet, facing the future on dry land. "I'm not much of a sailor," he said.

He sometimes wondered if he'd taken up golf in an unconscious attempt to avoid long hours bobbing on the water trailing a fishing line to catch the occasional salmon, or cramped in the cabin playing chess with his morose father. A round of golf took at least three and a half hours and precluded taking the boat out. His father, a dutiful parent, silently caddied for him in junior competitions. That was how he had met his second wife, Tobias's stepmother, Inge. Her daughter, Margrethe, and Tobias had been junior members at the same time and at the same club. Tobias was still a member there. The course wasn't as well-designed or well-tended as Skovlynd, but Tobias liked it. He thought he would ask Norbert if he was free to play with him.

And then he would put in a call to Nicholas Hove.

27.

FRIDAY: WEEK TWO

North Jutland Police District

Pernille Madsen wondered why her personal life had become so dull that she was glad to come to work on Great Prayer Day, when the rest of the country was on holiday. She had a caseload that kept her busy, but not so busy that she couldn't take a day off. She had turned down invitations from friends to spend the holiday weekend with them in Copenhagen. They were all couples with children. Pernille liked children, but she didn't want to spend the weekend in Tivoli Gardens. Besides, she wanted to find Jolene's attacker before it was too late. Before he went too far and killed someone.

She had identified three attacks in the last ten years in Scandinavia. All followed the same pattern. The victims were prostitutes. They were gagged with their own panties. They'd been filmed or photographed.

She read the file on the first known attack. Versterbro in Copenhagen. A hotel near the station. The victim had four broken ribs, a broken jaw, extensive bruising in the genital area. She had been found by the hotel manager. Manager? Did places like that actually have managers? Whatever he was, pimp or room-renter, he'd been questioned and cleared.

She opened the file on the second attack. The report was in Swedish, but she understood enough to see that the pattern was the same. The victim was a Sami working as a prostitute in Pitea, Northern Sweden. She had attempted to drown herself in the river after the attack but had been spotted by a tourist and rescued. Her injuries were similar to those of the first victim. The attacker's routine was the same. Plastic gloves, mask, camera.

Only a year between these first two attacks. Then a gap of seven years to the third attack. Stockholm. The perpetrator had contacted the victim online. She had gone to his hotel – one of the smartest in Stockholm. The bedside telephone in the room had been disconnected. The victim had been found, unconscious, by a hotel cleaner. No fingerprints, no DNA.

Smart bastard. But Magda is extracting your DNA from the hairs that Jolene yanked from your head. Well done, Jolene, thought Pernille.

She decided to widen the search. She would contact Europol to find out if there'd been similar sex attacks elsewhere in Europe. That would have to wait until Monday. And it would take time. The weekend stretched ahead. She might go to Tivoli Gardens after all.

East Jutland Police District

Tobias intended to enjoy his day off. He was in good spirits when he parked at his golf club. The manager, Christer Alsing, hurried towards him.

"Tobias, just the man I need. Can you come to the office and give me some advice?"

"I'm meeting a guest," said Tobias. "Can it wait until after we've played?"

"Not really," said Christer. "I'm leaving at five o'clock."

Tobias looked at the sky.

"No need to worry about rain," said Christer.

"My guest will be here soon," said Tobias.

"You can see the car park from the office. This won't take long."

Tobias reluctantly allowed himself to be ushered through the clubhouse door, into the office and into a chair in front of a computer screen showing the pond on the 14th hole at sunset.

Christer pulled up a chair beside Tobias and clicked the mouse. "Take a look at this."

From the bushes near the fourteenth green, a black shape emerged. It took Tobias a second or two to realise it was a human being – man or woman he couldn't tell – in a wetsuit, wearing flippers, goggles, scuba diving equipment and carrying what looked like an empty, white net. The effect was somewhere between hilarious and sinister. The figure flapped, penguin-like, towards the pond, adjusted a weight on his belt, entered the water and sank beneath the surface. The screen went black.

"The head green keeper hid in the trees," said Christer. "Waited for hours to catch him at it. Filmed it all on his smartphone."

Another image swam on to the screen. The creature in black broke the surface of the water, splashed towards the bank, crawled up through the reed bed and got to his feet clutching what looked like a giant bag of slimy frogspawn. Tobias wanted to laugh.

"Golf balls," said Christer. "He's diving for golf balls.

On private property. That's illegal isn't it?"

Tobias kept his face straight. "I'll get someone to look into it."

"We drain the ponds for balls every six months," said Christer. "We sell them in the pro-shop. The number retrieved was going down. That's how we twigged someone was stealing them. So what do you think we should do about it?"

"Put a CCTV camera there," said Tobias. "It doesn't even have to be a real one. That should deter the Creature from the Black Lagoon." His mouth twitched.

"Good idea," said Christer. "Thanks for the advice. Have a good game."

Norbert laughed when Tobias told him about the frogman. "But it's no joke for the club," he said. "Skovlynd has the same problem. They've lost revenue. The manager told me last week they got less than half the balls they usually retrieve. He's reluctant to put up a CCTV camera. Malling doesn't like the idea. Too many celebrity members not wanting their duff golf shots to turn up on YouTube."

They reached the fourteenth hole. The green was protected by trees on the right and the large pond on the left. Tobias and Norbert successfully avoided both.

"All square," said Norbert.

"This won't take long." Tobias walked off the green towards the clump of bushes from which he'd seen the frogman emerge. He squeezed through the bushes, clambered over a ditch and dropped down on to the road. He heard Norbert calling out,

"We're playing golf, Tobias. It's a holiday. You're off duty."

Tobias crouched to examine tyre marks in the grassy

verge. He climbed back up the ditch and pushed his way through the bushes to the green.

"He's smart, our frogman," said Tobias. "He doesn't go near the pond on the tenth. It's too near the clubhouse. We're at the far end of the course here and he can get to the road easily."

"Same with the ninth at Skovlynd," said Norbert. "There's an access road used by the green keepers at the back of the lake."

"He drives a van of some kind," said Tobias. "He should get his tyres changed. The two left ones are bald. Not so smart."

"A lot of people are finding life tough at the moment," said Norbert. "I admire his enterprise. I wonder where he's selling the balls?"

Tobias found the probable answer to that question on his way back to Aarhus after a satisfying dinner with Inge and Norbert. The light was fading from the sky when his headlights picked up a sign at the side of the road. *Golf Driving Range. 8am – 10pm daily. Lessons. Shop. Big Reductions. Next Left 2 km.* Out of curiosity, he took the next turn left and followed signs – *Lake Balls: 5 Lessons 80 kroner: Clothing bargains* – to a floodlit driving range.. The floodlights went off as he turned into the car park. The glass door to the shop was locked but an interior light was still on. Tobias could see a barrel-shaped metal basket filled with golf balls by the desk. *Lake Balls 5k each. 50 balls 200k.* He rapped the glass but there was no reply. The shop light went out. A car door banged. An engine revved. A white van came at speed from the back of the shop. It slowed as it passed Tobias. The window went down. A voice called out, "Sorry, mate. We're closed. Come back tomorrow." The van raced away before Tobias could speak.

It was raining when he got back to Aarhus and parked in the square. He left the golf clubs in the boot of the car and hurried to his flat. He switched on a light, shook the raindrops from his jacket and hung it on a coat hanger to dry. He lit the candle on the table by the window and squared the file that lay there. He selected a bottle of Monbazillac from the wine cabinet, poured himself a small glass, carried it to the table, sat down, opened the file and began to read.

Emily Rasmussen was vital to the enquiry. People remembered her. He thought of all contradictory adjectives they'd attached to her. Gentle, honest, musical, jealous, possessive, fierce. A warrior for the environment. A young woman in love. Like Agnes.

Lennart, by contrast, was a cipher.

The telephone rang. Tobias glanced at the number and saw it was Hilde. He closed the file, stood up and opened the door to the balcony. He could see Hilde silhouetted in the rain-streaked window opposite. He pressed the answer button on his phone.

"I was wondering if you'd like a nightcap," Hilde said.

Tobias hesitated. "Not tonight." And maybe not any other night, he thought. Time to move on. To Sofie? I ought to say something to Hilde.

"I wanted to tell you that Eric has got a shore job." She hesitated. "And I'm pregnant."

Tobias felt as though the blood was draining from his body.

"Don't worry, Tobias," said Hilde. "It's not yours. We were careful. The dates don't fit. Eric wanted a baby. Me too."

Tobias could now see her moving about in her flat, see her hand gently rubbing her belly.

"We're moving to a house," said Hilde. "With a garden. It was good while it lasted, wasn't it? Good for both of us, I think."

"Good luck," said Tobias.

"I wish you luck as well. I'm waving at you."

Tobias waved back. The light went out in Hilde's flat. He stood for a moment. There was the usual Saturday night noise from the square. The wet tiles on the cathedral roof glistened under the floodlights. Rain dripped from the lilac trees in the gardens below. He hoped Agnes wasn't tree-hugging and getting soaked. He picked up his phone and sent her a text. "Dry & studying or wet & tree-guarding?" He closed the balcony door. A response from Agnes flashed on his phone. "Dry & partying. Love you."

Tobias sat down again and opened the file. He took out one of the stills copied from the news footage of the demonstrations. Emily Rasmussen being arrested. She was looking straight at the camera. A policeman gripped one of her arms. She had the other raised in a clenched fist salute. A spirited girl. An attractive girl. But also neurotic and jealous, according to her step-father. Where was she now?

28

SATURDAY: WEEK TWO

Nicholas Hove got up from behind the desk in his office overlooking the harbour in Aarhus, shook hands with Tobias and said genially, "I haven't been interviewed by the police since my old days as an activist. Take a seat, Chief Inspector. I see you have to work on holiday weekends too. No rest for the wicked. What can I do for you?"

"It's about your days as an environmental activist," said Tobias. "Specifically, about a protest at Skovlynd in the late nineties."

"I remember," said Nicholas Hove. "The golf course versus Bechstein's Bat. The golf course won. Not surprising, given the amount of money Kurt Malling was willing to throw around."

Tobias raised an eyebrow.

"I don't mean money in brown envelopes," said Nicholas Hove smoothly. "Malling was a big donor to the library and the museum," he paused, "as well as the Conservative Party, of course. You know he's standing in the election?"

Tobias nodded.

"Is someone suggesting there were kickbacks?" said Hove. "Is that what this is about? It's a bit late in the day, is it not?"

"This is about a murder enquiry," said Tobias.

Hove looked surprised, but not perturbed. "Who's been murdered? Is it someone I know?"

"We found human remains in a bog at Roligmose," said Tobias.

"I read about that," said Nicholas. "Why do you want to speak to me?"

"We have reason to believe they are the remains of someone who was part of a protest against building the golf course at Skovlynd. Do you remember Emily Rasmussen?"

Hove looked shocked. "The reports said the remains were of a male."

"That's correct," said Tobias. "We haven't identified him yet. But we know his girlfriend at that time was Emily Rasmussen and she was part of the Skovlynd protest. We haven't been able to contact her. Can you help?"

"I remember Emily Rasmussen," said Hove. "I didn't know her well."

"Her boyfriend was called Lennart."

Hove closed his eyes in concentration, opened them and shook his head. "Sorry. I don't remember Emily with a boyfriend. There was a guy called Lennart who used to turn up at demos, but I don't remember much about him." He grinned. "I mostly noticed the girls."

Tobias took an envelope from his briefcase and shook three photographs onto the desk. He turned them to face Hove and straightened each one of them.

"Can you name the people in these photographs?" he asked.

Hove picked up each photograph in turn and studied it.

"I recognise my younger self, of course. But I have to think about the others. People came and went. Even Aksel."

"Who's Aksel?"

"He'd been on protests all over. He was a kind of green anarchist. He was the most committed of all of us."

"Is he in any of these photographs?"

Hove shook his head. "Aksel was good at avoiding being photographed. And avoiding arrest."

"What's his surname? Do you know where he is now?"

"I don't think I even knew it. I have no idea where he is now. Everything petered out after the arrests. We knew we'd lost. People drifted away."

He picked up the first photograph again. "The girls chained to the Hydrema are Emily Rasmussen and Gudrun Jeppesen," he grinned. "I had a bit of thing with Gudrun."

"Is Emily's former boyfriend in any of these photos?"

"Former boyfriend? Did Emily and he split up?"

"We assume so," said Tobias. "She didn't report him missing."

"They must have broken up," said Hove. "Do you know when he died?"

"About fourteen or fifteen years ago. We think no later than 1999. Probably just after the Skovlynd protest. Look again at the photos. Is he in any of them?"

"I don't recognise him if he is. As I said, I don't remember much about him."

"Are you still in touch with Gudrun Jeppesen?"

"We haven't spoken in a long time," said Nicholas. His grin was sheepish now. "I married a friend of Gudrun's. It was all a bit sticky."

"I'd like to talk to her," said Tobias. "Have you any idea where we might find her?"

Hove was silent for a moment. "I have no idea where she is now. At the time, she was sharing a house near the university." He paused. "I have an idea she went to live on an island."

"Keep the photographs," said Tobias. "Let me know if you remember anything else." He put his card on the desk.

Hove's secretary put her head around the door. "Kurt Malling has arrived," she said.

Tobias didn't hide his surprise.

"Politics makes strange bedfellows," said Nicholas Hove smoothly. "Malling wants my support for a wind farm project that's running into opposition." He laughed. "Bechstein's Bat strikes again." He stood up. "I hope I've been some help."

He escorted Tobias to the door. "If you get in touch with Gudrun, give her my regards."

Tobias found a Gudrun Jeppeson Holm in the white pages of the national telephone directory. She lived on the island of Aero. Was she even the right person? Was she at home?

Yes, she was the Gudrun Jeppeson Nicholas Hove had mentioned. Yes, she was at home. He could visit her.

Tobias made a quick calculation. It was nearly four hours to the ferry. Add another hour and a quarter for the crossing. Was it worth it? He could talk to her on the telephone. But that was never as good as interviewing someone in person. Assessing them.

"I'll be with you by five o'clock this afternoon," he said.

29.

Gudrun Jeppeson lived in a converted barn at the back of a cobbled yard in Aeroskobing, the postcard-pretty town on the east side of the island. Her sitting room was filled with wool in various stages of production. A loom stood in one corner. In another corner, knitted baby cardigans in blue, pink and yellow, hung from a rail. The table was covered with scraps of rainbow-coloured woollen garments attached to knitting needles.

"I remember Emily," she said. "She wasn't the kind of girl you'd forget." She swept up a pile of knitting from a chair. "Sit down."

She picked up a partly finished red jumper from the table, and settled herself in an armchair. A ball of red wool followed the jumper and fell on the floor. Tobias could barely stop himself from picking it up. He tried not to look at the jumble of knitting on the table.

"When did you last see Emily?" he asked.

"I don't think I've seen her or heard from her since the protest at Skovlynd." Gudrun knitted as she spoke.

"Did you expect to hear from her?"

"Not really." The needles clicked quietly. Gudrun scarcely looked at them, her fingers moved rhythmically as she spoke. "The group fell apart after the arrests. Nicholas Hove dumped me and went off with my best friend. She wasn't even part of the protest. She was always mainstream. They only met because I introduced them." Her mouth twisted in a smile. "She's the reason he's in politics." She laughed. "I met someone else and came to live here. I run a mail-order business."

"Do you remember Emily's boyfriend?"

Gudrun nodded. "Lennart? Thin boy. Played the guitar. Clung to Emily like a leech. He liked to play a Simon and Garfunkel song. '*Emily, whenever I may find her*'." She rolled her eyes.

"Do you remember his second name?"

Gudrun stopped knitting and thought for a moment. "Praetorius," she said. "Lennart Praetorius." She took up her knitting again.

At last. A name for Bogman. Tobias felt tired.

"How well did you know him?" he asked quietly?

"Not that well. He was quiet. He played his guitar. He didn't say much in discussions. Some of the group thought he was a police informer."

"An informer?" Tobias was wide awake again.

"We all thought there was an informer in the group. The police seemed to turn up at demos before we did. One time we organised a flying picket outside the developer's house."

"Kurt Malling's house?"

She nodded. "That was his name, yes. He had a big house on the coast. Hectares of forest." Gudrun's face tightened with disapproval. "We fell right into a trap. The police were waiting for us. Nicholas accused Lennart of being an informer. Lennart accused Nicholas. They had a bit of a punch up."

"A punch up?" Hove hadn't mentioned that.

"They thumped and kicked each other," said Gudrun. "Aksel intervened and calmed them down. But things weren't the same after that. We all got suspicious of each other. That was another reason the group split up."

"What about you? Did you think there was an informer?"

Gudrun nodded. "But I had no idea who it was. Some of the others thought it was Emily. She always seemed to have money."

"I've seen footage of her chained to a Hydrema digger, being dragged off, being arrested."

"She was never charged with anything. That was another reason some people thought she was an informer. Aksel thought the arrests might have been cover."

"What was Aksel's surname?"

Gudrun thought for a moment. "It might have been Schmidt, but I'm not sure. He wasn't around all the time. He floated about from protest to protest. He had links with groups in other countries. He warned us about informers. He told us about police infiltrating protests in England and Germany." She paused before adding thoughtfully, "He had a thing about Emily too."

Tobias raised an eyebrow.

"Emily was a good-looking girl. To tell you the truth, I was a bit jealous of her. I hated that Nicholas fancied her. There were times when I could have scratched her eyes out." She laughed. "Now I see him on television and wonder how I ever fancied him. But I never thought Emily was an informer. She was straightforward. Lennart too."

"Do you know where Aksel is now?"

"I've lost touch with most people from those days, sorry. Nicholas Hove might know."

"Why did he accuse Lennart of being an informer?"

Gudrun shrugged. "Maybe because Lennart was quiet. He listened. He didn't talk much. Nicholas thought that was suspicious. Maybe he was a bit jealous of him as well. All the girls liked Lennart. I liked him. He brought out a maternal streak in me. In all of us, I think."

"Did that make Emily jealous?"

"She didn't show it. But I remember her saying if Lennart slept with anyone else she would never forgive him."

"Do you think the punch-up could have been about that?"

Gudrun shrugged. "It might have been a factor."

"Do you know where Emily and Lennart went after the Skovlynd protest?"

"No idea." Gudrun shook her head. "They had a big blue van with a rainbow on it. I remember they went to Sweden in it. To an anti-nuclear protest. They travelled around a lot. They could be anywhere, if they're still together."

"They are not together," said Tobias quietly. "Lennart Praetorius is dead. Two weeks ago we found human remains in a bog at Roligmose in East Jutland. We also found a bracelet we know was bought by Emily Rasmussen for her boyfriend, Lennart. Thanks to you, we now know his surname and can begin tracing his next of kin."

Gudrun put down her knitting. She looked out at the rain falling in the courtyard. "That's so sad," she said.

"Are you in contact with anyone else from the Skovlynd protest?"

"I was there mostly because of Nicholas," said Gudrun. "When he we split up, I lost interest. I didn't keep in touch with any of them."

"Can you think of anyone else who knew Emily and Lennart?"

"Apart from Nicholas? No." She gave another of her crooked smiles. "Oddly enough, my husband has done some IT work for the golf course developer, Kurt Malling. Something to do with a wind farm project in Jutland. He tells me there's a lot of opposition from green activists." Gudrun picked up the knitting. She put it down again. "I've just remembered. My husband said the protests were being organised by some guy who'd been involved in protests all over Europe. England. Germany. Lapland. I thought he sounded a bit like Aksel. He was always going off somewhere else. He liked being where the action was." She picked up her knitting again.

"How did Malling react to the protests? Was he heavy handed?"

"I'll say. He hired extra security guards, as well as calling the police every time demonstrators turned up at the golf club or outside his house. That's if they weren't there already. Which is why we all thought there was an informer in the group."

"What was Emily like?"

"Attractive, strong-willed. Fearless even. She wasn't frightened of arguments. She stood up to Malling a couple of times."

"In what way?"

"I remember once or twice him coming up to us with the security guards and ordering us to leave. Emily said it was a public highway and we had every right to be there. She had some other reason for not liking him. I remember her saying 'I don't like the company he keeps.'"

"What kind of company?"

"I think she meant politicians and policemen."

Tobias turned down Gudrun's offer of coffee and a snack. He was hungry, but it would be dark soon and he wanted to catch the last ferry to the mainland. While he waited on the slipway, he sent a four-word text to Eddy and Katrine. "Bogman name Lennart Praetorius."

The ferry was approaching land when Katrine called him back.

"I've identified two males called Lennart Praetorius who fit Bogman's profile," she said. "One of them is definitely alive. He's a trade union official. We can rule him out. The other Lennart is registered at an address in Helsinger. He was born in 1977. Today is his birthday. Harry can check the dental records tomorrow but it all fits. He applied for a passport in 1993. It was sent to the Helsinger address. The electoral roll shows only two pensioners living at that address. Hanne and Jesper Hedegaarde."

"Famor and Mormor," said Tobias.

30.

SUNDAY: WEEK THREE

A frail, white-haired woman with a walking stick answered the door of the narrow terrace house not far from the harbour in Helsinger. Tobias and Katrine presented their ID.

"Mrs Hedegaarde?" said Tobias.

"Is this about my grandson?"

"Is your grandson Lennart Praetorius?"

She nodded. "You'd better come in."

Tobias and Katrine followed her slowly down a short corridor to the kitchen. They had interrupted a birthday party. Dozens of miniature Danish flags decorated a layer cake from which slices had already been cut. An elderly, bald man contemplated the slice which lay on a blue china plate on the table in front of him.

"It's Lennart's birthday," said Hanne. "We always have a cake on his birthday. We keep hoping he will be back one day to share it with us."

The old man got to his feet.

"These people are from the police, Jesper," said Mrs Hedegaard.

Alarm spread across the old man's face. He put his hand on his wife's arm. "It's bad news, isn't it?"

"Perhaps you should sit down," said Katrine.

Hanne leaned on her stick with both hands and drew herself up. "We'd rather face things standing up," she said.

"Two weeks ago we found the remains of a young man in a bog at Roligmose," said Tobias. "We think they are the remains of your grandson, Lennart Praetorius."

Hanne trembled but remained standing. Her husband put his arm around her shoulders.

"Are you sure it's Lennart?" said Hanne.

"We were able to match his dental records," said Tobias. "There was this as well." He took from his briefcase the Seiko watch and gave it to Hanne. She turned it over and read the inscription. "This is the watch we gave Lennart on his eighteenth birthday." She held it to her heart. "What happened? When did he die?"

"We are not sure," said Tobias. "We think he died more than twelve years ago. He was murdered."

The silence was electric. The elderly couple were rigid with shock.

Hanne spoke first. "How did he die? Who killed him?"

"He was hit on the head, probably with a rock or a stone," said Katrine. "We are trying to find who did it."

"The blow to the head was fatal," said Tobias. Get this over with. Please don't ask for more detail. I don't want to list the injuries to his ribs, his arm, his hand.

Hanne sighed. "I'll sit down now, Jesper," she said.

He pulled out a chair for her and indicated two other chairs at the table for Tobias and Katrine.

"Take the cake away, Jesper," said Hanne. "I can't bear the sight of it."

Jesper took the cake from the table and carried it out of the room.

Hanne was still holding the watch. "Can we keep this?"
Tobias nodded.

"Can we bury Lennart now?" she asked.

"Yes," said Tobias. "Someone from our victim support unit will be in touch with you tomorrow."

Jesper came back with a photograph album. He set it down on the table.

"Our daughter was a heroin addict," said Hanne. "She got clean long enough to have Lennart but not long enough to keep him. His father stayed around only long enough to have his name on the birth certificate. We never saw him after that. He was an addict as well. We had Lennart from when he was three months old until he was ten. Mette came and stayed from time to time but that was almost worse than her never seeing him at all. Then she said she was clean again. The court gave her custody. She took Lennart to live in Christiana. Of course it all broke down. She had to leave Christiania. They came back here. That only lasted a few weeks. Mette went to stay with friends. She was taking heroin again. She took an overdose. Accidentally, we are sure, we hope. I can't bear to think…"

Jesper squeezed his wife's hand.

"Lennart went a bit wild after his mother died. He stopped going to school. He said he wanted to find his father. He lived in a squat. He came back a few times, usually when he needed money. But he was a good boy at heart."

Hanne began to cry. Tobias produced a clean white handkerchief and gave it to her. She dabbed her eyes.

"Did he find his father?" asked Katrine.

"If he did, he never told us," said Jesper. He opened the photograph album and turned over the pages. He showed Tobias and Katrine a full-page photograph of a dark-haired smiling young woman with a baby.

"Mette and Lennart. That was taken at the christening."

He turned over more pages.

"This is the most recent photograph we have of Lennart. I took it one day he came to visit and helped me in the garden. He was seventeen."

Jesper fell silent.

Tobias and Katrine studied the full-length photograph of an intense-looking, dark-haired teenager, leaning on an upright spade.

"We didn't see him often after that," said Hanne. "He came every six months or so. He would turn up without warning and stay for a day or two. We would come down for breakfast in the morning and he would be gone again. Without a word," said Hanne.

"Once he didn't turn up for nearly a year," said Jesper. "He didn't even telephone. Then he just appeared on the doorstep one day."

"It was his twenty-first birthday," said Hanne. "He was here for his twenty-first birthday. He brought a girl."

"They came over on the ferry from Helsingborg. They had a van," said Jesper. "A blue van. They were living in it. They showed us. It had a bed and a folding table and chairs and a little gas stove for cooking. It was cosy. They were proud of it."

Katrine produced the photograph of Emily. "Was this the girl?"

Hanne and Jesper studied it.

Hanne sighed. "It was so long ago. But she was blonde and pretty, like this girl. Her name was Emily."

"Emily Rasmussen," said Tobias. "We know she was with Lennart in Lapland 1997 and 1998."

"I'd like to speak to her," said Hanne.

"So would we," said Tobias.

Hanne looked puzzled.

"She left home around the time Lennart was killed," said Tobias. "We're trying to contact her. So if you remember anything, anything at all that might help us find her, we'd like to know."

"She seemed a nice girl," said Jesper. "They stayed for one night. We had a lovely time. We had twenty-one candles and twenty-one flags on the birthday cake. We drank champagne. I gave Lennart one hundred kroner for his birthday. They left the next morning."

"We didn't take a photograph," cried Hanne. "Why didn't we take a photograph? We were so happy to see him."

Jesper put his arm around her shoulders. "Lennart came to see us a few months after that. With the girl. I asked if him if he needed money. He said no. But I gave him some anyway."

"Did they still have the van?"

Jesper nodded. "I think so. They only stayed a few hours. We had a brief telephone call from him. I don't remember when exactly. Maybe a week later. After that, we didn't see or hear from Lennart again. We waited for about a year. Then we went to the police."

"We waited too long," said Hanne. "We shouldn't have waited so long. Always hoping to hear from him." A sob escaped from her.

"The police told us they had no reports of anyone of his description being injured or killed. They said Lennart was an adult. He was twenty-one. They said sometimes people, especially men, left home and didn't return," said Jesper.

"As soon as we mentioned Christiana, they seemed to lose interest," said Hanne. "We mentioned the girl but we didn't know her second name. The police said they had no reports about a girl of that description being injured or missing either. We went back to the police a year later, when we still hadn't heard from Lennart. They told us the same thing."

"I'm sorry," said Tobias.

"If only we'd reported it sooner," cried Hanne.

"Maybe he was already dead by then," said Jesper. "And we didn't know. All those years hoping, hoping…and all the time…"

"They could have looked for the girl," said Hanne. "That might have helped."

"Without a name, or a photograph, there wasn't much to go on," said Tobias. "We're having difficulty finding her now. Do you have a photograph of Lennart which we can release to the press? Perhaps Emily will see it and come forward. We hope she might be able to tell us something." Such as whether or not she killed him, he added silently to herself.

"You can take this," Hanne detached the photograph of seventeen-year-old Lennart from the album, kissed it, gave it to Katrine. "Promise you will bring it back."

"I promise," said Tobias. He slipped the photograph into his briefcase.

"We can provide grief counselling as well," said Katrine. "Is there anyone we can call or fetch? A relative, or a neighbour perhaps?"

Hanne and Jesper looked at each other. They shook their heads.

"We'll call our priest," said Jesper. "We need to organise everything for the funeral. We want to say goodbye in the proper way."

"We've had fourteen years of sorrow," said Hanne. "Missing him. Hoping that he was alive. What fools we were." A tear ran down her cheek. "You can do one thing for us. Take away the cake. I can't bear to see it again."

Katrine sat in the car with the cake in a box on her knee. She turned an anxious face to Tobias. "I checked the missing males," she said. "I didn't find a Lennart Praetorius. I didn't include him in the list. I'm sorry," she said.

"It made no difference," said Tobias. "If we'd come here at the beginning, we still wouldn't have learned much about Emily. We need to find her. I'm convinced she's the key to everything."

"What will we do with the cake?"

"Take it back to the office. Remove the flags and candles and offer everyone a slice with their coffee tomorrow," said Tobias. He glanced at Katrine. "Has this job not hardened your heart yet?" He put the car into gear and accelerated away from the sorrow-filled house. "It will, Katrine, it will."

31.

MONDAY: WEEK THREE

Karl Lund called Eddy to tell him the contents of the underground bin in which the first bones had been found were now bagged, labelled and ready for inspection.

"They're in nineteen clear plastic bags," said Karl. "We can't keep them in the lab so we've put them in the garage. I've emailed you a list. Call me if you need me. Good luck."

Katrine had already printed off the list. She waved it at Eddy. They went down to the garage.

The forensics team had sorted the rubbish into categories – animal, vegetable, paper, plastic, glass, tin, cloth, miscellaneous. Paper, plastic and glass should have been in recycling bins, and to be fair to the inhabitants of the housing blocks nearest to the bin, the bags containing these materials were small and the contents easily checked against the list provided by Karl Lund. The uncooked vegetable waste, such as potato peelings, onion skins, carrot scrapings and banana skins, could have been composted, but since the inhabitants of these same housing blocks did not have gardens, the waste went to the bin along with scraps of cooked, leftover meat and fish. The bags of food waste did not smell as bad as Katrine had feared. What she took at first to be hard-boiled eggs in a separate bag – hard-boiled eggs in dustbins? And people complained about poverty? – on closer inspection turned out to be golf balls whose covers had split to reveal a yellow inner-core.

"A dead cat. Ugh," said Eddy, gingerly putting to one side a plastic bag containing the feline corpse and picking up a smaller bag. He glanced at the label. "This one's a dead budgerigar. The cat killed the budgie. The budgie's owner killed the cat in revenge. That's my theory."

"Three sets of dentures, two pairs of spectacles and a broken riding crop," said Katrine, putting a tick beside them on the list.

"A torn jacket with a swastika on the sleeve." Eddy shook his head. "The things people get up to in Gelleruparken." He held up a pair of pink silk panties in one gloved hand. "These look as though they were gnawed through. Ripped off by somebody's teeth." He thrust the panties towards Katrine. She wrinkled her nose in distaste.

Eddy replaced the panties and picked up a bag of letters, envelopes and wrapping paper. He handed the bag to Katrine.

"Get names and addresses from these. Check how many of them were questioned in the door-to-door. Uniform spoke to seventy-five people. There must be at least five hundred living in the block nearest the bin. I'll stay and finish checking this lot."

When Eddy returned to the office, Katrine was so absorbed she didn't hear his approach.

"I'm going to take a break," he said. "Fancy a coffee?"

Katrine didn't reply.

"I'm going to open the window and piss into the courtyard," he said.

Katrine granted him a quick smile before turning back to the screen. "I've made a list of the addresses. They were nearly all checked in the door-to-door. Here they are," she tapped a file on her desk, not taking her eyes from the screen. "I'm looking for Lennart Praetorius. I want to know when he was reported missing. I searched only for males aged twenty to twenty-eight missing between 1996 to 1999. That's what Brix said. I was worried I'd left him out of the list by mistake. The grandparents told us they didn't report Bogman, I mean Lennart, missing until a year after they'd last seen him." She shook her head. "I still think of him as Bogman."

"Me too."

Katrine scrolled down a list of names. "I can't find him in 1999."

"The wrinklies probably left it more than a year," said Eddy. "The older you are, the faster time passes."

"It must be flying past you, then, Eddy," said Katrine. She flashed a smile at him and continued scrolling.

"I've found him." She clapped her hands. "February 2nd 2000. Lennart Lars Praetorius. Helsinger. Reported missing by Jesper and Hanne Hedegaarde." She smacked her forehead. "I should have extended the search into 2000. But we got sidelined by Bruno Holst. The guy who turned up alive in Germany."

"Don't beat yourself up about it," said Eddy. "We wouldn't have identified him without the bracelet. Unless the grandparents mention it in the report."

"I'll ask Helsinger to send over the file," said Katrine.

"Tell them it's urgent," said Eddy. "Or you won't get it for ages. The boss is still waiting for the file on Emily's stepfather."

Tobias was in the library at Jyellands Posten, settling himself at a machine which magnified microfiches. The librarian had organised the newspaper's reports of the protests at Skovlynd golf in date order. The room was dark and quiet. The only sound was the click of the machine as it moved the microfiches into the frames.

There were ten brief stories – each two paragraphs at most – about the demonstrations at Skovlynd. The first report was from April 1996. The last was dated September 1998. There was a statement from the protesters, who called themselves the Green Brigade. The ten signatories to the statement included Emily Rasmussen, Nicholas Hove and Gudrun Pettersen, but not Lennart Praetorius and not anyone named Aksel Schmidt, or Aksel anything. None of the reports mentioned him.

One report quoted Kurt Malling: *"I too am concerned about the environment. My company is developing several green energy projects. This club will bring jobs to the area. It is supported by local businesses and services. Most of the forest will still be in place. Bechstein's Bat will not be affected."*

The newspaper had printed a letter in reply from Nicholas Hove: *"Our concern is not only about protecting the habitat of Bechstein's bat but about the widespread use of chemical pesticides and fertilisers on golf courses, the excess use of water for irrigation and the impact on the wetlands around Skovlynd."*

Tobias stood up and stretched. He began to think rooting through rubbish might be more interesting. All the roads to Emily seemed to finish in dead-ends. He sat down again and squinted into the viewing machine. A centre-spread about the protests clicked into view. This was better. There were ten paragraphs with names and quotes, and four large photographs.

Tobias zoomed in on a black and white photograph of Emily and Lennart – easily recognisable now – in the rain, hair plastered against their faces, holding up a dripping banner: TREES NOT TEES: SAY NO TO GOLF. No caption. The photograph said it all.

The second photograph, also in black and white, was a sideways view of Emily and Lennart, facing a tall man sheltering under a golf umbrella and flanked by police. It was captioned *'Stand-off'*.

The third photograph was a reverse of the previous one. Kurt Malling, under the umbrella, stiff with anger. *'Skovlynd developer Kurt Malling unmoved by protests'*, was the caption.

The fourth photograph showed three protesters dragging a sodden and muddy tent to the side of the road. *'Weather more effective than police. Storm sweeps away camp of the eco-warriors'*. Tobias enlarged it. Emily and Nicholas Hove. Who was the third man in photograph? Could it be Aksel?

Tobias printed the stories and the photographs and marked the date on each report. He wrote, "Aksel?" on the back of the fourth photograph and booked a motorbike courier to take it to Nicholas Hove.

32

TUESDAY: WEEK THREE

"She can't have vanished into thin air," said Larsen. He stared at the photograph of Emily on the board in the Incident Room. "She must have done something, somewhere."

"The story was on television last night, and in the evening papers, with Emily's photograph," said Tobias. "And Lennart's photograph as well. Last seen with Emily Rasmussen and so on. It was on television and in all the papers, local and national, this morning. It was on radio last night and again this morning."

"Fifty-three people telephoned last night," said Katrine. "Three were mediums, offering to get in touch with Emily through the spirit world."

Larsen rolled his eyes.

"One caller was sure Emily was living next door to her in Ribe. West Jutland sent three squad cars at midnight and wakened a kindergarten teacher who looked a bit like the photographs but was definitely not Emily."

"She looks like half the women in Denmark," said Larsen gloomily. "At least she's not a kiddy. We'd have thousands of calls and they'd all be useless." He waved at Katrine to continue.

"Ten callers wanted to know if there was a reward," said Katrine. "They didn't have any information."

"We haven't the budget for a reward," said Larsen.

"Fifteen callers thought they'd seen Emily in the last few days. Every location was different. She was spotted in ten different places on the same day at roughly the same time. Never at an address." Katrine glanced at her notes. "She was seen walking on the beach, in a café, in a cinema. One woman said she was with Emily at a bus stop when she vaporised in front of her eyes."

"These appeals always bring out the nutters, the chancers and the snoopers," said Renata. "Did any sane people call?"

"Fourteen women and two men called to tell us they'd met Emily in environmental groups at least ten years ago," said Katrine. "They were vague about dates but they all mentioned the Skovlynd protest. Ten of the women and one of the men remembered Lennart as well. All of them thought Emily had gone to join another protest somewhere. Lapland was mentioned, but also Germany, England and Estonia. None of them had anything concrete to add to what we already know."

"Nicholas Hove and Gudrun Jeppessen both mentioned an activist called Aksel. Possibly Aksel Schmidt, but Gudrun isn't sure," said Tobias. "Did anyone called Aksel get in touch?"

Katrine shook her head.

"Either she's dead, or she wanted to disappear," said Eddy. "It's not that difficult. You can buy a false identity online. Or she could just use cash, not buy a mobile phone in her own name. The things that trace you are mostly electronic."

"Any progress on the Hotmail and Facebook front, Renata?" asked Tobias.

"The request is with the US State Department. I'm still waiting for an answer."

"Can we hurry them up?"

"Only if we suggest she has some kind of terrorist link. That gets them moving double-double quick."

"Tempting," said Eddy.

Larsen stared stonily at him.

"Only joking," said Eddy.

"Emily was arrested at the Skovlynd protest," said Tobias.

"September 10th, 1998," said Eddy. "There's no video of the interview. She was released without charge."

"That's a pity," said Renata. "That might have helped with the Americans. They're jumpy about eco-terrorists."

"With good cause," said Larsen. "Nutters, all of them."

Tobias thought about Agnes. Passionate, naïve perhaps. But not a terrorist, and definitely not mad.

"Emily's fingerprints are on file. That's useful," said Eddy. "She can be identified even if she's changed her appearance."

"No sign of the blue van?" asked Tobias.

Eddy shook his head. "Even Kazakhstan has automatic number plate recognition. But the van hasn't been seen anywhere. It's vaporised as well."

"Her mother got an email from her on the twenty-fourth of September 1998, saying she was going away with Lennart," said Tobias. "We must find out where those emails are coming from."

"I'll ask Foreign Affairs if there's anyone I can speak to directly in the State Department," said Renata. She picked up her papers and slipped out of the room.

"Emily made the complaint about her stepfather before she went away," said Tobias. "There might be something useful in the file. Registry hasn't sent it over yet."

"Cuts," said Larsen gloomily.

"Her photograph went to all Swedish police departments," said Tobias.

"They're nomads aren't they? She could be wandering with the ruddy reindeer herds," said Eddy. "Living with Eskimos in the Arctic circle for all we know."

"We'll send her photograph and details to Norway and Finland as well," said Tobias. "In case Emily has gone to a different part of Lapland."

"Right." Larsen stood up to indicate the meeting was over. "Send them to the rest of Europe as well." He paused on his way out the door. "Send them to the whole bloody world while we're about it." The door swung shut behind him.

"What next?" asked Katrine.

"We need to find Aksel Schmidt or whatever his name is," said Tobias.

"I've looked on the national database," said Katrine. "The only Aksel Schmidts are all under twenty-five, which makes them too young at the time Emily disappeared. I've checked the list of green activists and can't find anyone named Aksel. He seems to have vaporised as well."

"Suppose all three of them, Emily, Lennart and Aksel were otter watching together, and there was some kind of argument," said Eddy. "A fight over Emily. Let's say they both fancied her. Aksel kills Lennart. He and Emily carry Lennart's body between them."

"Everybody said she was in love with Lennart," said Katrine. "Why would she help his killer?"

"Maybe he killed Emily as well," said Tobias.

"She sends emails to her mother. She has a Facebook page," said Katrine.

"So maybe Aksel is sending the emails," said Eddy. "To make everyone think she's alive."

"All the more reason to find him," said Tobias. "We might need those mediums after all."

He went back to his desk and sat for a while thinking. Was it possible Aksel had killed Emily? That he knew Emily well enough to have not only her email address but her mother's as well? That he sent emails so her mother wouldn't report her missing? It was probably worthwhile searching the bog again for traces of a second body. Another cost to the enquiry, but Larsen would agree it was necessary. His phone rang. It was Nicholas Hove.

"I've looked at the photo you biked to my office," he said. "I think Aksel is the guy on the far left, beside Emily Rasmussen. It's so long ago, I can't be certain. I've contacted a couple of activists I know. One of them told me he sees Aksel at demos from time to time. He doesn't know where he lives."

"What's Aksel's surname? Is it Schmidt?"

"He's not sure about that either. But he says Aksel is involved with some protest at the city hall next month. There's a European conference on the environment on the fifth of June. I'm speaking at it. My activist friend said something is happening. He doesn't know exactly what, but it's about climate change and it's intended to coincide with the conference." He paused. His tone changed. "I always had a soft spot for Emily. Let me know how she is when you find her."

If we find her, thought Tobias.

"Thanks," he said. "I will."

"And good luck with Aksel." Nicholas Hove rang off.

Tobias straightened the phone and tidied a pencil into the mug on his desk. It was a present from Agnes. A white mug with a green slogan: "Root For Trees!" A memory stirred. Agnes talking about trees. On the telephone. Was it on the night they found Bogman? Hadn't she mentioned someone called Aksel? Tobias reached for the telephone. He hesitated. He was reluctant to involve Agnes in the investigation. He picked up the phone and called her.

"Hi, Dad, I saw you on television last night, appealing for information about that missing girl. You looked great. Have you found her?"

"Not yet," said Tobias. "Where are you?"

"In college," said Agnes. "I'm between classes."

"So when are you back hugging trees?"

Agnes sighed. "I have an essay to write. I won't get up there this weekend."

"Where exactly is 'up there'?"

"About five kilometres inland from the coast, near Frostrup."

"How many of you are at the camp?"

"It varies," said Agnes. "Sometimes as many as fifty and sometimes as few as five." Her voice changed. Why the sudden interest, Dad? Are you trying to find out something for your colleagues? I've had the lecture. We're not breaking any laws."

Tobias took a deep breath. "This has nothing to do with trees, Agnes. It's about the missing girl. She's hardly a girl," he added. "She must be at least thirty by now. She was involved in a green protest around the time of her disappearance. And she had a friend called Aksel. He might know where she is now. He'd be about the same age. Didn't you mention someone called Aksel?"

"There are lots of people called Aksel. How do you know he's the right one?"

"I don't know," said Tobias. "But nobody called Aksel got in contact after the appeal. I thought maybe that was because he was up a tree with no television." He hoped he sounded matter of fact, not sarcastic.

"Don't be sarcastic, Dad. Yes, there's someone called Aksel supporting our protest. He came to the camp a couple of weekends ago. The weekend you found the body in the bog."

"What is Aksel's surname?"

"I don't know. I only know him as Aksel. He's a nice guy."

"Where does he live?"

"I've no idea, Dad."

"Does Magnus know where he lives?"

Agnes sighed. "I don't know. Ask him yourself. He's up at the camp. I'll get him to call you."

"Can you give me his number?"

"No, Dad. I can't do that without asking him first."

"This is urgent, Agnes. We need to talk to Aksel. He may be the only person who knows where Emily Rasmussen is."

"He may not even be the right guy, Dad. I'll tell Magnus it's urgent. OK? Now can we talk about something else? Something more cheerful?"

"So tell me something cheerful," said Tobias.

"I'm going to have lunch next week with the wind farm developer." Agnes sounded pleased. "Buying me lunch won't change my mind, but I'm glad he's taking the protest seriously. What do you think of that?"

Tobias thought Kurt Malling would be charmed by Agnes, would listen with every appearance of interest and would ignore what she said.

"I think you should go and enjoy your lunch," he said.

"There's no such thing as a free lunch, Dad. I know that's what you think."

"You're not nervous about it, are you?"

"They're all relying on me to put up a good show. I wish Magnus could come with me, he's better at explaining our objections."

Tobias wanted to say Kurt Malling would be instantly prejudiced against the bearded, be-studded Magnus. He bit his tongue.

"I'm sure you'll be fine, pumpkin," he said. "Where are you having lunch?"

"No idea. He's sending a car for me." She giggled.

"Very grand," said Tobias. "Have fun."

"You too, Dad. You don't have enough fun in your life."

Tobias thought that might be about to change.

When he got back to his flat, he was in the mood to listen to something joyous as well as ordered. The Six Bach Partitas, perhaps. He listened while he ironed a pale blue shirt and draped it gently over the back of a chair. He chose a brown leather jacket from a selection in his wardrobe. He didn't want to seem too formal, but he didn't want to be too casual either. He hadn't gone to dinner with a woman in ages. Was this a date? Did anybody use that term anymore? When was the last time he'd done this? His relationship with Hilde had never involved food. He'd taken the librarian in Silkeborg to a fashionable restaurant on her birthday, when she'd asked him to move in with her or move on. He'd moved on. He put on the blue shirt, buttoned it, adjusted the cuffs.

The track ended. The last notes of the piano died away. Tobias switched off the CD player. He hoped Sofie liked Bach.

He was meeting her at a canal-side restaurant not far from where she lived. As he walked there, he found himself thinking ahead to the your-place-or-mine-for-coffee conversation. He reined back his imagination. Easy now. Take it easy. Sofie could be seeing someone else.

She arrived two minutes after the waiter had shown Tobias to the table. She sank into the chair opposite him with a sigh of exhaustion.

"Hi, it's been a long day. I got back from France this afternoon."

"How was the chateau?"

"More dead animals on the walls than you could shoot in a lifetime. Tiger skins on the floors. Kurt loves all that. He's a hunter."

Of women as well, thought Tobias. He wondered again about Malling's relationship with Sofie.

"Was it all work and no play?" He hoped she'd been too busy for cosy dinners with Kurt Malling, or anyone else for that matter.

"Luckily my job sometimes combines both," said Sofie. "Kurt does a lot of business on the golf course. I get to play as well, naturally."

"So you played golf?" Who did she play with? Malling? "With Malling?"

"Kurt got one game in. He had to fly back for a board meeting about the wind farm on the north-west coast. I stayed on. I managed to play twice. Lucky me."

"With the clients?" Tobias aligned his knife and fork with the edges of the table.

"With two of our funders and Marcus Thomsen. He's a keen golfer. We played a four-ball."

"We should have a game sometime," said Tobias.

"I'd like that," said Sofie. "A two-ball. How often do you play?"

"Golf?"

"Or anything else," said Sofie.

"Not often enough," said Tobias. "I'm out of practice."

He straightened the spoon so it also lay exactly parallel to the edge of the table, adjusted the salt and pepper pots, re-positioned the narrow glass vase containing a single pink rose and the lighted candle in its crystal candlestick. The movement of his hands was careful and precise. He smoothed out a small crease in the white linen tablecloth and squared the menu card. He was conscious of Sofie's bemused gaze.

"I spent a lot of time in a boat when I was younger," he said, "A small boat. Everything had to be tidy."

"Shipshape," said Sofie.

He looked up and smiled. "Yes. Shipshape."

"You're a tidy person. You play tidy golf. You like things neat and simple."

"I don't like things out of place."

"Is that why you're a policeman?"

"Not really. But it's probably why I stay a policeman."

"So why did you join the police?"

"I had a wife and a young child and I needed a job. It was as simple as that. What about you? Why are you in PR?"

"There's a simple answer to that as well. I was at university with my friend Hannah. She started her own business and she asked me to join her."

They sat in silence for a moment. Tobias decided to plunge in.

"How well did you know Emily Rasmussen?"

"What?" Sofie was startled.

"Astrid Thomsen's daughter, Emily Rasmussen. She was the girlfriend of the young man whose remains we found in the bog at Roligmose."

Sofie stared at Tobias in shock.

"We called him Bogman," said Tobias. "But we now

know his name was Lennart Praetorius. He was murdered about fourteen years ago. Around the time Emily Rasmussen had a row with her mother and left home."

Sofie found her voice. "I didn't know, about Emily's boyfriend, I mean. I only knew Emily was estranged from her mother."

"Were you friends with Emily?"

"Are we having dinner or am I being questioned by the police?"

Tobias put up his hands. "Sorry, but this will save time. One more question and I'll stop and we can enjoy our dinner." And everything else that might follow. Easy now. "What do you know about Emily Rasmussen?"

"That's not a question, that's an order." Sofie sat up. "OK. Let's get this out of the way. I didn't really know her. I met her for the first time when Astrid and Marcus got married. Dad and I were guests at the wedding. Emily hardly spoke to me all day. Strange, unhappy girl."

"Why do you say that?"

Sofie shrugged. "She was all brittle and talkative one moment, morose and silent the next. I thought she was neurotic. But as I say, I hardly knew her."

"You suggested to her mother that Emily might be on Facebook."

"Did I?" Sofie thought for a moment. "Yes. I remember. It came up in conversation one evening. Not that long ago. In the last few weeks, I think. Kurt and I were having dinner with the Thomsens."

"Was it the night I met you? You were with the Thomsens. I was with Norbert Fisker and my stepmother."

"It was probably that evening. Kurt and Marcus were discussing the wind farm project. I was there as PR. Astrid came because Marcus wanted to cheer her up. She'd just had an email from Emily and it had upset her."

"And you suggested Astrid look for Emily on Facebook?"

"I can't remember if I suggested it first," said Sofie. "There was a general discussion about using social media. I think it was Marcus who said maybe Astrid should look for Emily on Facebook. She said 'I've heard people talking about Facebook but I don't know anything about it and I wouldn't know where to start'. He said he didn't know either. So I said to Astrid, 'I'll help you'. I went to see her the next day."

"And you found Emily's page?"

"I sat down with Astrid and we looked through all the Emily Rasmussens on Facebook. There were at least a dozen. Only about half of them had photographs, so we could rule them out. I thought it was going to be impossible, but as soon as Astrid saw the word 'Sápmi' she said, 'that's her'. There was no photograph, no personal details. But Astrid was convinced it was Emily's page because she lived in Lapland. Emily had been to Lapland. She told Astrid she loved it and she'd love to go back there."

Tobias nodded in satisfaction. It all fitted.

"I feel sorry for Astrid," said Sofie. "She's fragile. Whatever happened between her and Emily, it's cruel of Emily not to contact her."

"From what you and others tell me, she didn't want her mother to marry Marcus Thomsen."

"Perhaps she thought it was too soon after her father died."

"Perhaps," said Tobias. He paused before adding, "Do you think your father is re-marrying too soon?"

Sophie flushed. "Are we having dinner or is this another interrogation?"

"We're having dinner," said Tobias.

"Since you ask," said Sofie, in a hard voice, "I think Dad is re-marrying far too soon. He barely knows Inge. She picked him up on a cruise."

"That's hardly fair," said Tobias. "They're both widowed, they're both lonely."

"A geriatric knocking shop," continued Sofie. "There's nothing else to do on a cruise but drink, play cards and…"

The waiter arrived with the menus.

"They're not geriatrics," said Tobias. "I'd like to think I'd still be up for it when I'm sixty-five."

Sophie laughed. She opened the menu. The atmosphere eased.

Tobias heard a faint buzz. He swore softly.

"What's up?"

"I'm being called." He pulled the phone from his pocket. "Yes?" He listened for thirty seconds. He then sighed.

"Sorry, Sofie. I have to go. They've found a woman's body at the foot of high rise flats in Gellerupparken."

She stared at him in dismay. "Do you have to go this minute? Can't you at least stay and eat something?"

"I need to get there before they move the body," said Tobias. "I'm sorry. Can we do this another time?"

"Not if we never get as far as the first course," said Sofie.

33.

Tobias was still cursing his luck when he got to Gellerupparken. The estate had been the answer to housing problems in Aarhus in the nineteen-sixties but the concrete tower blocks, four and eight storeys high, had become a problem themselves. The area had high levels of crime and unemployment. Most residents of

Aarhus had never been to Gellerupparken. Some residents of Gellerupparken, on the other hand, had never been to other parts of Aarhus. They stayed within their own immigrant communities. The Left said this was because they feared racism. The Right said it was because they wanted to create a state within a state. The Left called the area culturally enriched. The Right called it crime-ridden. The national intelligence service, PET, had it constantly under surveillance. Tobias hoped whoever had died that evening was of no interest to PET. He disliked working with them because they were inclined to keep information to themselves. He hoped whoever had died had no connection to any of the Gellerupparken gangs. Dealing with the gangs was like wrestling with an octopus. He wasn't optimistic as he drove under a concrete walkway and headed towards the block where the body had been found, but the area was quiet. Four teenage girls wearing headscarves and swinging shopping bags strolled along the pavement. It was twilight. Tobias heard a whistle and saw there was a match on the floodlit football pitch watched by about thirty men. Further on, half a dozen nine or ten-year-old boys were kicking a football against garage doors. As Tobias drove past them, the ball smashed a light above the garage. In the side mirror Tobias saw the boys scatter. He turned a corner and saw the police cars and the white Forensics van outside one of the eight-storey blocks. He drew up behind the van. Eddy Haxen was talking to three women, their faces whitened by the blue lights of the police cars winking in the dusk. He acknowledged Tobias with a wave and pointed to a balcony on the top floor of the block. Tobias looked up; saw a camera flash; a tall figure in pale blue overalls; another camera flash.

Eddy broke off talking to the women and came to meet Tobias.

"We weren't going to call you," he said. "We thought it was a straightforward suicide."

They ducked under a tape sealing off thirty square metres of rough grass and concrete paving. A technician unfolded a portable floodlight. The brightness briefly dazzled. Tobias blinked; saw Harry Norsk crouching beside a broken body in a yellow T-shirt and black trousers, face down, one arm and both legs at an impossible angle on the blood-soaked grass.

"We thought she was a jumper, but there's something not right," said Eddy.

Harry looked up when they approached. "Hi, Tobias. There's a rip in the back of her T shirt." Harry looked up at the balcony. "I can't see anything that could have torn it on the way down. Of course it might have been torn already. But I don't think so."

"Karl's up there with Skaarup," said Eddy.

He nodded towards the women hovering beyond the blue and white police tape. "Those three said they heard a scream from somewhere above them, around nine o'clock. They were watching a programme that begins at nine and it had just begun. They were on the seventh floor. They ran out to the balcony. The one without the headscarf called the emergency services. They all rushed down here. They could see that she was dead. They don't know who she is. They could be saying that because they genuinely don't know, or because we're the police. I've got their details in case we need to speak to them again."

People appeared on balconies all over the block. At ground level, a small, silent crowd gathered in the dusk.

"I don't want to hang around here longer than necessary," said Eddy, "but you'll want to take a look at the flat she fell from."

Tobias hunkered down to look at the body. The back of the T-shirt was torn from the bloodied shoulder to the waist. He could see her skin.

"She landed on her back," said Harry. "Her left shoulder hit the ground first. She died immediately. Not more than thirty minutes ago. About nine o'clock, I'd say. Rigor mortis hasn't set in yet." He turned her over so that Tobias could see her face. It was unmarked, except for black and yellow bruising around her right eye.

"Someone gave her a black eye," said Harry. "Sometime in the last few weeks, I'd say. She's wearing a wedding ring."

"Look at the inside of her wrist," said Tobias. "I think that's some kind of name bracelet." Harry separated the gold chain from a mess of blood and bone. He peered at it. "Girlie," he said.

"Ah, fuck," said Eddy. "I don't believe it. The woman who skipped from the hospital was called Girlie." He banged his head against an invisible wall.

"Do you recognise her?" asked Tobias.

"I recognise the name," said Eddy. "Do you remember the illegal we let slip? The one in the hospital? She was called Girlie. Her face was pulp when I saw her. She'd been beaten up and dumped at the emergency room. But I think it's her."

"The only way we're going to know for sure is if the hospital kept her blood samples," said Harry. "Can I move her now?"

Tobias nodded. "Let's go and look at this flat, Eddy," he said. "Are you sure it's the one she fell from?"

"It's directly above. The door was closed but not locked when we got there. The place was a bit of a mess. We could see there'd been some kind of struggle."

They took the lift to the eighth floor. Eddy was grim-faced, silent. Tobias followed him down the walkway.

"There's an elderly couple on one side and a woman with three children on the other," said Eddy. "They say they heard nothing. It's possible. The wrinklies are deaf. Their television was blaring. The woman's children were yelling and running around."

A uniformed policeman lifted the barrier tape. Eddy and Tobias went into the flat. They negotiated their way through overturned chairs, plates and cutlery on the floor, remnants of chips, splatterings of what looked like blood, an overturned table, an unmade bed, a sofa. Tobias dipped his finger in a red splash, sniffed it. "Ketchup."

They stepped through an open glass door to join Karl Lund and Katrine on the balcony.

"Hi, Tobias," said Karl Lund. "Look what we've found." He held up a plastic bag containing a thin strip of yellow material. "It was caught on the edge of the balcony. She must have gone over backwards."

"Nobody jumps off a balcony backwards," said Katrine. "Somebody pushed her."

"She was wearing a name bracelet. Girlie. I think it's the same Girlie we saw at the hospital," said Eddy. "The Girlie I let slip through my fingers." He thumped the wall. A lump of plaster dislodged and fell.

Katrine put her hand on his arm. "Hey, we both let her slip."

"It bet it was the same fucker who killed her," said Eddy. "Sick bastard."

"Probably her husband," said Katrine. "We should be able to find him if he's here legally. Are there prints?"

Karl nodded. "I'll say. Busy spot. Prints everywhere. We should be finished by tomorrow afternoon," said Karl. Talk to me then."

"Call in the other teams for a door-to-door," said Tobias.

"I asked about that earlier, just in case," said Eddy. "They're here already. Alsing got a DNA match on the SmartWater in the Danske bank car. He's running a stakeout. Hoping to net the whole gang. They won't move from their positions."

Tobias thought for a moment. "OK. We'll do a couple of hours now, and start again tomorrow after Harry's done the autopsy. I'll take the smaller block opposite. You and Katrine take this block, alternate floors. Good luck."

"We'll need it," said Eddy.

He wasn't optimistic about finding out much in a door-to-door enquiry. In Eddy's experience, witnesses to crime in Gellerupparken were more frightened of the criminals than of the police. He began his enquiries on the seventh floor. No one answered his knock at half the flats and no one in the other half saw, or admitted to having seen, anything. He was about to begin what he was sure would be equally hopeless enquiries on the fifth floor when a woman wearing rimless spectacles and a black headscarf stepped out of the shadows near the stairwell. Eddy almost collided with her.

"There's a café bar on the south side of the square in Vesterbro," she said. "Meet me there in twenty minutes."

The lift doors rumbled open. She stepped inside. The doors closed. Eddy ran down the stairs to the fourth floor and found Katrine with her hand raised, about to ring a doorbell.

"I'm leaving this block to you," he said. "Someone wants to talk to me. Do as many doors as you can."

He was gone before Katrine could speak.

He found the café bar easily. A woman was sitting outside with her coat collar turned up. He glanced quickly at her. Youngish, short dark hair, no glasses. He went inside. The room was crammed with young people clutching glasses of beer. Eddy frowned. It wasn't where he'd expect to find a woman in a headscarf and he couldn't see her anywhere. He felt a hand on his shoulder. He turned and saw the woman who'd been sitting outside.

"You walked past me," she said. "Let's go back outside. It's quieter. Get yourself a beer if you want to."

Eddy bought himself a beer and followed her. It had grown chilly, as well as dark.

"I'm with PET." She turned her collar up again. "You can call me Linda. If you want to check me out, speak to your boss. I've been watching a retail unit and flat near that block. I didn't see the woman fall. But I know who she is and who might be able to help you."

"So tell me, Linda," said Eddy.

"The flat is a brothel. The Filipina worked there. Four other sex workers use that flat, plus another one five doors down on the right, going away from the stairwell and the lifts. They also use a flat in the block opposite. They're all illegals except for a big fat Nigerian. The business is managed by a Turk. He's legal. He's also one of our informants."

"So you let him run his brothel in peace."

Linda shrugged. "We leave him alone. He tells us stuff."

"Did he kill her?"

Linda shook her head. "He was playing football with a bunch of ragheads. The match started at eight. They were on the pitch at the time."

Eddy thought he would check for himself. He didn't trust PET. They always played their own game.

"The dead woman was beaten up once before," said Linda. "Our informant took her to the hospital."

"You mean he dumped her at the hospital," said Eddy. "We'll need him to identify her."

"You can't ask him," said Linda. "He can't get involved. Immigration will poke their noses in. It'll fuck up our operation."

"Are you covering up for him? Did he beat her up?"

"No and No. A client beat her up."

"How do you know? Did she tell you?"

"There's a bunch of leftie law students running an advice centre for women. One of them told me. She doesn't know I'm PET. She thinks I'm a community worker."

"What's her name? Where do I find her?"

"Irene Voss. The centre is in Bazar Vest. I don't have a number for it."

"There were two beds in Girlie's flat."

"Maybe they had some kind of rota. Maybe they play foursomes." Linda shrugged. "Who knows? It's not her usual place. She normally works in the block opposite."

"Why did she change?"

"No idea," said Linda. "Ask the Nigerian. She's legal."

"Where will I find her?"

"Maybe in the flat five doors down. Otherwise you could cruise and look for her." Linda smiled sardonically. "But she'll be hard to find in the dark."

"You could ask your Turkish tout."

"You're lucky I'm telling you anything. If the Turk thinks we've ratted on his set-up, we'll piss him off. If we lose him at this stage, heads will roll. I'll make sure it's your head and not mine."

"So why are you helping me?"

Linda shrugged. "Call it female solidarity. I don't like men who beat up women."

"Thanks." Eddy gave her his card, and an appraising stare. "You look good without the glasses and the headscarf. Can I get you a drink?"

"I have a partner in Special Forces," she said. "Can I give you a tip?"

Eddy nodded.

"I'd be a bit more subtle, if I were you." She smiled, put Eddy's card in her pocket, got up and walked away.

34

WEDNESDAY: WEEK THREE

Tobias woke before the alarm on his phone summoned him from sleep. He lay wondering what might have happened with Sofie if he hadn't been called to the crime scene in Gellerupparken. Would she have invited him to her flat? How long had it been since he'd spent the night with a woman? Hilde had always left his bed and gone home without spending any unnecessary time talking. Before that, he'd spent as few nights as possible in Silkeborg in the fussy home of Anna, the librarian. She, in turn, had disliked his Aarhus flat. "Spartan minimalism" she called it. How had they managed to sustain a relationship for six months? Sex, he supposed. He thought sex would be exhilarating with Sofie. If he ever found the time, and Sofie had the inclination. He picked up the phone. There was a butterfly in his stomach. He hadn't felt that kind of apprehensive flutter since the early days with Karren. Sex had been good with Karren. It was everything else that was wrong. Sofie's voice – even in a phone message it had a hint of laughter in it – told him to leave a message.

"Sorry about last night," he said briskly. "I'd like to see you again." He paused. "And by the way, she was pushed."

Eddy wakened with hunger pangs and thought he might make a hash of fried potatoes and eggs, until he discovered he'd no eggs, no coffee and no milk. He settled for a bread roll, with cheese and a dab of strawberry jam, in the police canteen.

He got two mugs of coffee – one for himself and one for Katrine – and carried them to the Investigations Room. Katrine was already at her desk, as usual. She looked as though she'd not only had breakfast but had gone for an early morning run as well. Eddy thought he might start going to the gym again. He set a mug of coffee on Katrine's desk.

"Thanks, Eddy." Katrine gave him a brief, distracted smile. Her gaze returned to the computer screen. "There's a message from Karl. They found a passport. Corazon Girlie Sanchez. Born in Manila. It's got a biometric chip so we can do a fingerprint ID. Plus Harry can check the blood sample with the hospital. But I'm sure she's the same Girlie we saw there."

"I'm still kicking myself," said Eddy. He settled on the edge of Katrine's desk.

"Me too." She took a sip of coffee. "Where did you get to last night?"

"A mystery woman in a headscarf asked to meet me in a bar." He paused for effect. "It turned out she was working undercover for PET. She told me Girlie's flat was a brothel. There's another one five doors down. Did you call there?"

"Nobody answered on that floor," said Katrine. "Except the old couple and the family we'd already spoken to."

"There's a sex worker who's legal, according to PET. She might talk to us. And there's a student volunteer in an advice centre who knows about the earlier assault on Girlie. Her name's Irene Voss." Eddy glanced out of the window. "It's going to rain. Where would you rather be on a wet day? In here, staying dry, or out there getting wet? He didn't wait for an answer. "Finish your coffee and get your raincoat. We're going to Gellerupparken to find Irene Voss."

The Women's Legal Advice Centre was tucked into a corner of the big, hangar-like market called Bazar Vest, beside a stall selling embroidered slippers and kaftans. There was a poster on the closed shutter: an emergency telephone number emblazoned across a shadowy male figure, arm raised threateningly over a cowering, shadowy female. Eddy rapped hard several times on the narrow door beside the shutter. A white-faced girl appeared.

"We're not open yet," she said.

"We're looking for Irene Voss," said Eddy. He showed his ID.

"I'm Irene Voss. Come in," she said distractedly. "I was going to phone the police. I need to show you something." Eddy and Katrine followed her down a short dark corridor into a small, high-ceilinged space crammed with a desk, several chairs, two large filing cabinets and a bicycle.

"Yasmina in the shop next door told me a Filipina fell from one of the blocks last night. I hope I'm wrong, but I think I know who it was."

"We found a passport in the name of Corazon Girlie Sanchez," said Katrine.

Irene cried, "Oh, no. I was afraid it was Girlie. I left my phone here last night. I found it on the desk this morning. I saw she'd sent me a message. A photo." She picked up a phone from the desk and handed it to Katrine. "Look at that."

Katrine saw the blurred, headless, image of a bulky male shape in a black sweater and trousers. The photo was timed at five minutes past nine the previous evening. She passed the phone to Eddy.

"I told Girlie she could call me any time. But when she called, I didn't have my phone," said Irene. "I feel terrible. I let her down. I was laughing my head off at the cinema when she needed me." Her eyes filled with tears. "If only I'd had my phone."

"You wouldn't have known what this was," Eddy was looking at the photo, thinking it didn't tell him much.

"Did you know her mobile number?"

Irene shook her head. "But I would have guessed it was Girlie." She pulled a tissue from a box on the desk and mopped her eyes.

"You'd have thought it was a mistake," said Eddy. "The kind that happens when people press a button by accident. I'm going to need this photo, OK?" He forwarded the image to his own phone. Then he wrote the number of Girlie's phone in his notebook.

"I might have called her," said Irene. She blew her nose.

"You'd have been too late," said Eddy. Had a phone been found at the scene? He didn't think so. "There can only have been a couple of minutes, maybe less, between her sending this and hitting the ground."

Irene winced.

"Why did you tell Girlie she could call you?" asked Katrine. "Why did she come to you? Was her husband beating her up?"

"Her husband's in Manila," said Irene. "They have three children. Girlie was sending money back."

"Money earned as a prostitute," said Eddy.

"She was desperate," said Irene. "She didn't want to be a sex worker. She answered an advertisement in the Philippines for a job at the UNICEF Depot in Copenhagen. It was a scam. She paid over all her savings to fly here. The job didn't exist. She applied for asylum. She'd no chance of getting it, and she knew that. She met someone who said she could get work here. It was sex work, of course."

"So it was a client who beat her up," said Katrine.

Irene nodded. "I told her to tell the police. She wanted to know if she reported the assault, would it help her request for asylum. I said it was unlikely. I offered to find her a place in a refuge but she said she needed to work to send money home. She told me she'd been to the hospital but I could see she was in pain every time she moved. She could barely see out of one eye. She was frightened as well. I gave her my number and told her she could call me anytime. What else could I do?"

"If you'd reported her to Immigration, she might still be alive," said Eddy.

"That's not our policy," said Irene, holding her head up. The colour returned to her cheeks. "Our service is confidential. If we reported people they'd never come to us."

"What did she tell you about the man who attacked her?"

"Not much," said Irene. "He picked her up down by the harbour. They went back to one of the flats she and other girls used for clients. It's in one of the blocks here. She didn't tell me where it was exactly. Maybe it was the one she fell from. I don't know. The client called himself Jon. They all do, apparently."

"What age was he?"

"She wasn't sure. She thought he was thirty at least, maybe older. But we were speaking English. She had very little Danish and her English wasn't that good either. I got her to fill out a form." She opened a drawer in one of the filing cabinets, leafed through a folder and pulled out a single sheet of paper. She gave it to Katrine.

Only six answers, on what was obviously a standard questionnaire, had been filled in: Name, Girlie; age 26;

country of origin, The Philippines; Married; immigration status, not divulged.

"Girlie told me another sex worker was attacked five months ago," said Irene. "She said all the working girls were nervous afterwards. The girl who was attacked was from Thailand. She didn't go to the police. Girlie said she went to Copenhagen."

"Do you know the Thai girl's name?"

Irene shook her head.

"Girlie never came back," she said. "Do you think she fell over the balcony when she was trying to get away from this man?"

Katrine imagined the scene. Girlie opening the door to a client, recognising him as the man who'd attacked her. Backing away. Trying to make a call for help. His cry of rage as he realised what she was doing, his bull-like charge at her, the phone flying from Girlie's hand.

"We think he pushed her," she said. "This is a murder enquiry."

35.

Tobias made himself a cup of coffee and switched his mind to work.

Two murders; two people who seemed to have vanished from Denmark, if not from the world; two sets of human bones which had materialised in rubbish bins in the city. He would leave Eddy to run the Girlie investigation. He would concentrate on Bogman. Katrine could assist them both. And the bones? The bones could wait until carbon dating told him how old they were.

He was sure Agnes had called or texted Magnus with

the urgent request to contact him about Aksel. He trusted his daughter. He didn't trust Magnus. On the two occasions they'd met, Magnus, in various subtle ways, had shown his disdain for the police. He would drive to the protest camp and find Magnus. The cadaver dog was going to Roligmose. He could stop there as well. See if the dog had sniffed out anything. The wind farm protest was in North Jutland Police District, where Pernille Madsen was based. He called her from the car, before he set off.

"The wind farm protest? We keep an eye on it," said Pernille. "They haven't caused any trouble so far. A patrol car drives up there from time to time." She gave Tobias the co-ordinates for the camp. "Why the interest? Anything I should know?"

"We're trying to trace a missing girl. Emily Rasmussen. She was the girlfriend of the victim we found in the bog. She was active in the green movement. They both were. There's a guy up at that camp who knew her. He might know where she is."

"I saw her details on our system. I saw the television reports as well. You were looking good, Tobias."

"Thanks." Tobias wondered how Pernille looked these days. She sounded just the same.

"So you identified your Bogman," said Pernille. "And now you're looking for his girlfriend."

"She's an elusive girl," said Tobias.

"Are you sure she's alive?"

"We're not sure about anything," said Tobias. "But she sends emails. We're waiting to hear where they're sent from."

"Thanks for your email about Bruno Holst. You closed that case. Well done."

"Thanks. What about you? You were working on an assault last time we spoke."

"Plus two burglaries and a domestic. We're at least one detective short."

"Cuts? Same here. There's a team on round-the-clock watch on the gang we're pretty sure did the Danske bank raid. Plus we've a detective on sick leave."

Tobias switched on his satnav and began entering the co-ordinates of the camp.

"The assault is taking most of my time," said Pernille. "The perpetrator is a nasty piece of work. I want to nail him and put him away for a long time. He gagged a sex worker with her own panties and nearly beat her to death. We have DNA and a thumbprint but it doesn't match any known offenders."

"Good luck," said Tobias.

"You too," said Pernille.

She switched her attention back to the report on the dead prostitute who had been found at Lonstrup. The prostitute who had been dumped in the sea at Hamburg. She had a feeling this case was connected to the cases the profiler, Matt Erikson, had found. She read the autopsy report closely. And there it was. The giveaway detail she thought might be there. Traces of silky threads found in the victim's teeth. Gagged with her own panties. She drummed on the desk with satisfaction. "You bastard. I'll get you yet," she said.

36.

A weather front was rolling in from the west when Tobias reached the forest track leading to the camp. "Save Our Trees: Say No to Turbines" proclaimed the banner strung across the track. Tobias drove underneath it and followed the track for a kilometre until it reached a clearing the size and shape of a football pitch. It seemed to Tobias that trees had already been chopped down to make space for the turbines. Logs were stacked in rows along all four sides of the clearing. Two canvas tents and a wigwam constructed from woven branches stood on the south side, sheltered from the prevailing wind. A wisp of smoke rose from a hole in the ground outside one of the tents. Tobias parked the car and got out. There was no sign of anybody. He walked towards the tents.

A girl with abundant blonde hair emerged from one of the tents. She was wearing green dungarees and hiking boots and carrying a large coffee percolator. She looked relaxed.

"Have you brought the charcoal?" She crouched over the hole in the ground, moved a metal cooking rack to one side, picked up a stick and poked at a smouldering charcoal fire. "We're running low." She pushed the rack back into place and put the percolator on it.

"I'm not here about charcoal," said Tobias. "I'm looking for Aksel."

The girl stood up. Her expression changed. "Who are you? Why are you looking for him? Anyway, he's not here."

Tobias produced his ID.

"This is a peaceful protest," said the blonde. "We're not breaking the law."

"I'm not here about your protest either," said Tobias. "I want to speak to Aksel about another matter. Can you tell me where to find him?"

She shrugged. "He comes and goes. I don't know where he is."

There was the sound of a vehicle coming up the track. A dark blue van turned into the clearing and stopped. A slim figure with long dark hair, wearing khaki trousers and a camouflage jacket jumped out. It was Magnus. He strode towards Tobias and the girl.

"If you're looking for Agnes, she isn't here, Chief Inspector," he said. "Is something wrong?"

"Didn't you get her message? She asked you to call me."

Magnus addressed the girl. "I got charcoal. It's in the back of the van." It was clear he intended her to fetch it. She went obediently to the van. Magnus watched her go. He tossed his hair back.

"Why do you want to speak to Aksel?"

"I'm investigating a murder," said Tobias. "He might know the whereabouts of an essential witness."

"I don't know where he is," said Magnus.

"But you know him?"

Magnus said nothing. He stroked his beard.

"You've been seen together," said Tobias. It was a shot in the dark.

"I might have known you'd be snooping on me," said Magnus.

Tobias felt like telling Magnus he was not important enough to be snooped on, but merely said, "Where can I find him?"

Magnus shrugged. "He's not here. He could be in Aarhus. He could be in Copenhagen. He could be in Sweden. He hasn't been here for a while."

Nor have many other protesters, thought Tobias. It seemed to him a feeble sort of protest. The turbines would probably win. He felt a pang of sympathy for Agnes. She would be disappointed.

The blonde girl came back carrying a large bag of charcoal. She dumped it beside the fire.

"Who is Agnes?" she said.

"Agnes is a green warrior," said Magnus. He looked uncomfortable. Tobias wanted to punch him.

An ancient bus lumbered into the clearing and stopped. Five young people dismounted, chatting and laughing. They dropped rucksacks beside the bus and headed towards the fire. Tobias guessed they were students. One of them called out, "Any coffee on the go? We've come all the way from Esbjerg."

The atmosphere lightened. The blonde girl said, "You're welcome. Coffee will be ready soon."

Tobias showed his ID to the group. "I'm looking for Aksel," he said. "It's not connected to this protest."

"Aksel who?" said a red-haired girl.

"I'm not sure of his second name," said Tobias. "It might be Schmidt."

"Where's he from?"

Tobias said he didn't know that either.

"You don't know much," said the red-haired girl. The rest of the group laughed.

"I wish I knew more," said Tobias. "Because I think he can help me solve a murder."

The group fell silent.

"A young man, a green activist, was murdered in a bog at Roligmose fourteen years ago," said Tobias.

"I saw something about that on television," said a skinny boy in the Esbjerg group.

"His girlfriend hasn't been seen since," said Tobias. "Aksel knew her. I think he might know where she is."

There was a general shrugging and mutterings of "Don't know him. Can't help you."

The percolator bubbled and gurgled. "Get yourselves mugs," said Magnus.

The students drifted towards the rucksacks. Magnus went into the wigwam.

"Aksel's in Aarhus," said the blonde girl quickly. "In Brabrand. The Gellerup part. First floor, end of a block near City Vest."

Magnus emerged from the wigwam with two mugs.

"I'll be off then," said Tobias.

He looked back when he got to his car. The students were drinking coffee and laughing again. Magnus and the blonde girl appeared to be having an argument.

37.

There was no sign of Karl and the Crime Scene Investigators when Eddy and Katrine emerged from the lift on the eighth floor of the block at Gellerupparken. The flat from which Girlie fell was still sealed off, but the Forensic team had gone. Katrine called Karl Lund.

"We finished at two o'clock this morning," he said. "I'll have preliminary results for you in a couple of hours. Busy spot, that flat. Some traffic. I'd say we have the fingerprints and DNA of half the men in Aarhus. Plus three boxes of condoms, three boxes of baby wipes, four vibrators, a two-litre bottle of massage oil, a feather duster, a set of handcuffs and a riding crop."

"Did you find her phone?"

"We found a phone in the bushes near the block. It's probably hers. We won't be sure until we match fingerprints."

"The killer's number might be in it," said Katrine. She crossed her fingers. "And Philippines numbers. We need to contact her next of kin."

It was not a call Katrine wanted to make.

Eddy had counted five doors down to the other flat that was used as a brothel. He rang the doorbell. There was no reply. He knocked. No reply. He thumped the door. No reply. He shrugged.

"She's probably sucking a dick somewhere else. Let's go."

They went directly to the Forensics laboratory. Karl Lund was dusting a mobile phone for prints. They watched him pass the phone under the UV lamp.

"Clean as a whistle," said Karl. "The screens on these phones are usually smothered in prints. But not this one. It's been wiped."

"It must be her phone," said Katrine. "Are there Philippines numbers in it?"

"No," said Karl. "Everything was deleted."

"Bastard," said Katrine.

"Clever bastard," said Eddy. "When a woman's assaulted, the bastard is usually too drunk or too stupid to get rid of prints or DNA. This bastard is different. My guess is none of the prints or fluid traces we found are his. I hope I'm wrong."

"You're right," said Karl. "If he wipes a mobile phone and deletes all the number before he throws it away, he won't leave prints anywhere else. He was probably wearing gloves." He paused. "I bet he's done this before."

"We think the same guy beat her up ten days ago," said Eddy. "He might have left a tiny trace of something, somewhere. But I'm not holding my breath."

Katrine took a gulp of air into her lungs before she

followed Eddy into the autopsy room. She had not yet rid herself of a gagging reflex whenever she entered that cold space that smelled of blood and formaldehyde.

Harry Norsk tipped something into a stainless steel bowl. Katrine looked away.

Harry smiled. "Hi, guys. I see you get a bit green around the gills, Katrine. A sip of brandy usually does the trick." He pointed to a small white wall cabinet with a green cross on the door.

Eddy grinned. He opened the cupboard, took out a half-bottle of brandy and poured a capful into a glass beaker.

Harry lifted Girlie's liver from the bowl and placed it on a set of scales.

"This unfortunate woman wasn't a drinker," he said. "I bet your liver isn't as healthy as that, Eddy."

Katrine was white-faced. Eddy gave her the beaker of brandy.

"She has extensive injuries and bruising," said Harry. "Five broken ribs, a black eye, bruising on her stomach and inner thighs. These injuries are all about ten days old. I'd say she was still in pain from them. She hadn't had sex recently. She was probably still too sore. There was no sperm in any orifice. No material or skin under her fingernails. Her neck was broken when she fell. That's what killed her."

We killed her, thought Katrine. If we stayed with her in the hospital, she'd still be alive. She glanced at Eddy. He was staring at the bloodless body on the stainless steel table.

"We'll catch him," he said. "We'll find the fucker who did this."

Katrine thought it sounded like a promise.

When she got back to the office, an envelope from registry was in her pigeonhole. Inside was a file labelled

Lennart Praetorius. She began reading it as she walked to her desk. She was still absorbed when Eddy looked over her shoulder.

"The grandparents mention the watch," she said. "That would have been enough to identify Bogman."

"But not who killed him," said Eddy. He perched on her desk. "Anything else interesting?"

"They hadn't seen him since May 1998," said Katrine. "They spoke to him on the phone about four months after that, perhaps longer. Their contact with him was intermittent. They went to the police again in February 2001. It's pretty much what they told the boss and me on Sunday. There's not much else. Lennart didn't turn up on any database. The only known address for him was the grandparents' house in Helsinger." She paused. "But this is interesting. His last call to them was from a mobile phone, a new one, the grandparents said. Lennart told them he'd only just got it. But he didn't give them the number. The call ended abruptly. Lennart said something like, "Oh, there's the ambulance coming down the track. That's Emily, back from the lily pond. Bye.""

"The lily pond? Sounds like a Chinese take-away," said Eddy.

"The police checked calls to the grandparents landline from mobile phones," said Katrine. "There weren't many. An electrician, someone from their church, a plumber and one number which was defunct." Katrine's voice slowed as she relayed the information to Eddy. "The phone company said the mobile hadn't been topped up and no calls had been made since the date of the call to the grandparents on September 21st, 1998. At 9.30pm." Her voice quickened with excitement. "They gave the co-ordinates of the nearest base station when he made that call."

Eddy sprang off his perch and gripped Katrine's shoulder as she brought a map up on her computer screen.

"Zoom out," he said. "Let's see what's nearby."

Katrine enlarged the area on the map around the base station. In the left hand corner of the screen they saw Roligmose.

"I'll call the boss," said Eddy.

Tobias was watching the cadaver dog, an incongruously cheerful golden spaniel, and her handler, a craggy, former Special Forces soldier, moving across the bog. The dog worked in twenty-minute bursts, straining on the leash, nose to the ground. The sun was low in the sky, below a bank of dark grey cloud. Tobias thought he could smell rain coming, in the way the spaniel, now making its way back to the dog-van, could smell a decomposing corpse. He heard the familiar buzz of his phone, put it to his ear, listened to Eddy telling him about Lennart's last call to his grandparents.

"Lennart must have made the call from Roligmose," said Eddy. "It's in the area covered by the nearest mast. The call ended abruptly. Lennart said, "Bye now. I see Emily coming back from the lily pond." There's a Chinese restaurant ten kilometres away called The Lily Pond."

Tobias pictured Lennart standing in the bog, talking on the phone. Was he alone, or with someone else? Emily bumping down the track in the blue ambulance with a Chinese takeaway supper, Lennart breaking off the call. And what then?

"So they were here at Roligmose on the twenty-first of September," said Tobias. "On their own, or with someone else. Astrid Rasmussen got an email from Emily on the twenty-fourth of September saying she was going away with Lennart. Did they split up after that, or…?"

"She'd already killed him, and skipped off to join the Eskimos," said Eddy.

38

THURSDAY: WEEK THREE

Eddy adjusted the viewing screen in the Incident Room and checked a set of images on his laptop. He looked around. Katrine was pinning photographs to a board on the wall. They were all copies of the images Eddy was going to show on the screen.

Chief Superintendent Larsen, Tobias, Karl Lund, Harry Norsk and Renata Molsing filed into the room and took chairs in front of the screen.

"Everybody here? Right? Let's see what you've got, Haxen," said Larsen.

The first image flashed on to the screen. A round face with regular features, bright eyes and smoothed back hair. Katrine thought it a face full of hope. She felt a rush of compassion for the young woman who thought she was on her way to a well-paid job and a better life, and found instead a sordid job and a brutal death.

"Girlie Corazon Sanchez," said Eddy. "Thirty-one years old. Victim of a scam that lured her to Denmark six months ago. When she had this photograph taken for her passport, she believed she was coming to a job at UNICEF in Copenhagen. The job didn't exist. She paid a fake agency thousands of dollars – we don't know the exact amount. The scam is still being investigated both here and in the Philippines. As far as we are aware, no one has been arrested."

Larsen uttered a short, sardonic bark.

The next slide showed Girlie's expressionless face in death; her bruised eyes mercifully shut.

"Girlie became a sex-worker in Gellerup," said Eddy. "Her pimp is a Turkish man who is also an informant for PET. Two weeks ago, she was dumped at the hospital. She'd been badly beaten. Skaarup and I interviewed her at the Sexual Assault Centre. She wouldn't say anything about her attacker. She seemed frightened of him. We thought, wrongly, it was her husband, her partner or her pimp. Unfortunately she left hospital before she could be interviewed again by us or by Immigration."

Larsen grunted. "Unfortunately is an understatement, Haxen. But I'll say no more. Immigration must take their share of the blame." He gestured impatiently. "Get on with it."

"She went to an advice centre and spoke to a volunteer called Irene Voss. She told Irene Voss she'd been attacked by a client. She was afraid if she went to the police, she'd be deported. Irene Voss gave Girlie her telephone number."

A third image flashed up. A faceless, bulky shape that almost filled the screen.

"Girlie sent this photo to Irene Voss. She must have taken it seconds before she fell, was pushed, from the balcony of the flat."

The balcony now appeared on the screen, followed by a close-up of the balcony ledge showing a wisp of yellow cotton snagged on the grey brickwork.

"We think the abusive client came back. Girlie recognised him and managed to take and send this photo.

We surmise he realised this. He wrestled the phone from her. There's evidence of a struggle."

Eddy clicked on the next image, the interior of the flat. Overturned chairs, plates, cutlery, the remnants of chips on the floor, the unmade bed, the sofa.

"Is that blood?" asked Renata.

"Ketchup," said Eddy. "We think she was eating when her attacker arrived."

"The meal was still in her stomach," said Harry Norsk.

The final image – Girlie's body, splayed on the concrete path – appeared on the screen.

"The immediate cause of death was a broken neck," said Harry. "She had broken ribs and multiple bruising from injuries sustained two weeks earlier. She would not have had the strength to fight back."

"And there's no possibility she could have jumped from the balcony to escape her attacker?" asked Renata.

""The fragment of cotton is from the back of her T shirt," said Karl. "An exact match."

"What about contacting her next of kin?" asked Renata.

"I've told the Philippine's Embassy," said Katrine.

"Is Irene Voss in danger?" asked Tobias.

"We don't think so," said Katrine. "The perpetrator deleted all the numbers from the phone. Plus he'll have looked at the photo she sent. He's unrecognisable. It's not much help to us, unfortunately."

"I don't want to hear that word again," said Larsen. "Tell me something useful."

"We can play around with the image and get some sense of his height and weight," said Karl.

"This is one clever bastard," said Eddy. "He wiped the phone. My guess is none of the prints in the flat will be his.

He probably wore gloves. He's done this before. Irene Voss said another sex worker, also an illegal, was attacked a few months back."

"Same perpetrator?" asked Larsen.

"We don't know at this stage, sir. We're trying to trace the sex worker. Apparently she moved to Copenhagen afterwards. We've alerted Immigration, and Vice."

"Needle in a haystack," said Larsen resignedly.

He thought for a moment. "Alsing's team is still tied up waiting for the Danske gang to assemble. He thinks they can bag the lot. I don't want to jeopardise that. You'll have to handle this on your own, Haxen. Skaarup can work with both you and Chief Inspector Lange. What I want to know is this – are the bones that keep turning up anything to do with this case? Are they the bones of sex workers murdered by this same perpetrator?"

They all considered this possibility silently for a few moments.

"We don't have duplicate bones," said Harry. "If we had two ulna, for example, instead of just one, we could see if they're a match, if we're dealing with one body or more. We should get the results of carbon dating by next week. Brix is trying DNA amplification. That should tell us if there is more than one victim. It can't help with identification, of course, unless we have DNA to compare it with."

"I don't want even a whisper outside this room that there could be multiple victims," said Larsen. "Got that? I'll brief the media centre about the Filipina. I'll have a word with Immigration as well. Keep me informed of developments. Right?"

He turned to Tobias.

"What's the latest on Bogman?"

"I've got an address for a green activist who knew Emily Rasmussen," said Tobias. "He might know where she is."

"Pigs might fly," said Larsen. "Let me know when you find her."

The meeting broke up.

Tobias, Eddy and Katrine headed for Gellerupparken. Eddy and Katrine in one car. Tobias in the other.

Eddy and Katrine went to the flat five doors down from the one Girlie had used on the night she died. Eddy rang the bell.

A statuesque woman in a yellow kimono opened the door. She yawned.

"Hi, honey. I'm Augustina."

Eddy tried to keep his eyes from her bust – it was as high as her cheekbones and shone like polished mahogany. He produced his ID.

"You're up early," said Augustina, with a slow smile. "You're looking for a special price? You guys are always looking for a discount." Eddy decided to let the remark go. He didn't much care if his colleagues bought sex. "You want to arrest me?" She flashed her teeth at him and was halfway through a rapid recital of her repertoire and prices before she noticed Katrine behind Eddy. She backed away from them. They followed her into the flat. It had the same layout and furniture as the one from which Girlie had fallen, except the table and chair weren't overturned and the sofa boasted two pink velvet cushions. Augustina picked up a cushion and held it to her like a shield.

"What do you want? I told you, I'm legal. You want to see my papers?"

"One of your friends was pushed over a balcony last night," said Eddy.

"I don't know anything about that. What friend?"

"Her name was Girlie," said Eddy. "You worked together, Augustina. She's dead."

Augustina clutched the cushion more tightly.

"Did you have a cat fight? Did you push her?"

Augustina stared at Eddy. She was clearly unnerved.

"Where were you last night, Augustina? Didn't you hear the commotion? Didn't you hear the sirens? Didn't you see the flat taped off? The men in blue suits collecting evidence? Five doors down, Augustina. Where were you when all that was going on?"

"I had an appointment," Augustina said. "Downtown." She swallowed. "I didn't come back until a few hours ago. I didn't see anything. What happened?"

"Somebody pushed Girlie off the balcony five doors down. Who might have done that, Augustina?"

Augustina was silent for a few moments. Her voice hardened. "You have to compensate me for all the business I lose because you guys are around," she said. "You understand?"

Eddy turned to Katrine. "I think we'll take Augustina down to Fredensgade right now as a material witness. Tell her what rights she has."

Katrine opened her mouth.

Augustina said quickly, "What do you want to know?"

"That's better," said Eddy. "Have you or any of the other girls had an abusive client?"

"Not me," said Augustina. "I'm too big and strong." She threw the cushion at the sofa. "And I'm legal. He picks on the smaller girls. And the illegals."

"He?" said Eddy and Katrine in unison.

"Who is he? Give us a name," said Eddy.

"I don't know his name or anything about him. I just heard about him. There were rumours. He beat up Girlie a few weeks ago. Before that I heard he beat up a Thai girl from another block."

"What's her name? Where does she live?"

"I don't know. She moved away."

"Where did she move to?"

"I told you, I don't know her name. I don't know where she went." Augustina shrugged. "People move around. She didn't work with us. She was in another block. I told you."

"Do you mean she worked for a different pimp?"

"I don't know who she worked for. She didn't work with me."

"How does this guy know which girls are illegal?" asked Katrine.

Augustina looked uncomfortable. "I heard he told the Thai girl he was a policeman working undercover to find illegal immigrants. He asked for documents. He said he wouldn't report her if they had sex for free."

"Aw, fuck," said Eddy.

"Did Girlie tell you that?" asked Katrine.

"I just heard, that's all," said Augustina. "Word gets about."

"You took Girlie to the hospital. Is that when she told you?"

"I don't know anything about that. It wasn't me took her. I don't know what you're talking about."

"You're on CCTV." This wasn't true, but Katrine guessed Augustina was the woman the ambulance driver had seen in the van which unloaded Girlie at the Emergency Room. "You can tell us about it here, or you can come with us to Fredensgade and tell us about it there. You found her, you called someone. Both of you took her to the Emergency Room," said Katrine.

"You called your boss," said Eddy. "The Turk. He doesn't like his girls getting involved with the police, isn't that right, Augustina?"

"Just tell us about the time you found Girlie and took her to the hospital," said Katrine. She exchanged a glance with Eddy.

"Maybe we should take you down to headquarters after all," he said.

"I'm sure that won't be necessary if Augustina talks to us here," said Katrine.

"I never saw who hurt Girlie," said Augustina quickly. "I never saw him. He was gone when I got there."

"So what happened exactly? Just tell us how you came to take Girlie to the hospital," said Katrine in a patient tone. "Take your time."

Augustina's shoulders dropped. She flopped down on the sofa and leaned back resignedly. "OK."

Eddy and Katrine sat down at the table. Katrine took out her notebook. Eddy set his phone to record the interview.

"I came back early and the door wasn't locked," said Augustina. "We usually lock the door when we have a client. Girlie was tied up on the bed. She was choking. The bastard had stuffed her panties into her mouth so she couldn't call out. He tied her hands with her bra. She was lucky I came back early. I took the gag from her mouth and untied her. I called somebody. We took Girlie to the hospital."

"What did Girlie tell you about this client? What did he look like? Where did she meet him?"

"He picked her up down by the docks. He said he was from Immigration checking on illegal workers. He wouldn't report her if they had sex. They came here."

"To this block," said Eddy.

"To this flat," said Augustina. "Girlie moved into the other one after she got attacked. She was frightened he'd come back."

Katrine put down her notebook and looked at Eddy. "We'll have to get Forensics here."

He nodded. "Is there somewhere you can go, Augustina? We need to check this place for evidence."

"Forensics have finished in the other flat," said Katrine. "Can you go there for a while?"

Augustina nodded wearily. She moved around the flat picking up her things and putting them into a holdall. She zipped it up. She was still in her yellow kimono.

"Do you want to change your clothes? We can wait outside," said Katrine.

"I'm dressed for work," said Augustina.

Katrine had a sudden thought. "What did you do with Girlie's clothes? Where are the bra and panties, Augustina?"

She looked blank. "I didn't do anything. Maybe I threw them on the floor. I don't remember."

"What was Girlie wearing when you took her to the hospital?"

"I put a robe around her, like this one." Augustina touched the neckline of her own garment. "That's all."

"The bra and pants must be somewhere," said Eddy. "Maybe the Turk knows. Maybe he threw them away. Or did Girlie pick them up when she came back from the hospital? Was she wearing them when she fell? I'll ask Harry." He took out his phone.

"I don't think she'd want to wear panties he'd handled, he'd stuffed in her mouth," said Katrine, recoiling in disgust. "I bet she threw them in the bin."

An image flashed into her mind – Eddy dangling pink silk panties from an orange-gloved hand.

Eddy froze, phone in hand. He stared at Katrine.

"Are you thinking what I'm thinking?" she said.

He nodded. "Let's go."

As they got into the car, Eddy said, "It's the last thing we need. A suspect from Immigration, working undercover."

"We don't know that, Eddy. It might just have been something he said, so he'd know who was unlikely to go to the police."

"And I'm the Emperor of Japan. Plus, if we need to talk to the Turk, there'll be a fucking great argument with PET because he's one of their touts. Larsen won't like any of this."

"My turn to tell him," said Katrine.

Eddy patted her knee. "We'll do it together." He switched on the engine and pulled away from the kerb.

39.

Tobias walked around the tower block nearest to City Vest Mall looking for the squat described to him by the blonde girl at the protest camp. Was Magnus having a fling with her? Tobias hoped so. If it meant Magnus had switched his attention from Agnes. It would be hard on Agnes but she was young and resilient. He wouldn't, couldn't tell her about Magnus and the blonde. But he could keep his fingers crossed.

He identified the squat easily. It was at the end of a block, on the first floor, exactly as the blonde had said.

Banners hung from the balcony. *Save the Whale. Save the Planet. Save our Trees. Action on Climate Change! Whoever You Vote For The Government Gets In. Capitalism Kills!*

Tobias walked across the road to get a better view of the flat. The door to the balcony was closed. Curtains were drawn on the windows. There was no sign of life. The flat beside it was boarded up. Further along the block, a dog barked briefly, its paws up on the balcony ledge, before dropping down out of sight.

There weren't many people about. Two men in turbans sat on a bench in a small park opposite the flats, enjoying the May sunshine. Sunshine, like snow, improved Gellerup, thought Tobias. The trees were in full leaf. A young woman wearing blue jeans, a long black tunic and a black headscarf, cycled unhurriedly along the pavement. A battered silver-grey Volvo, parked across the road from the flats, gleamed in the sunlight. The brand-new black BMW beside it shone like coal. Drug dealer's car, thought Tobias automatically. Agnes would say this was police prejudice. He could hear her saying, "Why shouldn't someone in Gellerup have a new car?" He smiled.

He climbed the stone staircase to the first floor. The doorbell on the flat dangled uselessly from wires. The letterbox was blocked by a short plank nailed to the door. Tobias thumped the door. Nobody came. He put his ear to the wood and listened. He thought he could hear voices faintly. Male and female voices. Could Emily be there?

He went back down the stairs and walked to the back of the building. A row of garages with grey steel shutters ran along the back of the block. Graffiti covered most of them. On the one below the squat, Tobias could make out two words, recently added he thought: *Police scum.*

Tobias tried to lift the shutter. It was locked from inside. He banged on it. There was no reply. He walked to the front of the building and looked up at the flat. He thought he saw a curtain move. He went back to the door and hammered on it again.

He heard the distant rattle of a steel shutter. An engine revved. He ran back down the staircase, in time to see a white van career around the far corner of the block and accelerate towards one of the principal roads through the estate.

Tobias sprinted back to the garage. The shutter was down. He could detect no recent tire marks, but it was a dry day. Damn. Rain would have made tire marks visible.

He went back to the door of the flat and hammered on it. He waited five minutes, put his ear to the door again and heard distant voices, laughter. He shrugged. If they wanted to play silly buggers, he would return with a search warrant.

When he emerged from the building, the grey Volvo and the two men in turbans had gone. The road was empty. He walked back to his car.

He was about to start the engine when his phone rang. He dug it out of his pocket and glanced at the screen. Agnes.

"Hi, Pumpkin."

"You don't trust me, Dad. You didn't trust me to ask Magnus to call you."

"I trust you, Agnes. I don't trust Magnus."

"He would have called you. Things that seem so urgent to you are not so urgent to Magnus."

"I have to follow my own timesheet, Agnes. I couldn't wait for Magnus to get around to calling me about a vital piece of information."

"Why don't you trust Magnus?"

Tobias thought of four reasons simultaneously. He has studs in his ears, nose and mouth; he hates the police; he hasn't got a job; he's screwing another girl.

"He doesn't like the police," he said.

"He told me he was going to call you. He would have called you. You didn't give him a chance."

"Some things can't wait, Agnes. I'm on a murder enquiry."

"You just don't like him. You're prejudiced because he's a full-time activist."

"Quite so. I'd prefer he had a job."

"He doesn't need a job," said Agnes. "He inherited money. He works for the planet."

So Magnus was a rich boy. Agnes hadn't told him that before. It didn't make Tobias like him any better.

"I need to talk to Aksel," he said. "Does he have a job?"

"Magnus says he's some kind of IT specialist. You see? I did talk to Magnus about him. I asked him to call you. He said he was going to. But you couldn't wait. You had to go up to the camp."

"Where does Aksel work?"

"He's freelance. He can work from home."

"Even if home is a wigwam?"

"The wigwam is for storing stuff, Dad."

"And you don't know Aksel's surname?"

"It's Schmidt," said Agnes. "Magnus told me that as well."

"Thanks for that, at least."

"But no thanks for going up to the camp, Dad. Now they'll all know my Dad's a policeman," said Agnes. There was a bitter note in her voice. "We have an informer in the camp. We went to block the road to stop some equipment getting into the forest. The police were waiting for us."

"Don't you think the police might have guessed you'd try to block the road?"

"It doesn't matter what I think," Agnes sounded bitter now. "They'll all think I'm the informer because my dad's a policeman."

"Does Magnus think that?"

"He trusts me. He knows I'd never betray the group."

"Why don't you give it all a rest for a while," said Tobias quietly. "There are plenty of others to protect the forest and the otters."

"If we all thought like that, nobody would protect anything. We'd go on destroying the planet. And it's not otters, Dad. It's bats. Bechstein's bat. And the trees as well. They're the lungs of the earth."

Tobias sighed. "So where are you now?"

"In Copenhagen. But I'm going up to the camp this weekend."

"I thought you had an essay to write?"

"I can write in a tent too." The smile was back in her voice now. "Relax, Dad. Smell the flowers. I'm fine and everything's cool."

Tobias sat for a while pondering how anyone could suspect Agnes of being an informer. Agnes who couldn't tell a lie, who hated dishonesty. Perhaps he should, after all, tell Agnes he thought Magnus was sleeping with the blonde girl at the camp. Maybe she knew already. The young seemed to share everything these days. Best not to interfere. All he could do is hope for the best. Which for him would be for Agnes to fall out of love with Magnus and into love with somebody else.

He put the key in the ignition. He paused. He picked up his phone and read again the text Sofie had sent him in reply to his apology.

"You owe me. Reception 7pm Royal Hotel. Be there."

He texted, "And dinner afterwards?" Maybe coffee at Sofie's place as well. He turned the key and drove back to Fredensgade in high spirits.

Eddy and Katrine were in Larsen's office when he went to arrange a search warrant for the squat.

"More trouble I suppose," said Larsen when he saw Tobias. "It usually comes in threes. I've just had Haxen tell me someone from Immigration might have killed a prostitute. And one of the key witnesses is a tout for PET."

"I need a warrant to search a squat in Brabrand, sir," said Tobias.

"It can wait," said Larsen.

"I'm close to finding Emily Rasmussen, sir."

"And I'm close to boiling point. Right?" Larsen's eyes were bright with anger. "I've had journalists on the phone for the last hour. More bones were found at the recycling depot. Someone tipped off the press." He spoke through gritted teeth.

"It must have been someone at the depot," said Eddy.

"Of course it's someone at the depot." Larsen glared at Eddy. "If I thought it was a member of the force I'd have them demoted on the spot." He drew a breath. "They've stopped the conveyor whatsit until this is sorted. I don't want any more complaints about men being paid to stand around and do nothing. I want this bones business cleared up, pronto. Right? Get up there straightaway, Lange."

Tobias knew it was useless to argue with Larsen when he was in a temper.

Larsen turned to Eddy. "I don't want anyone, apart from Chief Inspector Lange, to know someone from Immigration might be involved until I've spoken to Renata Molsing and

Internal Affairs. And I mean anyone. Right? Now get on with it."

"What about PET, sir?" asked Eddy.

"I've already had them on the line wanting assurances you won't pull in this Turk for questioning. They don't want to upset him. Hah! Upset away, Haxen if you have to. I won't have PET swanking all over us."

Tobias thought he sounded almost cheerful at the prospect of a row with the notoriously self-regarding Intelligence Service.

"A fine kettle of fish," growled Larsen. He had calmed down. "We can sort out the warrant in the morning. Off you go." He waved them away.

"Good luck, boss," said Eddy, when they were safely outside Larsen's office. "If you find any pink panties in the rubbish, let me know."

40.

Tobias drove through three police checkpoints on his way to the city waste disposal depot. Larsen was clearly determined to keep the media at bay. A television crew had managed to get through to the third checkpoint. Tobias ignored their pleas for information. He drove to the recycling area, parked beside the Forensic van and went into the shed.

Harry Norsk and Karl Lund were standing over a static conveyer belt looking at six white bones and a small olive-green canvas bag. It looked like the kind of bag a fisherman might use for bait. The supervisor stood about a metre away, looking anxious. Half a dozen men in yellow overalls sat on the ground, their backs to the wall, looking bored.

Tobias raised his hand in a general greeting and went to join Karl and Harry.

"What can you tell me?" he said.

"Not much," said Harry. "Except I'm fairly confident these are human bones. I'll run the usual tests, of course, but," he picked up a long thin bone in his gloved fingers. "This is the humerus, the bone that runs from the shoulder to the elbow."

The supervisor's eyes were as round as saucers. His jaw visibly dropped.

"The bones that turned up ten days ago were the ulna and the radius," said Harry. "They're the bones that run from the elbow to the wrist. I can't say yet whether this bone," he waved the humerus like a flag, "was attached to them, but my guess – and it's only a guess – is that it was."

"Meaning all the bones are from the same body," said Tobias.

"I think so," said Harry. "I'm sending them to Brix." He paused. "There's one strange thing. These bones have been cleaned."

"Cleaned? What with?"

"Probably hot water and detergent," said Harry. "That's what I use. There's hardly a trace of dust on them. They can't have been in the skip for long." He picked up the second bone and dropped both bones into a clear plastic bag. "There's not much I can do here. I'm taking them back to the lab."

"They were in a skip at Viby," said Karl. "Building materials for recycling mostly." He waved at the assortment of cupboard doors, plastic shelves, window frames, bricks lying further along the belt. "And some other stuff, as well as the bones."

"People are always dumping things in skips," said the supervisor. He was composed now. "The Viby skip had two broken bicycle wheels, crisp packets, cigarette butts, old videotapes, you name it. A busted beach ball. Even a couple of golf balls. But as soon as I looked in the bag and saw the bones, I stopped the belt straightaway." He fidgeted. "When do you think we can start up again?"

Tobias looked at Karl and raised an eyebrow.

Karl picked up the canvas bag. "We're done here. All the other stuff, the bicycle wheel etcetera, is in the van", said Karl.

Tobias turned to the supervisor. "You can start up again whenever you like."

The supervisor grinned. "My boss at city hall will be happy." He put two fingers into his mouth and whistled. The men in yellow helmets got to their feet.

Tobias and Karl left the recycling shed and walked to their vehicles. Behind them, the conveyor belt jerked into life.

Eddy and Katrine were in the basement garage looking for the bag they hoped contained Girlie's panties.

"They were in the same bag as the jacket with the swastika," said Eddy.

"I think this is it." Katrine held up a bag. She put it on the ground, opened it, plunged her gloved hands into the contents and pulled out the pink panties. She sat back on her heels and grinned at Eddy.

Katrine dropped the panties into a plastic bag. She and Eddy went to the Forensic lab. Karl wasn't back from the recycling yard. Eddy attached a note to the bag and left it on Karl's desk.

They met Renata Molsing on their way to the Investigations Room. She waved a sheet of paper at them.

"I've had a reply from Hotmail. They've sent me a list of the IP addresses and the ISP host sites for the Emily

Rasmussen emails, along with the geolocations. Plus the date when the email address was set up. Here you are." She handed the paper to Eddy. "Good luck."

Eddy glanced at it. He whistled. "She gets around," he said. "Sweden, Norway, Germany, France."

When Tobias got back from the recycling centre, he found Eddy and Katrine going through the geolocation list.

"Emily's email was set up at an IP address in Skandeborg on the 24th of September 1998, the date of the first email to her mother. The twelfth of April emails are all from Internet cafés or open broadband hubs in public places," said Eddy. "Seven of them are in Denmark, including the most recent one: three from Copenhagen, one each from Odense and Fredericia, two from Aalborg. Two are from Lapland. Pitea in Sweden Lapland and Hurtigruten in Norway, to be precise. One is from Hamburg. One is from Arles in France. Two are from Stockholm."

"I'll check to see what was happening in those places around the date the emails were sent," said Katrine. "If there were green protests. Something that might have attracted Emily."

"Larsen has sorted out a search warrant for the squat at Brabrand," said Tobias. "We'll go in tomorrow morning. Let's do catch-up on everything else."

He led the way to the Investigations room. The photographs of Girlie were still pinned to the board. Her round features, bright-eyed, alive. Her bruised face, eyes closed, dead.

Tobias straightened a chair and sat down. Eddy perched on a desk. Katrine stood gazing at the photographs.

"We spoke to a prostitute who worked with Girlie," she said. "Her name's Augustina. She and the Turk took Girlie to the hospital after the earlier attack. Same perpetrator. According to Augustina, he gagged Girlie with her panties. He beat her up. He filmed her."

"We found the panties," said Eddy. "At least we think they're her panties. There could be DNA as well."

"Probably only Girlie's," said Katrine. "He wore gloves."

"If we're lucky, he wanked all over them," said Eddy.

Katrine made a face.

"Even a DNA match is no good unless we have someone to match it to," said Tobias.

"Larsen said if we got DNA he could ask all the males in Immigration to take DNA tests," said Eddy.

"Let's talk about the bones," said Tobias. "This last lot were dumped in a skip at Viby. They were in a canvas bag. An olive-green bag, with a shoulder strap. The kind of thing a fisherman might use. We'll put a notice up near the skip with a picture of the bag. Did you see anyone put this bag in the skip? That kind of thing. It's a long shot, but someone might have seen something. Can you arrange that, Katrine?"

She nodded. "I'll do that right away."

"I'll see you both in the morning," said Tobias.

41.

Tobias disliked receptions but he had to attend them from time to time. Award ceremonies, visits by the National Commissioners, visits by members of the Royal family, foreign police delegations, meet-the-press evenings – he loathed them all equally. He had developed a strategy for coping. He made a mental list of the people he had to converse with in case Larsen asked him what he thought about so-and-so, or what so-and-so had said about some aspect of policing. He worked his way through the names. When he had ticked off everyone on the list, he went home.

Tonight's reception was different. It had nothing to do with work. It was a corporate social affair. Sofie and Hannah were entertaining potential clients of a manufacturer of golf equipment. Tobias didn't need to ask himself why he was going to the kind of event he would normally avoid. The reason was standing beside a hefty bag of golf clubs, her high heels digging into a thick mat in a near-luminous shade of green with a small white circle on it. The mat was attached by a cord to a large screen showing a well-known Danish professional golfer continuously sweeping a golf ball into the blue distance. Sofie was surrounded by men. She was smiling, gesticulating, nodding her head in answer to questions Tobias could not hear.

A man stepped out of the audience and stood on the mat. Tobias saw that it was Norbert, loyally supporting Sofie's demonstration of what appeared to be a machine to measure? – Improve? – the golf swing. Sofie stepped off the mat and handed Norbert a golf club. He swung the club. A set of numbers replaced the golfer on the screen. Sofie clapped her hands. Another man stepped out of the crowd. Tobias recognised Marcus Thomsen. Sofie gave him a club. He swung it. Another set of numbers flashed on to the screen. Marcus Thomsen looked smug. Sofie said something. There was general laughter and applause.

Now Sofie saw Tobias. She smiled and called out to him.

"Come and have your swing analysed."

Tobias hesitated. If he refused she would think him churlish. She would accuse him of false modesty. A space opened for him. He stepped on to the mat, took the club, swung it. Another set of numbers. More applause. Tobias didn't wait to decipher the numbers. He retreated into the crowd. Someone tapped him on the shoulder. He turned. It was the Commissioner. He was asking if Tobias was a member of the East Jutland Police Golfing Society.

"I'm keen for someone from the district to play on the national team. You could be that person, Lange. Good PR today." He clapped Tobias on the back before going to join Kurt Malling, who was talking to the golf professional whose image was still on the screen, hitting balls with the regularity of a metronome.

Tobias scanned the room for familiar faces and saw Inge. He made his way to her side. They were joined by Astrid Thomsen. She greeted Tobias in a friendly manner but he detected an underlying nervousness.

"Are you still trying to find Emily?" she asked in a half whisper. "Have you any news?"

"We are in the process of tracing where the emails are coming from," said Tobias. He hesitated. "You know that if we find Emily, we can't make her contact you? Or even tell you where she is without her consent."

Astrid nodded and bit her lip. "I just want to know that she is well and happy."

Inge put her arm around Astrid's shoulder. "I know Tobias is doing everything possible," she said.

Marcus Thomsen approached. "I hope you're not upsetting my wife. This is hardly the time or the place."

"He's not upsetting me," said Astrid. "He says he'll soon be able to tell me where the emails are coming from. But I know he can't make Emily contact us if she doesn't want to."

Marcus nodded. "She's an adult." He added, in an aside to Tobias, "Even if she still behaves like a child."

The Thomsens moved away.

"Norbert and I are going to *Rigoletto* next week," said Inge. "Thank you again for the tickets." She smiled. "I thought you hated this kind of corporate thing, Tobias. You're a keen golfer, I know." Her smile broadened. "But I suspect that's not the main reason you're here." She glanced across the room at Sofie, now ushering people towards rows of chairs at the far end of the room. "She will keep you on your toes, Tobias. Good luck."

Music burst from loudspeakers. Two models, a man and a woman, in golfing clothes, pranced along a catwalk. Inge said she hated standing for a long time. She was going to sit down and watch the fashion show. She signalled her intention to Norbert.

Tobias stayed on his feet and backed slowly towards the exit, hoping to sit in the foyer until the fashion show was over.

"Hi Tobias," said a familiar voice. Tobias turned and saw Christer Alsing.

"Thanks again for your advice about the frogman stealing the balls in our pond," said Christer. "He hasn't been spotted since. We'll know roughly how many he stole when we drain the pond."

"How often do you do that?"

"Once a year in the summer, when the water level goes down naturally. That's what most clubs do. I reckon frogman took about fifty balls every time. He could probably get fifteen kroner each for the top brands, and ten kroner for the others. It was a nice little earner for him. All he had to do was clean off the mud and weed out a few duff ones."

A light shock ran through Tobias. He saw again in his mind's eye the frogman flapping across the grass, the net filled with golf balls, the tyre tracks, the white van roaring away from the driving range, the bend in the road, the sign: Lake Balls. Heard again the words of the waste depot supervisor – 'people are always dumping stuff in skips. Even golf balls.'

"I have to go," he said. "I've just remembered something. It's important. Sorry."

"No problem," said Christer pleasantly. "I'm going to sit down and watch the show."

Sofie must have sensed something. Tobias saw her turn and stare. She got up from her chair.

"I have to go," Tobias said when she caught up with him.

"Don't play games with me, Tobias," she said. Her eyes were like stones.

"No games. This is urgent." His mind was already elsewhere. He had the phone to his ear. He had walked to the reception. He needed a car. Eddy was saying, "What's up, boss?"

"I have to get to a driving range," he said. "Pick me up at the Royal Hotel. It's about the bones."

42.

They got to the driving range at nine o'clock. It was dusk. The shop was brightly lit. Behind it, floodlights from the range lit the night sky. The thwock and thock of golf club on golf ball was the only sound. White balls flew through the air like shooting stars.

The shop was garishly lit, but empty. Three walls were

lined with shelves neatly stacked with golf clothes. A wide door in the fourth wall led to a bank of machines which dispensed practice balls. A man in a yellow baseball cap pulled a lever to restock the machines. The balls made a noise like distant thunder as they rattled down a chute. The man glanced over his shoulder at Tobias and Eddy. "I'll be with you in a minute," he shouted over the drumming of the balls.

Eddy picked up a couple of golf balls from a half-full barrel beside the counter and juggled with them. The man in the baseball cap came back into the shop. He wore a badge: Jesper Erikksen: Manager."

"Can I help you?"

"Where do you get your lake balls, Jesper?" asked Tobias.

"You'd like to buy some? They're good value."

"I'd like to know where you get them," said Tobias.

"What does it matter?"

"It matters to us," said Eddy. "We're police officers."

Jesper asked, "Is this some kind of joke?"

Tobias produced his ID. "We're investigating a crime," he said. "Can you tell us where you got the lake balls?"

"It's not a crime to sell lake balls," said Jesper.

"It is if you put on a frogman suit and dive for them on private property," said Tobias.

"This is some kind of wind-up," said Jesper. "I don't go diving for golf balls. Or anything else for that matter."

"So where do you get your lake balls, Jesper?" asked Eddy.

Jesper looked uncomfortable. "From various suppliers," he said.

"And where do these," Tobias paused, "various

suppliers," another pause, "get their supplies?"

"I don't know," said Jesper. "You'll have to ask them."

"In which case," said Tobias, "you'll give me their names and contact details."

Jesper shifted uneasily. "I ought to ask him first."

"Him? That sounds like just one supplier to me," said Eddy. "Supplying you with stolen goods."

"I know nothing about any stolen goods," said Jesper. "I buy in good faith."

"And you don't think it's suspicious to pick up your supplies in a car park at Viby?"

This was a shot in the dark by Tobias but it hit the mark. Jesper flushed, then paled.

"You can tell us his name here, or you can tell us at police headquarters," said Tobias. "Your choice."

"His name is Afrim Bushati," said Jesper. "He's from Albania. He lives in Gellerupparken."

"What's the address?"

Jesper wrote down the address on a piece of paper. He pushed it across the counter to Tobias. "He'll know that I told you. He won't like that."

"He won't like being behind bars either," said Eddy. "And if you warn him that we are looking for him, you'll find yourself behind bars as well."

They left a subdued Jesper Erikksen and drove to the address in Gellerupparken. On the way, Tobias spoke to Larsen, who was pleased at apparent progress on the bones case but sceptical about the connection between the bones and stolen golf balls.

"I don't want to look like an idiot, Lange," he said.

"Neither do I, sir. But it's our best lead," he didn't say only lead, "so far."

Larsen allowed Tobias three officers from Armed

Response. They arrived, with Katrine, in an anti-riot transport vehicle. Arrests could be difficult in Gellerupparken.

The address for Afrim Bushati was on the first floor of an eight-storey block near the underground bin in which the first bones had been found. The entrance was on a walkway. There was no back door, but a balcony gave on to a wide alley at the back. Tobias directed two armed response officers to take one end of the walkway each. The third officer he stationed, with Katrine, at the back of the building, under the balcony. He and Eddy went to the door of the flat. The lights were on. Tobias knocked on the door. Eddy flattened himself against the wall, his Heckler and Koch 9mm pistol in both hands.

A dark haired woman in a pink tracksuit opened the door. Behind her, Tobias glimpsed a short corridor leading to a brightly lit room.

"I'm looking for Afrim," said Tobias.

"Who is it?" a man called out from inside the flat. Seconds later a short, stocky man came to the door. He was drying his hands on a grubby white towel. The woman slipped past him and went back into the room.

"Who's looking for him?" asked the stocky man.

"Police," said Tobias, showing his ID.

The man pushed the door against Tobias and ran back into the flat.

He picked up a chair and flung it at Tobias and Eddy in pursuit. He ran on to the balcony and vaulted over the wall. Tobias and Eddy got to it in time to see him scramble to his feet and run no more than ten metres before being brought down by a hefty shoulder tackle by Katrine. The Armed Response officer, slower because of his protective armour, arrived in time to help her handcuff Afrim.

"She's fit," said Eddy admiringly.

They went back into the flat. The woman had drawn herself into the smallest possible space on a sofa, knees drawn up to her chin. Her hands, clasped around her knees, were covered in an assortment of gold and silver rings. Tobias assumed she was Afrim's wife. She was watchful but silent as Tobias and Eddy glanced around the room.

They went into the narrow kitchen. Six red plastic buckets filled with golf balls sat on the floor. Water had recently drained out of the sink leaving a residue of suds and small bones, like chicken bones.

"Harry says it's hard to tell the difference between chicken bones and human finger bones," said Eddy.

"Better get these to him," said Tobias.

Eddy took a pair of rubber gloves and a plastic bag from his jacket pocket. He put on the gloves and began picking the bones out of the sink.

The woman on the sofa spoke. "Afrim is a good man," she called out. "He's done nothing wrong."

Tobias went to the kitchen doorway.

"So why did he run away?"

"He's a good man but he's also a stupid man. He thinks you'll throw him in jail because he finds and keeps the golf balls people are stupid enough to lose."

"We'll throw him in jail because he has human bones in his kitchen sink," said Tobias. "Because he dumped human bones in the bin fifty metres from here. Because we think he killed someone."

"Afrim wouldn't hurt a fly," said the woman. "He found

the bones in a lake when he was diving. I told him he should go to the police but he was worried he'd be deported."

"So he's an illegal immigrant," Tobias said heavily.

"He's an asylum seeker. He has a shite job making sandwiches in a factory. Eight at night until six in the morning. Earning peanuts. He was a diving instructor in Albania. He hit on the golf ball idea when he saw a golf tournament on television. He didn't make a lot of money. Just enough to make life a little easier."

"Why isn't he at work?"

"Thursday and Saturday are his nights off."

"When did he arrive in Denmark?"

"About eighteen months ago. I met him shortly after he got here."

"What's your name? What's your relationship to him?"

"Grete Kjaer," she said. "We live together."

Tobias turned. Eddy was peering at something in the sink. He lifted out the inset drainer, a small round metal container which allowed water to drain while capturing dregs and particles of food waste. He held it out for Tobias to inspect.

"Take a look at this."

Captured in the mesh of the drainer was a silver ring.

Tobias called out to Grete Kjaer. "Are you missing any of your rings?"

She spread her hands, examined her fingers.

Eddy had the ring in his hand. He held it close to his eyes. "It's engraved on the inside." He squinted. "Together Forever," he said.

Tobias and Eddy stared at each other.

"Fuck," said Eddy.

Tobias said nothing. His brain had built a picture

of Emily Rasmussen, a mysterious will o' the wisp, an elusive warrior in the ecological wars of the planet, fighting developers, living with reindeer. He had not envisaged her finger bones in a sink in Gellerupparken. A great weariness settled on him.

"I have all my rings," said Grete Kjaer. "All present and correct."

"Take a statement from her, Eddy" said Tobias. "I'm going to speak to Afrim."

If what Grete Kjaer said was correct and Afrim was an asylum seeker who'd been in Denmark less than two years, he could not have met Emily Rasmussen, unless she'd been living undetected in Aarhus. He could not have killed her, chopped her up and dissolved her flesh in acid. For how else could he have dumped her bones in bins in the city? Unless those bones belonged to someone else.

The anti-riot van was still parked below the balcony. Afrim sat in the back, handcuffed, behind a metal grille. Katrine was talking to him through the grille. Even in the dim interior light of the vehicle, Tobias could see that Afrim was trembling.

"Why you arrest me? I lose my job. You arrest me, I lose my job."

"A woman was murdered, here in Gellerupparken, on Tuesday night," said Katrine. "Where were you on Tuesday night between eight o'clock and nine o'clock?"

Afrim trembled more violently.

"Stealing golf balls is a crime," said Tobias. "But not as serious a crime as murder. Where were you on Tuesday night?"

"At the factory," cried Afrim. "I work at the factory."

"We can check that," said Tobias. "If you are telling the truth, you have nothing to fear."

"You ask my supervisor," said Afrim. "He tell you I good worker. I always on time."

"Why are there bones in your kitchen sink, Afrim?"

"I found them in the lake with the golf balls," said Afrim.

"Which lake?" asked Tobias. As the words left his mouth the answer came into his head.

Afrim spoke it. "The lake at Skovlynd," he said.

43.

FRIDAY: WEEK THREE

The draining of the lake on the ninth hole at Skovlynd Golf Course began just after sunrise. The manager, who lived in an apartment above the clubhouse, was wakened by Tobias and Eddy at five o'clock, minutes before the arrival of the crime investigation squad. He stood on the terrace in front of the eighteenth green from where he could see the lake on the ninth and the police vehicles driving over the fairway. He was horrified.

"You're going to drain the lake? We have a competition tomorrow," he said. "You can't close the course."

"You have human remains in your lake," said Tobias.

The manager was shocked into silence.

"Were you here when they created the lake?" asked Tobias.

The manager nodded. "It was the last thing they did," he said. "It was just after I joined the company. I joined in August 1998. The lake was filled in September or October. I could tell you exactly by looking through the invoices."

"That would be helpful," said Tobias. "Were the protests still going on?"

"They were at it right up to opening day," said the manager. "Then they sort of faded away. Battle lost, I suppose."

"When did you last drain the lake?"

"July last year. We try to pick a dry spell in the summer, when the water level is low." He looked and sounded unhappy. "I have to speak to my boss." He moved away and spoke quietly into his mobile phone.

Katrine arrived at the Thomsen's house a few minutes before eight o'clock. She wanted to get there before Astrid Thomsen heard news reports about bones being found in the lake at Skovlynd. Before the inevitable speculation that they might be the bones of her missing daughter.

She recognized Katrine immediately. Her face brightened. "You're going to tell me where the emails were sent from. I know it. Have you found Emily? Come in." She held the door open. They went into the wide hallway.

"Is your husband at home?" asked Katrine. "It might be a good idea to get him."

Astrid Thomsen's face went white. "It's bad news, isn't it? You've come to tell me something bad. That's why you want Marcus here. Tell me. Is she alive? That's all I want to know. Is Emily alive?"

Katrine was silent. She put out her hand tentatively.

Astrid Thomsen uttered a high-pitched scream, like a rabbit caught in a trap. Katrine caught her as she crumpled.

Marcus Thomsen came bounding down the stairs. "What's happened? What have you said to her?"

He took Astrid from Katrine and helped her into a chair. He stroked her hair with one hand and keyed a number into his phone with the other. "I'm calling a doctor."

"We've found remains in the lake at Skovlynd golf course," said Katrine. "We think they could be the remains of your stepdaughter, Emily Rasmussen."

Astrid moaned again. Marcus continued to stroke her hair.

"Are you sure? I will be extremely angry if you've come here and upset my wife over a case of mistaken identity. Emily has been sending emails. We're sure she's alive somewhere."

"We found a ring with the remains. We know it's a ring Emily's boyfriend, Lennart Praetorius, gave to her."

"She could have given the ring to someone else," said Marcus.

Astrid lifted her head. "Yes," she breathed. "That's possible."

"The only way to be certain is to take a DNA sample from you for comparison," said Katrine.

"How long will it take to get a result?" asked Marcus.

"Two or three days," said Katrine. "Maybe less. I can take a sample now. It takes only a few seconds. I just need to brush a cotton bud on the inside of your cheek."

"Do it," said Astrid. "But I still think Emily is alive. And I will go on thinking that until you prove to me that she's dead."

The doorbell rang. Marcus Thomsen went to admit the doctor while Katrine took a buccal sample from Astrid, who was sitting up but was still deathly pale.

While the doctor busied herself with Astrid, Marcus Thomsen walked with Katrine to the car.

"I don't want to believe the worst," he said, "But if this is Emily, do you have any idea what happened? Did she drown?"

Katrine hesitated. "There's a crack in the skull," she said. "The pathologist thinks it was caused by a blunt instrument. Whoever it is was killed by a person or persons unknown."

"Emily mixed with some unsavoury types," said Marcus. "Anarchists. Anti-this and anti-that. Have you any suspects?"

"Did Emily ever mention someone called Aksel Schmidt?"

Marcus shook his head. "When my wife is strong enough, I'll ask her if she's heard of him. I'll get in touch." He shook hands with Katrine. "Good luck, Inspector."

44.

Kurt Malling arrived at Skovlynd just before nine o'clock. The noise of his car door slamming reverberated around the concrete sides and bottom of the lake, now empty of water. Tobias, crouching near a crack in the concrete and clad, like the Forensic team, in blue protective clothing, knew it was Malling before he looked up and saw him standing behind the tape which encircled the lake and the white Forensic tent.

Malling had his hand up, as though to call a halt. His mouth opened to speak but closed again as one of the forensic team walked past him carrying a clear plastic bag full of bones. Malling's hand dropped. He looked shaken.

Tobias acknowledged his presence with a nod and focused again on what Karl Lund was saying.

"There was an earth tremor last year. In the early hours of the morning. It would have been enough to crack the concrete basin. Especially if there was already a weakness."

Tobias remembered someone telling him protesters had drilled into the concrete lining of the lake. Who had mentioned it? Nicholas Hove? Norbert?

"My guess is the body was buried in a shallow grave before the concrete was poured," said Karl. "With just enough soil to conceal it. When this crack occurred, the bones floated up. When did they last drain the lake?"

"July last year," the manager said.

Karl nodded. "That figures. The tremor was in August. The epicentre was south-east of Anholt, on the seabed. The seismologists measured it at 4.4 on the Richter scale. That's pretty strong by Danish standards. And enough to turn a hairline crack into a fissure half a metre wide. We widened it to get at all the remains, but the whole thing will have to be replaced anyway."

Tobias instinctively glanced up to where Malling was standing, ashen faced.

He used the iron rungs in the side of the basin to climb out onto the fairway. He went into the tent where the bones had been assembled on a trestle table. Harry Norsk had a paper-white skull in his hands.

"Hi, Tobias. If you include the bones from the bins and the finger bones you found in the sink, I have accounted for all of the skeleton." Harry weighed the skull gently in one hand. "This is female. It's lighter. The forehead is vertical. The vault is flattened. I understand you already know who it is?"

Tobias nodded. "Emily Rasmussen. We're almost certain. We found a ring with the finger bones. We know it was given to her by our Bogman, Lennart Praetorius."

Harry's finger traced a line on the skull. "There's a split in the cranium. Probably caused by a blunt instrument. And the mandible is fractured. Possibly with the same blunt instrument, although a fist could have done it. I've seen boxers with this kind of jaw fracture. Males, not female."

"Is there anything else you can tell me now?"

"There's one strange thing," said Harry. "Look at this stuff in the skull, behind the jaw." He turned the skull upside down so that Tobias could see gossamer filaments, like a spider's web, behind the teeth. "I'll get an opinion from Brix, but I think this is the same stuff we found with Bogman. Polyethylene terephthalate. Did you notice the Linden tree by the lake? Linden trees like alkaline soil. Remember what Brix told us? Alkaline soil preserves bones and rots flesh and natural fibres. You're looking at polyester fibres which didn't decompose. But why are these fibres in her jaw?"

"Maybe she was wearing a scarf, or a cap," said Tobias. His brain was already scanning his memory for the photographs of Emily in the newspaper, the pictures of her on videotape. All the images which came to mind were of Emily with blonde hair streaming behind her in the wind, or plastered to her face by the rain.

The Politi team had taken over an office in the clubhouse. Malling, with some grace, sent in a pot of coffee. When Katrine arrived, Tobias and Eddy took a coffee break. Karl joined them.

"I found this." He tipped a gold locket and chain from a clear plastic bag on to the table. "The seal on the locket was tight. The photographs are hardly damaged." He opened the locket so the others could see the round photographs of a man and woman. The woman was clearly Astrid Thomsen.

"The man must be her father," said Katrine.

"There can be no doubt now that it's Emily," said Tobias. "But we'll wait for the DNA confirmation before formally notifying the Thomsens."

They sat in silence for a moment.

"OK," said Tobias. "Let's go over what we know, and more importantly, what we don't know."

"Who sent the emails?" asked Eddy.

"Emily's killer," said Tobias. "To prevent her being reported missing. To cover up the fact that he'd killed her." He adjusted his coffee spoon so that it was aligned with his pen and notepad.

"He didn't bother to do that for Bogman, assuming it's the same killer," said Eddy. "And we can't be sure of that either."

"He didn't bother because there wasn't anybody to report Bogman missing," said Katrine. "Except Emily. And she was already dead."

"All that time we wasted, thinking she was alive," Katrine continued. "I imagined her leading some kind of nomadic life in the tundra. I thought we'd find her eventually."

"We did," said Eddy drily.

They were silent again.

"We won't know which of them died first until we know the age of the bones in the lake. Even then, it won't be exact." Tobias gazed at the notepad on which he had written two questions: who wrote the emails? where is the ambulance? He felt weary.

"What about the ambulance? Where is the ambulance?" he said.

"Maybe he disposed of it in a lake somewhere, like Emily," said Eddy. "Is there another lake on the golf course?"

Tobias shook his head.

"Are we assuming it's a male killer?" asked Katrine.

"Blunt instrument in both cases. Not a female weapon. And there are no women in the frame," said Tobias.

"There isn't anybody in the frame," said Eddy. "All we can be sure of is that Emily Rasmussen is dead. We don't need DNA to tell us."

"That reminds me," said Karl. "I have the result on those panties. Nada. Nothing. Only Girlie's saliva, blood, vomit, urine."

Tobias was suddenly alert. Voices, words, were darting around his brain. Harry's voice. "Why are these fibres in her jaw?" Pernille's voice on the phone. Where was that? In the car. What was she saying? He had been fiddling with the satnav, only half-listening. Something about panties.

"Pernille Madsen is investigating an assault in Aalborg. She said something about panties." Tobias shut his eyes to concentrate. "Panties and DNA. I'll give her a call." He was wide awake again. "OK. Either Emily sent some of the emails and the killer sent the rest. Or the killer sent all the emails. Either way, he needed access to Emily's address book, or he was with her when she wrote emails to her mother. And he dumped the ambulance."

"And created the Facebook page," said Eddy. "That was probably set up at some Internet café as well."

"I've gone through all the cafés and hotspots the emails were sent from," said Katrine. "I looked to see what was happening near them around the same time. There were demonstrations at the Shell refinery in Fredericia. I can check if Aksel Schmidt was among those arrested. In Norway and Sweden there were protests about oil-drilling near Pitea and Hurtigruten," said Katrine. "One of Malling's companies, as it happens. No arrests, so no names. There was a protest about a ship in Hamburg carrying nuclear waste. No arrests. And there was an anti-bullfighting demonstration in Arles, Provence. I haven't got a list of arrests yet. I started with the most recent email. It was sent three weeks ago, April fourteenth, from Hirtshals There's a protest camp in the forest near there."

"Hirtshals is not that far from Aalborg," said Eddy.

"I know," said Tobias. "And Asksel Schmidt has been to the camp."

They all paused for a moment to take in this information.

"Let's bring him in," said Tobias.

45.

The warrant to search the squat was on Tobias's desk, along with the long-awaited file on Emily Rasmussen's complaint against her stepfather. Tobias picked up the folder and put it down again. It was probably redundant. He hesitated. He never liked to leave a stone unturned. He picked it up again and took it with him. He would read it later, if he had a moment to spare.

They drove to the squat in two cars. Tobias and Eddy in one car, Katrine in the second car. Tobias parked at the front. Katrine parked at the back. Tobias and Eddy went to the door in the side alley. Tobias knocked on the door. Nobody came. He hammered on the door. Still no response.

Eddy shouted, "Open up. Police. We have a warrant to search these premises." He took his gun from his shoulder holster.

"Stand away from the door," he shouted. "I'm going to shoot out the lock."

A voice from inside cried, "Stop! I'll open the door."

Eddy lowered his gun. The door opened. A girl of about eighteen stood there. She wore blue jeans, a red T-shirt and a red bandana.

"What do you want? Why are you harassing us?"

"We're looking for Aksel Schmidt," said Tobias.

"He's not here," said the girl. "I'm the only person here."

Eddy pushed past her into the squat.

"You won't find anybody," the girl called out.

"Where is he if he's not here?" asked Tobias.

The girl shrugged.

"You can tell me down at headquarters, if you prefer," said Tobias.

"They've gone to North Jutland to stop developers cutting down a forest," said the girl. "I don't know where exactly."

Eddy bounded down the stairs behind her. "I've had a look around. There's nobody here."

Katrine joined them. "Nobody at the back either."

"I told you so," said the girl. "They're in North Jutland. Saving a forest."

Tobias hoped Agnes wasn't there. Had she said she was going there at the weekend? He couldn't remember. They'd had a scratchy conversation the last time they'd spoken. With any luck, Agnes had classes on Friday and wouldn't get to the camp until the evening, or the following day. He supposed she travelled with Magnus on the back of the motorbike. He never liked to think about that.

"OK, Eddy. Let's go," he said.

It was midday when they turned off the main road and onto the track running through the forest to the protest camp. The trees were cloaked in a light mist. The ground was damp and cut with deep tyre tracks. It looked as though at least a couple of lorries had taken the same route earlier.

As they got nearer, Tobias heard what sounded like faint cries. He rolled down the window and heard several loud bangs, like firecrackers.

"Sounds like a bit of riot, boss," said Eddy.

Two police officers in riot gear jumped out onto the track in front of the car.

"What the fuck," said Eddy, braking hard.

"P E T," shouted one of the officers.

Tobias waved his ID at him.

The officer strode up to the car. "We're raiding the camp. It's a pre-empt before a climate change demo next week. Get your car out of the way." He pointed to a sidetrack into the forest.

"We've come to speak to a suspect in a murder case," said Tobias.

"We're arresting them all," said the officer. "You can take your pick. Keep out of the way in the meantime"

Eddy turned into the sidetrack and parked. He and Tobias got out and headed through the forest towards the camp. The air was filled with shouts and clanking, clinking, rattling noises and more firecrackers. Then there was the sound of vehicle doors being slammed shut.

They emerged beside a television crew hurrying towards the noise. Tobias recognized the blonde reporter with the red spectacles. She clearly thought he and Eddy were journalists as well.

"They phoned us an hour ago when the police arrived," she said. "I think we've missed most of the action."

When they reached the clearing, Tobias saw what looked like planks of wood and power tools – was that an angle grinder? – being loaded into a police van. An officer emerged from the wigwam carrying what looked like fluorescent tubes and a tin of paint. Tobias flashed his ID.

"Peaceful demonstration, my arse," said the officer. "We found forty riot shields, fifty paint bombs, half a dozen hammers and hundreds of firecrackers in there," he jerked his head back towards the wigwam.

The PET officer who'd stopped the car came up to Tobias and Eddy. He pointed to a police wagon where a dozen or so activists sat on benches.

"If who you're looking for is in there, you can have them."

Tobias and Eddy ran to the arrest vehicle. Tobias felt his stomach tighten. Magnus was sitting, scowling, at the end of a bench. There was no sign of Agnes. Tobias relaxed.

"Which one of you is Aksel Schmidt?" he asked.

Silence.

"I want him," said Tobias, pointing at Magnus. The PET officer reached into the wagon and hauled out Magnus.

Tobias led him out of earshot. Eddy followed.

"Where's Aksel?"

Magnus was silent.

Eddy lifted him off his feet by the collar of his jacket and set him down again.

"Tell us where he is or I'll toss you back into the wagon."

Tobias said, quietly, "We want to talk to him about a murder. The murder of a young activist."

Magnus paled. He was clearly shocked. "Aksel saw the police vans coming. He ran into the forest with Agnes."

Tobias could feel his heart thumping. His imagination raced ahead of him. Stop it. Calm down. Think. He pulled out his mobile phone and called Agnes.

"Dad?" Her voice shook.

"Where are you? Are you alright?"

"We were raided."

"I know."

"You know? How do you know? Were you part of it? Did you know about it in advance?"

"I knew nothing about it. Where are you?"

"I'm on the main road near the camp. Walking to Aksel's motorbike."

Tobias began running to the car, talking as he ran.

"Stay where you are, Agnes. Wait till I get to you."

He could hear Agnes speaking to Aksel, hear the note of puzzlement in her voice.

"Don't go with Aksel," he shouted into the phone.

Eddy caught up with him as he got to the car. He started the engine. Eddy jumped into the passenger seat. They turned onto the main road and saw Agnes and Aksel, hand in hand, close to the trees, heading for a motorbike parked on the verge. Tobias had his gun in his lap.

Tobias braked beside the motorbike and jumped out, gun in hand. Aksel halted. He pulled Agnes around in front of him and held her close with one arm.

"Move away from him, Agnes," said Tobias.

Aksel tightened his grip on her. "Don't move. They're over the top. It's just a demo. They can't even arrest us. We're just having a walk in the forest, admiring the trees they want to destroy."

"Move away, Agnes," said Tobias quietly. Did Aksel have a gun?

Aksel put his other arm around Agnes and clasped her shoulders. No gun. Relief flooded through Tobias. Eddy came up beside him.

"Put your guns away and we'll talk," said Aksel. He was still holding Agnes. She was pale and rigid.

Tobias lowered his gun. Aksel suddenly shoved Agnes, hard, so she almost fell. Tobias instinctively reached out for her. Aksel turned and ran into the forest.

Tobias shouted, "Get into the car, Agnes."

He followed Eddy in pursuit of Aksel, running, weaving, almost slipping on wet ground, through the trees.

Aksel turned to shout at them, "You're making a mistake." He tripped, fell, cried out, "Fuck!"

When they reached him, guns at the ready again, he was lying on his back holding up a badge. Grinning.

"I'm with PET," he said. "You nearly blew my cover."

Eddy grabbed the badge. Checked it. Gave it to Tobias.

Aksel groaned and got to his feet.

Tobias gave him back the badge. "What were you doing with Agnes?"

"None of your fucking business."

"She's my daughter," said Tobias.

"I know," said Aksel. "I'm with PET, remember?"

Eddy put his hand on Tobias's arm. A signal to take it easy.

"Don't worry. I wasn't fucking her. We were on guard duty. Agnes spotted a police vehicle. Aalborg. Fucking amateurs. She shouted a warning but our vehicles were already three-quarters of the way up the track. All we could do was run for it. You should be grateful she hasn't been arrested."

He looked so self-satisfied, Tobias wanted to punch him, put him on the ground again.

"We're taking you in for questioning. About Emily Rasmussen."

Aksel looked surprised. "Emily Rasmussen? That's a name I haven't heard in a long time."

"Are you carrying a firearm?"

"Don't be ridiculous," said Aksel.

He looked bored while Eddy patted him down.

"No gun, boss."

"OK," said Tobias. "Take him in."

Eddy and Aksel travelled back to Aarhus with PET.

Tobias walked back to the road. Agnes was standing

beside the car, white-faced, anxious. He thought she was probably still in shock. He held her for a moment before gently pushing her into the car.

"What's happening, Dad? Why are you here? Why were you chasing Aksel?"

"He's wanted for questioning," said Tobias.

He started the engine. For the first twenty kilometers neither he nor Agnes spoke. When they reached the motorway, she began to say something.

"I don't want to discuss your foolishness, Agnes," said Tobias. "You're an adult. You make your own choices. I trusted you to make sensible choices. Instead you involve yourself with idiots. That bloody wigwam was full of paint bombs, and power drills, and planks and riot shields and wire cages on wheels."

"They're for building a three dimensional map. To put on wheels for the demonstration. To show what global warming is doing. Denmark will disappear when the ice melts, Dad. And we'll be responsible if we don't do something to stop it."

"And firecrackers?"

"They won't harm anyone. They just make a noise."

"Tell that to the judge," said Tobias. He overtook the police wagon. Magnus was in it. Good.

"I haven't been arrested," said Agnes. "They'll see I'm in the car with you. Now they'll all think I'm a police spy. I'd rather be arrested."

"And get a criminal record? And have that on your CV? Grow up, Agnes."

Silence fell again. Tobias felt tired. He'd not had much sleep. He switched on the radio and found P2Klassik. The sound of a symphony orchestra flooded into the car.

"I thought you only listened to police radio in the car," said Agnes.

"Don't be smart with me, Agnes."

They were forty kilometers from Aarhus when she spoke again.

"What has Aksel done? What's so important you had to drive all that way?"

Tobias considered saying he thought Aksel might be a murderer. He was tempted to say Aksel was a member of PET. Instead he said, "I can't tell you. Not yet. Where do you want to go? To the train station? To your Mum's house? To the apartment?"

His phone rang. Tobias glanced at the screen and saw it was Karren. He punched the loudspeaker.

"Tobias, have you seen the news? That camp in the forest has been raided. They've found weapons. Paint, power drills, all kinds of stuff."

"Police propaganda," muttered Agnes.

"Has Agnes been arrested? Hans Frederik is beside himself. You have to do something."

Tobias pulled the phone from its holder on the dashboard and gave it to Agnes.

"You speak to her."

"I haven't been arrested," said Agnes. "I'm fine, Mum. I'm with Dad. Bye for now." She put the phone back in its holder. "Take me to the station, Dad. I'm going to Copenhagen. I have an essay to finish."

46.

Larsen and Renata Molsing were with Eddy and Katrine in the Investigations Room when Tobias got back to headquarters.

"You've arrested someone from PET," said Larsen,

"Inspector Erik Bak, working undercover as Aksel Schmidt, a freelance IT consultant. He has had this alias for some time. I have Inspector Bak's service record." He waved two printed pages. "Why have you arrested him?"

"We haven't arrested him," said Tobias. "He's come in voluntarily for questioning."

"He's in the interview room," said Eddy. "Drinking coffee."

"What have you got on him?" asked Renata.

"He knew Emily Rasmussen," said Tobias. "He was part of the Skovlynd protest against the golf club. He has moved about from protest to protest since then."

"That's his job," said Larsen.

"We know the hotmail account of Emily Rasmussen was either set up by whoever killed her, or taken over by that person. The emails came from places where there were protests and demonstrations going on at the time," said Katrine.

"Harry found traces of polyester in the jaw and skull of the skeleton in the lake at Skovlynd," said Tobias. "Girlie was gagged with her panties. The same perpetrator told a Thai girl he beat up that he was a police officer working undercover." Tobias paused. "And if you give me a moment to make a phone call, I might have more."

"I hope so," said Renata. "Because what you've got is all circumstantial. It doesn't justify keeping him in custody."

"Make your call," said Larsen.

Tobias picked up the phone to called Pernille Madsen as soon as he reached his desk.

She was in the lab with Magda Johanssen when the switchboard put the call through.

"You mentioned a case to me," said Tobias. "The perpetrator had gagged the victim with her panties. You have DNA."

"Not yet," said Pernille. "I'm in the lab now. We'll have a DNA profile by tomorrow." She glanced at Magda for confirmation. Magda nodded. "We have a partial thumb print which we're pretty sure is the perpetrator's. But it doesn't match any sex offenders, or anyone else for that matter, in the database."

"We're questioning someone in connection with two murders," said Tobias. "The first victim was assaulted a few weeks before she was murdered. Her attacker used her panties as a gag. We think he came back and murdered her. We found the skeleton of an earlier victim, years back. Probably twelve years back. We think it's the same perpetrator because there were polyester fibres in her jaw. What else can you tell me about your case?"

"There's a clear modus operandi," said Pernille. "He uses black strips of cloth, plastic gloves, he gags the victim with her panties, he photographs or films them, and he picks on prostitutes." She took a deep breath. "I've found four similar attacks in Europe in the last ten years. Not counting the latest one in Aalborg." She recited them. "Esbjerg ten years ago, Pitea in Swedish Lapland, nine years ago, Stockholm two years ago. Arles in France last year. And the body washed up at Lonstrup, the one we think went into the sea at Hamburg a few months ago, had traces of fibres in her mouth as well." She drew breath again. "What are the dates of the murders you're investigating?"

"The first one is Emily Rasmussen. We found her skeleton. We think she was murdered in September 1998, or maybe a short time later. The second victim was murdered four days ago in Gellerupparken."

"And you have a suspect?" said Pernille. "Good work. I'll send you the thumb print and the files with photos."

"Thanks, Pernille." Tobias hung up.

He went to the viewing area from where he could see and hear Eddy and Katrine interviewing Erik Bak, aka Aksel Schmidt.

"You've told us you last saw Emily Rasmussen in the summer of 1998," said Eddy. "Which month?"

"I can't remember. July or August, I suppose. I can't be sure. It's so long ago."

"Emily Rasmussen was in Sweden during July and August 1998," said Katrine.

"Then maybe it was later," said Asksel Schmidt. He sounded irritated.

"So, after January 1999?" said Eddy.

"I can't remember. I was moving about from group to group. And the membership of these groups shifts and changes all the time."

"Have you been undercover with green activists all the time?"

"Pretty much," said Aksel. "Except for March and April last year. I was on a Europol training course in Norway."

"Where were you two weeks ago? April eighteenth to be precise," said Katrine.

Erik Bak shrugged. "I'm not sure. Probably in the squat."

"Did you sexually assault a prostitute in Gellerupparken on that day?"

"Definitely not," said Erik Bak.

"Did you subsequently murder the same prostitute?"

Erik Bak sat up. He was less relaxed now. "What?"

"Did you also sexually assault a prostitute from Thailand, who worked in Gellerupparken?"

"I've never sexually assaulted anyone," he said.

"The man who beat and assaulted the Thai sex worker told her he was an undercover police officer," said Eddy.

"So?"

"You work undercover in Gellerupparken. You were with green activists in places from which emails were sent to Emily Rasmussen's mother. Emails intended to make her think Emily was alive, when in fact she was dead."

"What places? What emails?" Eric was clearly rattled.

Tobias put his head around the door of the interview room and beckoned to Eddy and Katrine. They joined him in the viewing room from where they could see Erik Bak, fidgeting.

"Here's a list of sexual assaults, similar pattern, over a period of at least ten years," said Tobias. He handed the list to Katrine. "Find out where he was at the time of each attack. Have you fingerprinted him, or taken a DNA sample?"

"Not yet," said Eddy.

"We should have the DNA profile tomorrow. Pernille Madsen is sending over a print as well. It should be here by now. If it matches, we've got him."

"Go home, boss," said Eddy. "Relax. Get some sleep. Skaarup and I can deal with this."

Tobias was tired. He had been up since before dawn. It was now almost nine o'clock in the evening.

"See you tomorrow," he said.

"With any luck we'll have it all tied up and we can all take the day off," said Eddy.

"I'll take the files home, just in case," said Tobias.

Sofie telephoned as he was parking the car in the square below his apartment.

"I saw the news reports," she said. "The skeleton in the lake at Skovlynd. The speculation it might be Emily Rasmussen."

"We can't be one hundred per cent sure until we get the DNA results."

"You think it's Emily?"

"I can't say yet," said Tobias.

"You know it's Emily. I can tell from your voice."

Tobias didn't contradict her.

"Astrid is in a terrible state. She telephoned me. She wants to go on believing Emily is alive."

"Have a drink with me this evening. It's a beautiful evening."

"I can't. Sorry."

"Tomorrow?"

"I'm going to France tomorrow evening. Kurt is entertaining some potential partners in his chateau business. He wants me there."

"Why?" Was he sounding jealous? He didn't want to sound jealous.

"Are you jealous?" Sofie laughed. "He needs me there because I speak French."

"What's the name of the chateau?"

"Chateau Sentout. It's near Arles. We're flying down tomorrow. Me, Kurt, Marcus and the architect. The usual suspects." She paused. "I'll be back on Tuesday evening. We can do something then if you like."

Third time lucky? Tobias smiled. "That would be nice. Dinner? I'll book something."

"Text me on Tuesday," said Sofie.

47.

Tobias sat for a moment before getting out of the car. The files were in the pocket of the door. He picked them up, carried them to the apartment and set them down on the table by the French window. It was dusk. The sky above the rooftops was rose pink shading to indigo. He stepped onto the balcony and inhaled the cool night air scented with lilac and cherry blossom. He left the balcony door ajar when he went back into the room. He chose Scarlatti sonatas played by Mikhail Pletnev to accompany his methodical movements around the kitchen as he assembled a supper of Beemster Very Old cheese, a handful of walnuts and a slice of dark rye bread. He felt relaxed. Was it the music? Was it the sense of a job finished? He looked forward to a good night's sleep after an exhausting day.

He woke in the middle of the night. Something was bothering him. What had been dreaming about? He couldn't remember. An idea, a word, something, was darting about in his brain, eluding capture. What was it? There was air in the room. He slept with the window open. He was neither too hot nor too cold. He tried an old trick for dealing with his rare bouts of insomnia – playing a Bach prelude in his head, imagining the precise fingering, the weight of each note, the tempo. It was no use. He could not concentrate while the gadfly thought was in his head. He got up.

He poured himself a whiskey, added a dash of water, and stood on the balcony to drink it. The buildings all around were dark, the cafés and bars in the square had closed. The lights had gone out in the buildings all around, even in the cafés and bars in the square. The floodlit spire of the cathedral stood out against the night sky and the moon rode high above it. It was a night for romance, and he was alone. He imagined Sofie in a four-poster bed in the French chateau. Where was it exactly? He sat down at the table and opened his laptop and searched for Chateau Sentout, near Arles. The result flashed onto the screen.

Chateau Sentout is a castle in the commune of Saint-Desir de Provence in the department of Bouches-

du-Rhône in southern France. In 1994 it was listed as a Monument Historique.

The chateau was built in the 1680s by Gerard Peltier who built boats (barques)which transported wine on the river Rhone. His son, Jean-Marc Peltier, planted vineyards on the property and was ennobled by Louis XV for supplying wine to the new light infantry regiments. The chateau was the principal residence of his descendants until the late 19th century when they began using it as a summer residence only. The chateau gradually fell into a state of disrepair.

Wine production declined after the Second World War. The last official harvest was in 1980. In 1990 the chateau, by now almost in ruins, was sold to a construction company which intended to build housing to serve the expanding city of Arles (15km). The plan was opposed by the local commune and the French Heritage Society and the chateau was designated a Monument Historique. The new owners have promised to restore the building and maintain its special architectural character.

There was a link to a photograph in a local newspaper. It showed a handsome baroque style building with turrets and mansard roofs. The walls were standing. The rooves had fallen in. Scaffolding covered half of the building. Nobody could possibly stay there. So where did she stay? The nearest big town, he supposed. Arles. That was the gadfly word his brain had been chasing. He had come across it in the files.

He opened the file and found the list Katrine had compiled, matching the ISPs of the emails to green protests. The Shell refinery in Fredericia; oil drilling in Pitea and Hurtigruten; nuclear waste in Hamburg; the wind farm near Aalborg; bullfighting in Arles. She hadn't identified anything near Esbjerg and nothing in particular in Copenhagen, but there was always some kind of protest going on in the capital.

He was sure Pernille Madsen had mentioned Arles. Wasn't it one of the places where a prostitute had been assaulted? Gagged with her panties, like Girlie and, every instinct told him, Emily Rasmussen.

He searched the file for the list Pernille Madsen had sent from Aalborg. Yes! Arles leapt out at him. Arles, April fifteenth, a year ago. Amina Okonjo, an illegal immigrant working as a prostitute, had been found by a physiotherapist leading a group of heart patients on an early morning walk. She had two black eyes, broken ribs and a ruptured spleen. She told the police she'd been gagged with her own panties and punched and thumped by a client. He didn't speak French. Her pimp had driven her to the clinic and dumped her in the grounds.

The cathedral bells rang out. Tobias started. Normally his brain filtered out the constant ringing of the bells. Another, recent, memory was dislodged. Erik Bak: "I was on a Europol training course in Norway."

Tobias pulled Erik Bak's service record from the file. There it was in clear print. April ninth until May eleventh. *Bergen: Weapons Training and Surveillance Methodology*. Erik Bak could not have assaulted a prostitute or sent an email from an Internet hub in Arles on the fourteenth of April.

There was one other person who could have sent that email.

Tobias opened the file on Emily Rasmussen's complaint against her stepfather. Words sprang at him as he read. Gagged. Blood. Bruised. Tied up. Vomit. Fear. Dead.

He poured himself another whiskey and went on reading.

The telephone call from Emily Rasmussen to the police in Skandeborg was logged at 8am. Emily told the officer who took the call that she had found violent sexual pornography on her stepfather's laptop. She had gone to her stepfather's study to consult an atlas. She thought he had gone to work. The laptop was open on his desk. She glanced at it and saw a photograph of a woman bound, gagged, her face covered in blood. The picture changed. Now there was a different woman on the screen. She was gagged and spreadeagled. Her thighs were covered in blood. She appeared to be dead. She clicked through more images: women gagged and bound, their faces beaten to pulp, bruises on their stomachs and inner thighs, vomit in their hair, blood trickling from their noses.

Emily heard her stepfather speaking to her mother downstairs. She ran from the study to her room. Her stepfather went into the study. Emily went downstairs and telephoned the police. She told her mother what she'd seen and what she had done. The two women went upstairs to confront Marcus Thomsen. He flew into a rage, accused Emily of lying and slammed the study door. Emily and her mother waited outside the room until the police arrived approximately fifteen minutes after the call was made. Marcus Thomsen denied having images on his computer. He said Emily was jealous and delusional. The police checked the laptop, a Gateway Solo 9100, on the spot. They found no pornographic images. Emily said Marcus Thomsen must have switched laptops. The police searched the room. No second laptop was found. Emily was so insistent, the police continued searching, even taking up the floorboards. They then searched the rest of the house. No laptop was found. Emily was interviewed by the police. She stuck adamantly to her story. A police psychologist could find no evidence of schizophrenia or any mental disorder. Marcus Thomsen had no police record. Nor could the Skandeborg police find any reports of assaults on women.

Tobias closed his eyes to think. Could Emily have invented something which so exactly matched the modus operandi of the man who killed Girlie? And the Russian prostitute he dumped in the sea at Hamburg? Who almost certainly killed Emily?

It was like one of those locked room mysteries by Agatha Christie. The Mystery of the Missing Laptop. Could there have been a second laptop?

Tobias went out on to the balcony and took three deep breaths. The gardens below were early-morning still. A movement caught his eye. The fountain in the lily pond had sprung into life. Where had he seen a lily pond mentioned? He went back inside and leafed through the file on Bogman. It was in the notes on Lennart's grandparents. His last words to them on the phone: "Bye now. I see Emily coming back from the lily pond." The call was logged at 21.30 on the twenty-first of September 1998. Tobias frowned. It would be dark at that time in September. The headlights would have been on. Lennart couldn't have seen who was driving the ambulance. Lily pond. Lily pond. He closed his eyes again and conjured up the house in Skandeborg. Judge Hendrikson's house, where the Thomsen's had been living when Emily disappeared. He saw again the gardener gazing into the pond at the side of the house. "*The same bloody heron has been taking the fish.*" The pond had been there when the Thomsen's lived in the house. Where had Thomsen's study been?

He picked up his phone and called Sofie.

"Tobias?" She sounded sleepy. "Why are you calling me at this time? Is something wrong?"

"I need to know something urgently," he said. "When exactly did Kurt Malling buy the chateau in Provence? It was near Arles, wasn't it?"

"What?"

"When did Malling buy the chateau? Was it in April last year? Did Marcus Thomsen go with him?"

"We all went. I mean the team working on the project. Kurt, Marcus, the architect and me."

"When was this? It's important."

"Wait a moment. I'll get my diary."

Tobias was aware of his heart thumping.

"April," said Sofie. "We went down on April twelfth and stayed until the sixteenth."

"Where did you stay?"

"In a hotel in Arles."

"Does Kurt Malling have business interests in Hamburg?"

"I believe so, yes. What is this about, Tobias? Why are you interrogating me at six o'clock in the morning?"

"Does Malling have interests in Lapland?"

"I think his company is doing oil exploration up there. What's going on, Tobias?"

"What flight are you taking this evening?"

"Kurt shares an executive jet. We're all going in that."

"What time?"

"Six o'clock from Aarhus. What is this about, Tobias?

"I'll tell you on Tuesday," he said.

Tobias phoned Eddy.

"It can't have been Asksel, or Bak or whatever he calls himself."

"I know," said Eddy. "It didn't match the print Pernille Madsen sent over. We let him go. What now?"

"I have an idea," said Tobias. "I need to speak to Larsen."

48

SATURDAY: WEEK THREE

Y ou disturbed the judge on his safari holiday, and now you want to disturb the peace and quiet of his weekend by putting a frogman in his lily pond?" Larsen put his head in his hands. He looked up again. "This is just a theory, isn't it? You don't even know if the pond is below the window of Thomsen's study. In fact you don't even know if his study was on that side of the house."

"It all fits, sir."

"It all fitted Eric Bak too."

"Thomsen was in the same places at the same time. He could have sent the emails. He obviously knew his wife's email address. I am convinced he had two laptops. One for everyday use. One for viewing the pictures he took himself, and possibly even sold on."

Larsen sighed. "It's plausible."

"My theory is that Emily Rasmussen guessed he'd thrown the laptop into the pond," said Tobias. "She went back in the ambulance to look for it. Thomsen saw her and murdered her."

But not before he subjected her to the same kind of treatment he gave the other women. An unwelcome image swam into his head. Emily Rasmussen, gagged, bound, beaten.

"Thomsen knew concrete was being poured into the lake at Skovlynd," said Tobias. "I think he drove there in the ambulance and buried Emily's body in a shallow grave. He knew that Lennart would come looking for her. That Lennart knew Emily had gone to look for the laptop. So he drove to Roligmose and killed Lennart as well. Then he drove back to his house."

"So where's the ambulance?"

"I don't know, sir. He must have got rid of it somewhere."

Larsen sighed. "OK. Take whatever and whoever you need. I'll call Judge Hendriksen."

Tobias drove to Skandeborg. Karl Lund and his team and two divers from the Frogman corps followed him to Judge Hendriksen's house.

Arne Hendrickson was pacing his front lawn when Tobias arrived.

"We've got guests," he said. "You'll have to come back later."

His wife hurried out of the house. "Arne," she cried. "Don't send them away. Our guests will love the excitement of it all. It will be the talk of Skandeborg. They'll be dining out on it for weeks. You won't disturb us at all, will you Chief Inspector? We'll watch from the dining room window." She took her husband's arm. He allowed her to steer him back into the house.

The pond was surprisingly deep. One diver supervised as the other plunged and rose four times, emerging with, variously, a warped bicycle wheel, an empty paint tin, a broken baseball bat and finally and triumphantly, a mud and slime-covered laptop.

Gasps escaped through the dining room window. Tobias was uncomfortably aware of an audience as he and Karl Lund crouched to look at the laptop. Karl Lund wiped the surface with a gloved hand.

"Gateway Solo 9100. It's the same make," he said.

"He must have bought two of them at the same time," said Tobias. "Can we get any data off this do you think?"

"Not a chance," said Karl. "Not if he chucked it in here in 1998."

"It's evidence all the same," said Tobias. Enough evidence to make an arrest.

"It proves there was a second laptop." Tobias stood up. "The ambulance must be in this area. Thomsen must have driven it back here. It's the only way he could get back to his house from Roligmose after he killed Lennart."

"There's a lot of forest around here," said Karl. "And a lot of water. Plenty of places to hide an ambulance. I'll need more men if we're going to search the area."

Tobias called Eddy.

"We've found the laptop. Get over to Thomsen's house. Don't make the arrest unless you see him leaving the house. We're going to look for the ambulance. I want to have everything in place when we bring him in." After that, the thumbprint and DNA would seal the bastard's fate, he was sure of it.

He looked around. The driveway ran from the front gate to the house with lawn on either side. It widened in front of the house before curving around the far side. He walked to the open dining room window and spoke to the judge's wife who was standing with two equally transfixed guests. He recognised one of them as the Hendriksen's neighbour, Mrs Jacobson, her face lit with excitement.

"Is it possible to drive down to the lake from the house?" he asked.

Mrs Hendriksen shook her head.

"You used to be able to drive down," piped Mrs Jacobsen. "When the Rasmussens lived here we used to drive down to the lake so that Emily and her friends could water-ski from the jetty. But that stopped after Marcus married Astrid. He complained the teenagers were driving down on scooters and making a racket, even after Emily left. He planted leylandii to stop them."

"Can we walk down to the jetty?"

"There's a footpath at the back of the house," said Mrs Hendriksen.

50.

An audience of half a dozen, not counting police and forensics officers but including the Hendriksens and Mrs Jacobsen on her walking frame, watched the diver lower himself with rope and hooks into the dark waters of the lake. Watched him surface ten metres from the edge of the jetty. Heard him shout, "There's a vehicle on the lake bed."

After that, it was a matter for police launch and hydraulic equipment.

At three o'clock in the afternoon, the ambulance, brown water spilling from it, rose out of the lake and was deposited on the jetty. The bodywork was rusted and crumbling but the rubber tyres were intact.

Waves of relief and exhilaration washed over Tobias.

Eddy and Katrine were parked outside the Thomsen's house when he phoned to tell them the laptop and ambulance had been found. Eddy reached over and hugged Katrine. "The bastard's nailed," he said.

Astrid Thomsen answered the door to them. "Have you news for me? Have you the DNA result?"

"We will have news for you very shortly," said Katrine gently. "First, we need to speak to your husband."

"He's at the airport," said Astrid. "He's flying to Paris."

Eddy could barely conceal his astonishment. They'd been watching the house since midday. "When did he leave for the airport?"

"He left early this morning. He had some business in town. His flight isn't until five o'clock. You can give him a call if you like. He probably hasn't boarded yet."

Eddy pulled out his phone.

Katrine said, "I think we should sit down and have a talk, Mrs Thomsen. I need to explain some things to you. And I have something for you." She had Emily's locket and ring in her bag. She hoped they would bring some comfort. She shepherded Astrid Thomsen back inside.

Eddy was already speaking to Tobias. "Thomsen left the house this morning. He's at the airport. He's on a commercial flight to Paris, according to his wife."

Tobias was on the motorway south of Aarhus. The airport was a further half hour away. "Call the airlines. He must be going via Copenhagen. Find out which flight he's on." He stepped hard on the accelerator.

He ran into the terminal building holding the phone to his ear, listening to instructions from Eddy.

"He's booked through to Rio de Janeiro. His Copenhagen flight is leaving from Gate 5. They're boarding now. I'm trying to get hold of the airport director to ground the flight."

Tobias ran through security waving his badge. He ran to the departure gate. It had closed. He ran past a startled stewardess, bounded down a staircase and burst through double doors on to the runway. The whine of the jet engines deafened him. The steps were still at the plane. Thirty metres to go. He overtook Eddy, bent double, holding his side. Twenty metres. He thought his heart would burst. The marshallers were signalling. Ten metres. The engines roared. Tobias leapt on to the steps, clawed his way to the top, hammered on the aircraft door. Vehicles screeched across the tarmac. At least one was a police car. Katrine jumped out. The engines died. Tobias hung, exhausted, on the rail of the steps. The door of the plane opened as Katrine reached him. They walked together into the plane and arrested Marcus Thomsen for the murders of Lennart Praetorius, Emily Rasmussen, Girlie Sanchez and Ludmila Akulova. Katrine thought it was the proudest, most satisfying moment of her life.

Tobias left Eddy and Katrine to take Marcus Thomsen to headquarters. He would interview him in the morning. For now, he was exhausted. He was going home.

The light was on when he let himself into his apartment. Agnes was sitting at the table typing on her laptop. Books were strewn over the table. She looked up. "Dad?"

"Hi, Pumpkin. I thought you were in Copenhagen." He resisted the urge to gather up the books and arrange them in structured piles.

She shrugged. "I have all my stuff for my essay. I decided to stay." She paused. "I saw the news on television. You've arrested someone for the murder of the boy in the bog, and his girlfriend." She hesitated. "Was it Aksel?"

Tobias shook his head. "No. It was Emily Rasmussen's stepfather."

"I'm glad it wasn't Aksel. I'd hate to think I'd been friendly with a murderer. Maybe he's the informer. Is he? I know you won't say. They all still think it's me. It's not the same anymore. The suspicion. The talking behind my back." Tobias saw that she was close to tears. "I'm sorry, Dad. I feel all we've done, tried to do, has been turned into a hideous joke. And I've managed to fall out with you and Mum as well."

Tobias took her in his arms and hugged her.

"You can't stop your parents loving you, Agnes."

He thought about Astrid Thomsen and Emily. About how Thomsen had compounded his terrible crimes by estranging mother and daughter. Astrid would probably never forgive herself. He hugged Emily closer.

"What about a duet, Pumpkin?"

"You choose this time, Dad."

Tobias glanced at the books on the table. There would be time enough to tidy them away later. Life was too short to waste moments like this. He wondered if Emily would be buried with Lennart. Together forever.

He opened the piano stool. "What about the Schubert Fantasy in F minor?"

Haunting, dark, questioning, and quiet at the end.

Made in the USA
Lexington, KY
21 January 2017